ALSO BY ROB HOERBURGER

**My Name Is Love:
The Darlene Love Story
(with Darlene Love)**

Why Do Birds

a novel

Rob Hoerburger

71 SONGS LLC, NEW YORK, N.Y.

71
SONGS

71 Songs, New York, New York

Cover design by Rachel Willey
Interior design by Ben Grandgenett
Back-cover photograph by Colin Bridgham

Manufactured in the United States of America
ISBN 978-1-5323-8152-2 (Paperback)
ISBN 978-1-5323-8153-9 (E-Book)

For Casey and Rockboy

ROB HOERBURGER

No one sings like you anymore.
SOUNDGARDEN, "BLACK HOLE SUN"

1. New York City, Spring 1982

She was down to her last five million. Most of it was tied up in stocks and bonds, and there were a couple of properties back in L.A., but she still had enough ready cash to last several months in New York. Enough, that is, to pay for the hotel suite and the doctors. They'd told her she might need as much as three years to recover, but she was determined to lick this thing by Thanksgiving. By then she'd be ready to record again. And by the end of next year, the money would start flowing back in the right direction, and the curtain on her second act would finally rise. She'd go back to L.A. and show them all.

But it was still only May, and she had some work to do. The only figure she cared about today was 54 — which was the precise number of steps down to the subway platform, the number of steps that lay between her and the finale. For a second, just a second, she was tempted to race down. But before she could start to descend, she got caught in the spokes of memory. Suddenly in her mind she was brushing her hands along the cinder-block walls of her high-school stairwell, all big-boned and bounding, on the way down to the vinegary-smelling cafeteria. The phantom taste of the soggy grilled-cheese sandwiches and full-fat chocolate milk she used to inhale before band practice had barely left before the voices, more recent, kicked in, first in two-, then four-, then six-part harmony, finally overdubbed into a finger-wagging chorale of doctors and family members and friends and fans chiming and chiding, "Not in your condition." O.K., then. She'd take her time.

In high school the other girls had played flute, clarinet, the occasional bassoon or even tuba. She played drums. Why had she taken them up? The usual answer she gave, in countless interviews across more than a dozen years, was that she wanted to get out of gym class. Then, when she showed some facility for them, it was because she wanted to be close to him, to be a part of *his* destiny. And though she may have never become a heavy hitter like Ringo or Buddy Rich, even when it soon became abundantly clear that her primary talent was singing, she never lost her innate sense of rhythm. As her band teacher told her over and over again, she knew how to count.

She wasn't the first famous female drummer. There was that girl from the Velvet Underground with the funny first name — what was it? Mel? Moo? Mao? She could never remember. She wasn't too familiar with their music. The brother was, though; he had all kinds of wacky records — Frank Zappa, the Grateful Dead, Zeppelin. She did actually meet Lou Reed, the Velvet Underground's guitarist and lead singer, once, when they crossed paths in some recording studio or at some club. She knew that weirdo hit of his from 1973, something about the wild side. She knew everything that was in the Top 40 that year. How could she forget? It was their best year: three Top 3 hits and two platinum albums. "Your songs always make me happy," Lou Reed said to her from behind his shades, "because they're so . . . sad." Well, she didn't know about that, but she thought it was cool that they shared a birthday, or so *Billboard* said.

1973. Almost a decade ago.

Now she was in New York, alone. It was her second extended stay. The first one, during her and the brother's hiatus at the end of the '70s, she lived there on and off for six months to record a solo album and experienced the city as if through binoculars — she could see it up close but never really touch it, removed and refracted as it was by limos and doormen and producers and valets and flunkies and second engineers who ran interference for her and then sent her the bill. She never learned to hail a cab, never explored the broad streets or the back alleys, never really saw the unimaginable and so never imagined it. She never ordered for herself when they all went out for dinner, she and her new band and the production team.

When she was young, eating out meant Howard Johnson's or roadside joints with Formica counters and ripped banquettes, and she could have just about anything on the menu. Over the last few years, though, as the menus moved up a few rungs on the social ladder, along with her dinner companions, she cared nothing about the fine points of piccata or francese, beurre blanc or demi-glace or crème fraîche, because it all ended up in the same place. She let them order away, pushed around whatever was on her plate and then signed the credit-card slip. It was just like lip-syncing, this pretending to eat, lip-eating. She could be very convincing. Between recording costs, the suite at the Plaza, all the uneaten dinners, she spent something like half a million. And then the damn record never even came out.

Now, three years later, she was standing by the subway entrance on 42nd and Seventh, at the city's serrated edge. Shiny sprigs of her brown hair squeezed out from under her Yankees cap. As a kid she was a pretty decent softball player. When they lived back east, before they moved to California, she was usually picked first for the neighborhood games, and the brother usually last. Even though he was older, she often defended him from the neighborhood bullies who taunted the gawky, horn-rimmed piano prodigy that he was. One time she even slugged a greaser who was pushing him around, and after that they left him alone. But then, when she was about 13, the parents decided he would have a better chance at fame in California, and so the family moved. She gave up baseball for the drums, and then, once it became obvious that his voice wasn't going to sell many records, she concentrated on singing. It was just another way of coming to his rescue.

But those were the days of baggy sweatshirts and muddied Keds. Now her Nikes, a new pair for the new week, shone a bright, unscuffed white, broken only by their aqua swoosh. The 24K miniature gold records on her charm bracelet, pulled to its very farthest clasp and still loose on her wrist, clinked against the subway railing. Her tan merino sweater, size 0 and roomy, was layered over a white long-sleeve button-down, which was turned up at the cuffs but still covered her Rolex. (She remembered the first time she saw one, on the wrist of her best friend, F., and thought it was a man's watch. Now her own Rolex was one of her most prized possessions.) Her Gucci rope belt wound halfway back around itself through the loops of her pressed jeans. It was a little warm for the day — May 10, a Monday, and more than a little warm for the sweater. But taking it off was not an option, not even to wrap around her waist. It gave her the illusion of bulk.

She should have been an easy mark for the purse snatchers, palm readers and three-card-monte gamers who, taking one look at her, might have seen a month's work done in minutes. Yet somehow she walked the city with impunity. Times Square, the subway, Central Park, all of New York and the accompanying boogeymen and pervs and crackheads she'd been warned about, were just fun-house attractions to her, like the spinning windmills and felt-banked baby moats of miniature golf, hazards that she had to concentrate and aim her way past. Her ears, as usual, were the first line of defense. She could instantly absorb the city's polyphony, identify its movements and incorporate anybody's foot pattern — the wigglers and the waddlers, the inchworms and the gallopers and the high-heel stompers, the stilt and crutch walkers, and immediately move a step ahead or fall a step behind as necessary. What her ears didn't do, her eyes did, those two brown bulbs that, as the rest of her face turned in on itself over the years, became positively fierce. They were hidden behind her giant Ray-Bans, the same kind that became necessary when they were on tour, not that anyone recognized her anymore, really.

There were plenty of obstacles for her to clear during that crosstown jaunt to the subway, most of them involving food. There were the lunchboxes streaming toward her like torpedoes from either direction, black half-domes tucked under the sweaty armpits of brawny plumbers, electricians, pipe layers, jackhammer riders, on the way home to their suburban split-levels. These forbidding shells would have been emptied hours ago during the morning lunch breaks, but she could still see the damage in the workers' protruding guts: oozy, gooey sandwiches as big as shoes; half pies and guzzled Big Gulps; the caked residue on the work boots that was most likely neither Sheetrock nor plaster but rather errant confectioners' sugar from jelly doughnuts. It was like looking in the mirror to her, encountering all those potbellies, even though she hadn't eaten food like that for years.

Now that the weather was getting warmer, there were more smells, more sights, more sounds for her to navigate: the hot-dog carts, the speared rotisserie chickens in the Korean delis turning up on every corner, the garlic-and-butter sauce at the upscale lunch haunts on Madison, the shattering sizzle of corner grills and their mini Vesuvii of sausage and peppers and onions, the clackety clack of the roach coaches crawling back for the day to wherever they lived and then reloading every night with muffins, croissants, danish, bagels, bialys, buns, bear claws, half-moons. The cheaper the food, she knew, the wider the hips. One reason she liked the subway so much was that it seemed about the only place in all of New York where she couldn't smell anything cooking.

She could have taken a cab to the subway station, of course. But she was trying to stay on a budget, more or less. And she had time to kill: She didn't need to be on the platform until 3:20. Besides, walking across Manhattan proved — to her, at least — that she wasn't weak. At the corner of Sixth and 44th, she ran into a character she'd seen before: He was usually under cardboard and newspapers and army blankets — like the kind her father used to have in the back of his station wagon — grease-stained mechanic's pants and a moth-eaten Holy Cross sweatshirt hanging off his pole frame. He was guarding his shopping cart, festooned with punched-out stuffed animals and pinwheels and mops and brooms and American flags, like a going-out-of-business sale at an amusement-park kiosk. There was a plastic bag full of foul-smelling, empty beer cans. And, acting as license plates, there was a 45 record on each end of the cart. The back "plate" was always some Vietnam anthem like "Light My Fire" or "All Along the Watchtower." The front "plate" changed weekly. Today it was Chris Montez's "The More I See You," a loungy hit back when she and the brother were starting out in the business and always one of their favorite records. When they signed their first big recording contract, with the very same label, she remembered thinking it would be great if they ever got to be as big as Chris Montez.

Had there been such people on the street during her last stay in New York three years ago, wheeling their entire lives around with them? She couldn't recall. In the slow-baking heat today, the man was topless when he stuck out his coffee can, and she couldn't help staring at his torso, a patina of sweat trickling down the taut skin caked with soot and sun, hopping from one rib to the next. She gazed at him in wonder and awe. How did he get his body to look like that? She reached into her purse to pull out a five, and then the light changed; he snatched it from her hand and rolled the cart up Sixth Avenue, chanting, "Tit for Tet, tit for Tet," spittle dribbling down his unshaven chin.

Her own march resumed. She would ask about his diet another day.

So caught up in this reverie was she that for once she didn't notice someone else noticing her. Aside from the inconvenient lack of recent hits, the main reason she wasn't recognized very much was the fact was that her appearance had changed so radically — a kind of natural plastic surgery whittling her down until she had become her own doppelgänger. Still, she caught the attention of a scruffy man in a hooded sweatshirt across Sixth Avenue — or the green from her purse did — making him lift his head from the racing form he was studying and follow her, just catching the light. Her snow-white Nikes kept her in sight amid the heavy foot traffic. The sun was starting to beat down now with some attitude. Yet as she did with her sweater, he kept his sweatshirt on.

She pushed up her sleeve and checked her watch: 3:14, still plenty of time to make the platform. She planted her left heel, swathed in the micropillows of her new sneakers, on the first step of the dun-colored concrete and continued one by one, keeping a steady rhythm. Halfway down the stairs she realized that she had left her neat new bag of tokens on the nightstand at her hotel. Now there would be an unscheduled stop at the token booth. She couldn't see buying another whole pack, so when she got to the front of the line, she asked for just one, only to realize she had given her last small bill to the cart man. She pulled a wad of 50s from her purse. And that's when she heard a voice from behind her and felt a tap on her shoulder.

"A word of advice, ma'am," spoke the soft baritone of the man who had tracked her, who now flashed an NYPD badge and identified himself as an Officer Logan. He seemed surprised at how quickly she snapped around, her torso only barely stronger than dry kindling, beneath the broadish plank of her shoulders, as the two of them moved off to the side of the booth. His fingers were stung by bone. She seemed familiar somehow. "Don't flash a roll of bills like that, all right?" he said. "You might as well just dump them out your window."

After years of world travel, of meeting and performing for big shots in entertainment and government (twice at the White House), she had acquired the language of adulthood. Yet in this small crisis she reverted to the response she had when her first six-figure royalty check arrived, or when she saw Petula Clark (Petula Clark!) perform one of their own songs on TV: "*Man. . . .*" What would the mother think if she knew her daughter had been stopped by a New York undercover cop?

As she stuffed the change from the 50 back into her purse — 49 singles, a quarter and an eviscerating look from the token matron — the officer flipped his badge back into his sweatshirt and got ready to shift back down into his disguise. Then, catching a glint from inside her purse, he leaned in for a second look. She pulled out a small paring knife that he seemed to be fixated on.

"You really think that little thing would protect you?"

"Oh, that," she said, in clipped dismissal, discreetly checking her watch; the longer she stayed there, she thought, the likelier it was he'd recognize her. 3:18. "It's for this," she said, and pulled a whole lemon from the bottom of her bag. She had been carrying around lemons for years, once she discovered their diuretic effect, their tart capacity to subtract calories. You never knew when someone might press a drink or a snack in your hand; the lemon helped keep it from catching.

The officer passed the knife back to her just as his beeper began sounding, and by the time he picked his head up to issue her one more friendly warning, she was gone, having slid into the roll of the crowd headed toward the downtown platform. "Lemon," he said out loud, catching a lingering trace of it in the air. "She'd have a better chance with that than the knife."

The platform had just emptied, filling the train mostly with school kids in premature summer clothes, short shorts and tank tops, weather vanes in mesh and spandex. Every fourth or fifth one of them was plugged into one of those new portable tape players — Was that how they'd be listening to our next hit? she wondered — when she saw the keyboard, only 60 or so keys, small enough to fit in a duffel bag, the plastic microphone stand and behind it a one-man band with a three-ring body. As the train pulled away, exposing the grimy tiles and the graffiti balloons, she hid behind the newsstand — "Original Charlie's Angels Nix Reunion" blared the pink shock of some gossip magazine. She remembered the times — two — she had been on the cover of *People,* one of them her wedding day.

She took in the singer's camouflage colors, the sunglasses that were the deep mahogany of his skin, the silver hoop earrings in triplicate on each side of his face. His shoebox was half-full with loose change and single dollar bills, but he hadn't started to break down his "stage" yet, so she knew she hadn't missed the finale.

She had first taken in his show a few weeks earlier, when, on a lark, she decided she'd ride the subway to Times Square. She hadn't been on one in years. As the crowd poured out of the train, she found herself paddled in the direction of this busker, who was singing "Just the Two of Us," the smooth Bill Withers hit from a year or two ago. Most of the performance was this sort of light jazz or R & B — until the final song. After a few weeks she realized that, while the rest of the set changed, the finale never did, and so she kept going just to hear that one, the one that had changed everything for her, for them.

It was that feather duster of a song that nobody thought would be a hit, not even the marquee songwriters who wrote it. It was passed to her and the brother as, essentially, sloppy thirds after it had already been recorded by a couple of the biggest names in the business, to little effect, and after even their own label boss, H., the handsome trumpeter and vocalist, had tried and abandoned it (he couldn't quite hear himself singing those fluffy lines about angels and moon dust and hair).

After the brother worked up a different arrangement, a slow shuffle, it sped to No. 1 so fast they were still scraping together shake money for Bob's Big Boy when they got the news. The next spring, when the name of the song was found inside a few awards envelopes, no one was more shocked than they were, except perhaps the other nominees. Now, some 12 years later, here was this blind, black behemoth of a man, a jazz and R & B singer no less, his voice a shade deeper than, say, Lou Rawls's or Arthur Prysock's, singing it amid the rattle and hum of the New York City subway system.

She hadn't worked with many black musicians in the course of her career, save for that last time in New York, during the solo sessions. One night after they finished recording, the studio crew presented her with a mocha cake in the shape of a phallus. She sliced it up for them, in a deep blush, somehow forgetting to leave a piece for herself. She had never been prouder in the studio. But then, of course, the album was shelved. "It's a white girl trying to sound black," someone said.

No subways arrived to disrupt the finale, and she stayed for the whole song, mouthing the words along with the busker, sometimes even singing along softly, closing her eyes once or twice as she rediscovered the lilt of the melody, the halting cadences — her idea back then, on the record — reigniting the aroma of it, which had naturally dimmed over the years and the hundreds of times she had sung it. It was in fact the second time today she'd heard the song in public. She'd been out walking earlier when she picked up the scratchy sound of a radio playing somewhere, tuned to WABC-AM. The promotion guys at their label always said that your song wasn't really a hit until it was played on WABC. Since then she and the brother had had lots of songs played on WABC, a couple that were even bigger on the station's surveys than they were nationally.

Today, though, WABC was going all-talk at noon, and in the morning it was playing one song from each year in a retrospective of its Top 40 glory days. When the D.J., a kind of lechy guy who once said of her, "Have you ever seen this girl's legs?" got to 1970, he played that very song, their first big hit. No lechy comment this time. Well, she figured, it was an honor to have one of the last songs played on WABC. Now she guessed she and the brother would have to start concentrating on videos.

When the busker finished, she crept up past the magazine stand and in front of his shoebox, holding her breath, and dropped a 50, folded six times, into it, before taking several giant steps backward away from him. One day, maybe, she'd get up the nerve to tell him he was always late on the downbeat.

2. Queens, N.Y., Spring 1982

Sib Kelly pressed her cheek against the gray metal pipe holding up the basketball hoop in her driveway. She had just finished drills of layups, jump shots and three-pointers and needed to steady her legs, take a swig of Gatorade. She was starting to feel every second of the almost 48 hours she'd been awake, ostensibly from celebrating her pending college graduation; but her fatigue was pretty constant these days anyway. She hadn't been able to sleep more than a couple of hours a night for months. She told her father, who had been suspicious of her late nights right away but said something to her

only a few weeks ago, that she was cramming for finals and also trying to catch as much as she could of the last weeks of WABC-AM,
the legendary Top 40 station, which was going all-talk at noon that
day. Forget the fact that by March she could have neglected to turn
in another exam or paper and still graduated magna cum laude, or
that WABC had been pretty lame for years, drifting away from true
Top 40 after the disco crash into pallid adult contemporary. The station couldn't even play the No.-1-selling record in the city in the
last weeks — Joan Jett's "I Love Rock 'n' Roll" — because it was
too raunchy for the suits left to preside over the final days. So the
countdown stopped at No. 2 those last few weeks. But her father, she
thought, would worry less about her lack of sleep if she had a neat,
clean reason, and school and WABC for now were providing it. It
figured that her insomnia would catch his attention just when he had
stopped the accidental clanging of pots, the absent-minded jingling
of keys, the unconscious clodhopping on the stairs, almost nine years
after her hearing had returned.

It was already hot for 8:00 on an early May morning, and as Sib
— short for Siobhan — massaged the back of her neck with the
cold bottle of Gatorade, she stared down at the concrete around the
base of the hoop pole. The squiggles she noticed the last time had
deepened and widened into mini-fissures. She was surprised her
father hadn't troweled them over by now. Maybe this was a sign that
he was finally thinking about selling the house, now that he could,
if he wanted, retire from the Post Office and the block had become
a kind of widow's row. Most of the other men — WWII or Korean
veterans like him — had died or divorced their wives, and no one
really took care of their small lawn plots anymore the way he did.
Some of those widows had fled the big South Asian influx in the
neighborhood — Sib could smell the curry even this early in the
morning, and she chortled softly when she remembered the four of
them, her mother and father and her brother, Kieran, and her, going
to an Indian restaurant in Manhattan when she was about 7 and

how she thought they would be eating corn and squash and turkey and how she cried when it turned out not to be corn and squash and turkey at all and how it was her father with his big, soft hands and calm, ruddy face who soothed her and told her it was O.K., they'd make her spaghetti, while her mother just sat placidly, as she usually did, waiting for the storm to pass. Sib had been like that all the time — fidgety, squealing, unsatisfied, suspicious — in restaurants when she was a kid; now, particularly since she had gone to college, she could and did eat practically anything. Indian food, the kind from India, was one of her favorites.

She dribbled to the end of the driveway and looked for her father down the street. She had waited until he left for 7 o'clock. Mass at the Church of the Immaculate Conception to at least allow him the illusion that she was sleeping, then threw on her shorts and a tank top and hit the hoop. She had propped up the old transistor, the battery compartment held in place with Scotch tape, against the screen in the kitchen window, and when she paid attention she could hear the voice of Dan Ingram, one of WABC's longtime jockeys, the guy with the leer in his voice, reviewing the golden age of Top 40, year by year. When he got to 1962 he speculated that "The Loco-Motion" wasn't really by the singer listed on the record label, Little Eva, a supposed baby-sitting singing sensation, but rather one of the songwriters, Carole King, in disguise. She thought of how she was still listening to Carole King's mammoth-selling *Tapestry* album way after it was out of fashion, after the punks and the disco queens had kicked the singer-songwriters out of the pop penthouse. In the early '70s, when King and James Taylor and Joni Mitchell and the rest ruled, there hadn't been *any* music in Sib's ears.

From the end of the driveway, she saw her father emerge from down the block, as if on a wave out from the chiaroscuro of traffic and sleepy buildings. His shoulders, still quietly broad and thick from all those years carrying a letter sack, came into focus first, then the fluid stride of his long, unarthritic legs and, as he reached the corner, his wedding ring, meat-and-potatoes gold shooting off a laser of sun. She wondered again how long he was going to keep wearing it. The fingers of his left hand clasped a neatly creased white bakery bag, and *The Daily News* was comfortably tucked under his right arm.

It was her father's day off, but still he had risen early — it was his habit, after years of being one of the first out on his route; no one ever called to complain that Roy Kelly's mail was late being delivered. In an hour he'd managed to go to the stationery store to get the newspaper and to the bakery and almost be home. Daily Mass was usually express, but Sib hoped that maybe just once he'd spend a few extra minutes in the bakery to talk to Mrs. Donovan, whose husband had died five years before and who always threw an extra kaiser roll in his bag, an extra crumb bun on Sundays. His prompt return suggested to Sib that he'd had little more use for flirting with Mrs. Donovan than he would have with the extra roll, which he usually saved until the end of the day and, having not eaten it, wound up breaking apart and throwing to the birds.

"Short homily at the I-Mac, Pop?" Sib said as her father drew near. He was wearing a variation on a theme: navy Windbreaker, light blue button-down shirt, navy- blue T, black knit trousers, Thom McAn oxfords with thick soles, bifocals with black frames. Put a few postal insignias on and he could have been on his route again. All those years of walking had kept him not only fit but well oxygenated. His hair was still a thick, swarthy salt-and-pepper cushion between his scalp and old age. No wonder Mrs. Donovan had the hots for him.

"No homily," he said. "Maybe Father Felix had an 8 a.m. tee time." Roy knew that Father Felix probably couldn't tell a 9-iron from a mashie niblick, probably couldn't pronounce either in his heavy South Asian accent. This was her father's way of being inclusive, of protecting himself from the grumblings among the parish elders about foreign priests, the "Indian incursion" or the "curry suckers" who were taking over South Queens, from the churches to the 7-Elevens. Roy also knew that Father Felix was Sri Lankan, not Indian, but when he listened to neighbors and parishioners rant he had stopped trying to correct them, instead just nodded quietly, partly out of his nonconfrontational nature and partly because, after all the help he got from the neighborhood during the rough patches after the accident, he owed them some tolerance of their bigotry.

Sib considered her father considering her, basketball under her arm, hair drooling rivulets of sweat and secondhand smoke from Whelan's, the pub on North Conduit Avenue — "a bar for young plumbers and electricians," as she once described it to him (to which Roy once replied, "Do they bring their tools?") — where she and her friends had been out the night before. In his eyes she saw her own sagging from lack of sleep. In her mind she wandered the precincts of his that belonged to her, a 21-year-old daughter who had no idea what kind of job she wanted, not that there were many jobs anyway, now that Reagan's honeymoon was over and money was drying up everywhere, and what was her field, anyway — "communications"? And why at her age did she have only male friends? In her-his final disappointing summation, she would probably never get any further in life than the "high twelves" of her SAT scores, which meant she'd be smart enough to survive but never sharp enough to accomplish anything great — or dumb enough to develop some unintellectual talent that would make her rich or save her from some ranch-house fate on Long Island reserved for girls who at her age still lived with their fathers and were virgins and had bodies like coat boxes.

She played this game all the time, just to give her imagination a workout. In reality, as they stood in the shade of the maple at the bottom of the half-sloped driveway and her father wiped the bead of sweat from his own forehead, she was seeing a man looking at an old picture and registering the same reassurance every time. He found that reassurance in her eyes, the same sunset glisten of his mother, or the spaldeen bounce at the back of her tied auburn hair, the same as his wife's, even in its drip-dry condition, or the shy, slowly cracking smile that seemed to reach only halfway then lingered, like her brother's — the smile that was never in a hurry to come or go. It was the look, with only seasonal variations for clothes, setting, temperateness, that she'd seen every day since she'd woken up after the accident, the look that said, "I'm glad you made it."

"Wanna shoot a few, Pop?" she said, firing the ball toward him, knocking *The Daily News* out from under his arm. He caught it with his right hand and, bakery bag still curled in his left, hooked it back to her.

"Sorry, that was your mother's game," he said. Her father had never hesitated to talk about her mother and brother, even during the time when Sib could only read his lips, sort of throwing her into the deep end of grief right away. And now Sib was never knocked off balance by the mention or memory of them.

Her father heard the last few bars of "The Loco-Motion." "That's the one by the baby-sitter, right?" Roy said.

"Yeah, Pop, you big showoff." Her father always did know his history, even musical. And 1962, the year the song came out, was the kind of cakes-and-ale year that was easy on his memory. He was 33. He had a wife and two young kids and a good job and a new home. There was a Catholic in the White House, and the National League had returned to New York. What was there *not* to remember?

"Come in for breakfast when you're ready," he said, then suppressed a smile. "I think I've got an extra roll."

"One day, Roy Kelly, Mrs. Donovan is going to collect for all the extras," Sib shot back.

"Siobhan," he said in mock sternness, "she's a churchgoing woman." He was playing the prude because he knew she expected it.

"So, maybe she'll ask for a biblical exchange. You know, a roll for a roll."

Roy's back was to her now and she couldn't see him blush, the same blush he gave her mother when she first saw him playing baseball in the money leagues on a field of cement and weeds, just back from Korea and a solid .280 first baseman, and complimented his swing. They were married two years later, after a courtship spent in the city's sports arenas, and 11 months after that her brother, Kieran, was born.

Sib headed back up the driveway behind her father and watched him go in the detached garage behind the hoop. She never followed him into the garage; it was a place she could only explore alone, because the grief, which was diffuse enough now most everywhere else, still grew like ivy behind her father's neat rows of tools and drawers of nails and nuts and bolts and stacks of grass seed and fertilizer. The nails where the bicycles had hung had receded into the wall, and you could still see the rusting heads, like little pimples that couldn't be expunged no matter how you pulled and picked and scrubbed.

She heard her father put down the bakery bag and the paper and rattle something from its resting place.

"What are you doing, Pop?" she called from the side door of the house.

"Just pulling out the trowel. Maybe I'll get to those cracks today."

Sib rolled the basketball back into the garage, grabbed the radio and headed up to shower. By the time she got into the bathroom, the WABC recap was up to 1970, and when Sib heard the song the D.J.s were playing to represent that year, she shuddered and flipped the radio off. All these years later, she still couldn't stand to hear it. She turned on the shower and hoped that the noise and hard stream of water from the showerhead would wash away those first few sickening bars of the song. By the time she was finished and turned the radio back on, WABC was safely into the mid-'70s.

3. Queens, N.Y., Late Spring 1982

It was Andy Logan's first day off in weeks, and as he lay in his boxers and stretched his calves, long, solid, husklike ovals he had developed from years of running on soccer pitches, under the top sheet, he remembered that early Saturday morning at the seminary — where he went several years ago for a weekend "exploratory" retreat — when, with no meetings or prayer groups and time to run across the open fields, losing himself in the endless space in front, behind, on either side of him, the space to spare, it felt like the devil's naptime.

Birdsong was trilling softly now, nudging him out of slumber, and he felt a lazy breeze floating through his garage apartment in Bellerose, in the kind of neighborhood where things happened, it seemed, on an alternate soundstage. Bellerose was part of Queens but just a Frisbee toss and a tailwind away from the Long Island suburbs. Lawns were mowed, sidewalks repaved, Little League games played, Christmas trees decorated or menorahs lit, everything in tidy squares and the occasional relaxed curves, with a minimum of noise or mess. Andy rented from a middle-aged couple whose kids, two boys and a girl, or maybe two girls and a boy, like the town itself, were a bit phantom, now-you-see-them-now-you-don't, the bikes in the driveway sometimes there, sometimes not, their kid noise coming through on a damper pedal. This apartment, this neighborhood, were a good fit for an undercover cop or a single guy or a 360-days-a-year librarian or recovering somebody or anybody really who didn't want too many questions asked.

A few rosebushes were in full bloom under Andy's window, and their fragrance was commingling with his man-scents and the lingering fragrance of Dial soap. He'd showered before he went to bed, something he never did when he had to work the next day. On workdays he wanted to wake up and smell the assignment behind him, which gave him a leg up, at least in mind-set, on the assignment ahead. But with the smoke and the stale beer and the sweat from the bars and discos he'd been circling and casing on Northern Boulevard gone, the scruff shaved away and circled down the drain in his bathroom sink, the smells were rousing him. His right hand wandered down the treasure trail to his navel and grazed the small tuft of chestnut-brown hair on his stomach, then started under the waistband of his boxers. This was something else he never did while he was on call, but now that he was off for a few days, he could relax.

Before he could really get started, though, her face came back into his mind. He'd filed it away, put it on a kind of constant snooze alarm, while he was finishing his assignment that day in Midtown a few weeks ago, but now it met him again as if by appointment. He hadn't been able to figure out why he thought he recognized that strange woman in the subway — the tumblers had been only half falling, the way they did at precinct functions or family reunions when he backslapped and glad-handed colleagues or distant relatives whose faces he sort of knew but whose names deserted him, like calculus equations after he'd taken the A.P. test and gotten his course credit.

After he thought about her for a few minutes that morning in bed, though, something clicked. It couldn't be, he thought. What would *she* be doing there, on the streets of Midtown alone, no sign of a retinue or autograph hounds or flunkies or shields? Surely if it had been she, somebody else in New York besides him would be on her tail. He'd lost track of her while he was in college and hadn't heard her on the radio in a while. Still, she was about the most popular singer around for a few years when Andy was in high school. And, Andy thought at the time, the finest. A voice so low and so clear, so pure and yet broken somehow. Full of youth and vigor and yet older than dirt, hope and despair fighting to a draw. Utterly guileless. A voice with space in front, behind, on either side of it. A voice with space to spare. Someone like her wouldn't be so accessible on the street. Famous people, even the ones not trying to be incognito, still had enough invisible force fields around them, transmitting from a friend, a dog with a long leash, an attitude. Her defenses, he thought, had too many cracks in them. But when he was face to face with her, he was so distracted by the boniness, the spectral projection of her, that he never quite made the connection.

Andy got out of bed and, still in his bare feet and boxers, padded over to the hall closet. His bachelor flat was small and well swept, clear open lines and pathways in seemingly every direction. A couple of bookshelves, a narrow sofa, a solid, uncomplicated remnant, in deep leagues of indigo, on the floor in front of it, a crystal vase that he always cleaned but almost never filled on

his small oak dining table. On a side table, a 3-by-5 picture of
his parents — both schoolteachers, retired in Florida now — on
their honeymoon in the Catskills, his father full-haired but still
studious in glasses and a car coat, his mother with a wavy coif and
lipstick that shone even in the black-and-white tones. His cupboards, like everything else in his place, were roomy, half stocked
with bachelor food: cereal, soup, tuna fish, boxes of pasta and Irish
tea. Beer and milk and O.J. that stood unclustered in the fridge.
Across from the couch in the living room there was a decent sound
system that his parents gave him for his 16th birthday, ahead of its
time in that it was components and not one of those tinny-sound-
ing things that folded up like a suitcase. The linen-white walls
were empty and unstained and warm.

From the closet he pulled out a box of albums and singles he'd had
since he was a teenager. He didn't buy records that often anymore,
but he took care of the ones he did have, and he had carted them
all with him over the years. Looking at record collections was for
him still better than looking through one of his yearbooks or photo
albums, so vested were these records with memories; his included
More of the Monkees (sixth grade and a tall, dark young dynamo of
a teacher named Mr. Marino); *Blood Sweat and Tears* (pimples and
his first jockstrap); *No Secrets* (while the guys at school fixated on
the subject of "You're So Vain" and on Carly Simon's pokey nipples,
he was taken by the jazzy, elegant chords of "The Right Thing to
Do"). As he flipped through the albums, with worn spines but otherwise in mint-minus condition, he got almost to the end before he
found the ones he wanted. They were by the only artist, a girl-boy
duo, with two entries in his collection. One had a silver-and-blue
cover and the two of them in a wedding-like picture on the cover,
her dress lacy, his hair shaggy but somehow kempt. The other one
had a flap, all the same color, with just the duo's name — their family name, as they were brother and sister — stamped on the front in
a curvy logo. Andy jokingly used to call it the "Tan Album," mock-

ing not it but the Beatles' "White Album," which he never liked. Too unfocused and weird for its own sake. Too strung out.

Thinking of the "White Album" distracted Andy from the woman for a few minutes, bringing him back to a Christmas Eve when he was about 13 and hanging out with his cousin Tom, who was a few years older, with stringy blond hair, a thin but flabby frame, a hippie in waiting. Their families had just come back from Midnight Mass. "God, wasn't that endless?" Tom said. "All that stink from the incense. And the folding chairs" — when they got to the church, all the pews were already filled with the once-or-twice-a-year Catholics, whom the pastor, Father Monaghan, called "the irregulars." So Andy and Tom and their families had to sit way in the back on metal chairs with worn padding on the seats and kneelers. "I still have a dent in my ass," Tom said, and then pulled a flask from his back pocket and offered Andy a swig.

"No, thanks," Andy said, neutrally, no syllable emphasized, no judgment passed, wondering though if it was really the flask that caused the dent.

"Smoke?" Tom said. Again Andy declined. "Weed?" Tom said. "C'mon, there's got to be at least one vice there. I know, you must jerk off by now." Andy had in fact started having wet dreams — "nocturnal emissions," his health teacher called them, and when his mother started seeing the stains in his underwear when she did the laundry, she told Andy's father that it was time for "the talk." Which consisted of Andy's father saying to him, one fall day when they were out raking leaves, "How's your hygiene?"

"It's fine, Dad."

"Good, keep it that way."

Cousin Tom wouldn't let the matter drop. "If you don't jerk off yet, you will soon. By the time I was your age I was up to like, four times a day. Hey, you want to rub one out now? We probably have time before breakfast."

Tom slid his hand down between his legs, threw his head back and started a slow, stoned stroke. Andy felt a rustling underneath his dress pants. But he didn't want to defile Christmas by masturbating with his cousin. And he was more interested at that moment in Tom's record collection, a small aisle of albums jutting out on the side of his bed. "Mind if I flip through these?" Andy said. It was mostly trippy stuff — the Doors, Iron Butterfly, Janis Joplin, Sly and the Family Stone. An occasional Supremes or Temptations collection. And of course, the "White Album."

"Janis Joplin, I saw her on *The Ed Sullivan Show*," Andy said. "She's kind of a screamer."

"Oh, brother, she's the blues, the truth," Tom said. "You'll see, when you get older, after you start smoking weed and wanking regularly." Andy, though, much preferred Dusty Springfield, the British pop singer who had a hit out then called "A Brand New Me," all low lights and gently lapping voice, as opposed to, say, Joplin's overhead, overheated glare. He thought about trying to explain that to Tom, but by then Andy could smell the bacon frying and his mother's cinnamon rolls heating up in the oven downstairs. "I'm going to eat," he said, leaving Tom rubbing his crotch and going on about the blues, the truth.

Andy lost track of Tom when he disappeared into Canada a few years later to outrun the draft.

Andy opened the flap of the "Tan Album," and there was the idyllic sunbeamy-meadowy shot of the two of them. He studied the woman, standing behind the man. "Geez, it couldn't have been her," he said out loud. "She's too big, too full-faced." He figured that the woman he'd seen in Manhattan a few weeks back would had to have lost almost a quarter of her body weight to have actually been the singer. But something made him look again. *Maybe*. Then he stared at the album with the silver-and-blue cover; still, he still wasn't sure.

He pulled the record out of the silver-and-blue jacket, untouched for years in its inner sleeve, put it on the turntable, returned to his bedroom and crawled back under the sheets, picking up where he left off, his hand working in the tempos of the songs on that first side. He started in the small, soft thicket of his chest hair, carpeting pectorals that were solid platforms beneath, pushing his fingers through along with the passionate cleanliness of the album's opener, a big hit single, featuring a vibrant tambourine, then gaining even more steam next with the bubbly but short Latin number, slowing down for the seaside ballad, gathering some momentum again with the perky countryish tune and the goofy Beatles cover, until he came to the last song, the one that started it all for them, and, in a way, for him. It was the song that he had hummed or whistled to himself over the years in locker rooms — high school, college, police academy — as he absent-mindedly cast, or had cast upon him, sidelong glances.

His morning fullness now couldn't hold out much longer. Andy waited for the second verse, so that what was happening in his bed would be the opposite of what was happening in the song: stars shooting back into the sky.

By now the devil was out cold.

4. Queens, N.Y., Summer 1982

The good sisters would be at table, sometimes two, sometimes three, sometimes all four, dispensing their advice for living a clean life, for being closer to God:

"If you die within 24 hours of Easter, you go right to heaven."

"Everything was fine until they moved to Linden Boulevard."

"If only he'd left 15 minutes sooner."

"Ask the Little Flower."

"You have to cut the corned beef across the grain."

"Sundays you get a break from Lent."

"She thought Social Security was Welfare."

"Don't ever drive through Bethpage."

"It happened because he ate meat on Good Friday."

"Why would *The Enquirer* print it if it wasn't true?"

"It happened because they had relations during Lent."

"We buy only Ronzoni and Bumble Bee and Boar's Head."

"Is that Carmen Miranda?"

"Her husband was very sick."

"We always went to the mountains."

"That house in Ditmas must be worth a quarter of a million now."

"That's not music nowadays. I don't know what to call it, but it sure isn't music."

"It's in God's hands."

"If only. . . ."

The sisters who dispensed these morsels of experience and wisdom were the Rooneys — Sib and Kieran's mother, Genie, and their aunts, Maddy, Constance and Bern — and the kids had heard variations of them practically all their lives, spoken in one or the other's kitchens over individual chalices of beer and consecrated bowls of pretzels. Sib called them the aunts' greatest hits, and in fact they had become repeated, almost chanted, played and replayed and drilled down to their barest grooves, so often that the original context was frequently lost. Some of them stood on their own — Ronzoni and Bumble Bee and Boar's Head (and Hellmann's), always. But who had moved to Linden Boulevard? Who owned the house in Ditmas, and why was it lost? Who had the willies about Bethpage, a town on Long Island? Carmen Miranda, they knew, was the default response whenever some Latiny-sounding woman was on TV. "Is that Carmen Miranda?" came a voice from the kitchen. But mostly these life lessons were spoken with little or no back or front story, caught on the fly as Sib and Kieran and maybe their cousins passed through. For Sib it was like how the words "supreme" or "shangri-la" evoked the names of singing groups, how "avocado" was a paint color, the words detached from their original meanings. Kieran had two names for them — the Incauntations; the Commauntments.

After the litany, the sisters would often break into song. Some ancient thing like "Sidewalks of New York" that would inspire giggles and eye rolls from Sib and Kieran. Sib didn't giggle anymore, though, at the thought of those old songs; she knew that someday Barry White and Donna Summer would be in heavy rotation at nursing homes, favorites at the Saturday-night wheelchair roller-disco party.

The sisters' voices were going through Sib's head as she was getting dressed up for the first time since graduation, readying herself for what she had been dreading: a round of job-seeking in Manhattan. Where was the Commauntment to get her through that, putting on makeup and a skirt and nail polish when she would rather be shooting hoops? Aunt Bern, who at some point worked at the cosmetics counter in Alexander's department store, once tried to give her some tips — go light, start from the inside and work out, "Just like tossing a salad," her happy-go-lucky husband, Uncle Billy, would chime in — but Sib always treated the eyeliner brush or the pancake puff like a lacrosse stick, and so her face, on the rare occasions when she did wear makeup, was always raining colors. She didn't have too much more success, either, at least in her own eyes, with clothes. For someone who excelled at anything physical, who could run a six-and-a-half-minute mile and sink 100 consecutive foul shots and dig sizzling ground balls deep out of the hole at short and fire them to first, she was all thumbs when it came to putting on a dress. In her mind the dresses always clung, accenting, underlining, she thought, her thick frame, while sports always made the awareness of it go away. Aunt Maddy often bought her frilly clothes for Christmas and told her she'd grow out of this discomfort with all the "feminine pleasures." But Maddy's gifts almost always stayed in the boxes. Sib had even worn gym shorts under her First Communion dress.

Once Sib got to high school, her father would take her to a mall on Long Island, where there was a store that sold clothes for bigger-framed girls. They would have dinner on a weeknight and then drive out; she told him she wanted to go then so that she didn't have to waste their Saturdays. But she knew that by going at that time of the week and night, she probably wouldn't run into any of the girls from school. Her father went along with the ruse, but he knew.

Three of the sisters were gone now. Maddy from a stomach cancer that was discovered too late. "If only she'd gone to the doctor sooner." Bern, found dead in her bed one morning of unspecified causes, though at the wake Sib heard someone say it was a broken heart. "If only Uncle Billy hadn't left." And her mother. *If only.* . . . Just Constance, who never married, was left, in her late 70s and retired for decades from the phone company and still in Brooklyn. "Live a little less when you're young," Sib could hear her saying, as if someone had dialed "O" for life advice and she were dispensing another Commauntment, "and you'll live a little more later." Or as if Constance's early investments of virtue, of talc and cabbage and the daily Rosary, of avoiding Bethpage, were now paying the dividends of dotage.

Sib hadn't slept much, again, the night before, the normal insomnia compounded by the job-search stress. Reruns of *Mary Tyler Moore*, *The Uncle Floyd Show*, a few chapters of *East of Eden* got her through most of the night, but now she could see the damage in her eyes, the premature droop, for that time of day, for her age. "The radio," Sib thought, usually the universal cure; in those first months after her hearing came back years ago, even the static between the stations had a symphonic ring.

But these days the radio was letting her down. WABC, the great musical behemoth of her youth, was gone now. The FM stations were all stratified: synthy Brit stuff or post-disco reductionist dance-soul or soulless rock or adult contemporary. "Ebony and Ivory"? Lame.

Toto? All pop and no fizz. "Don't You Want Me?" A nice beat but overall a big drone. Sib turned and turned and turned the dial with one hand, blow-dryer in the other, as she searched for something to help her wake up. Finally she landed on one of the more recent songs that she really loved: "Forget Me Nots," by a jazzy R & B singer named Patrice Rushen. There were so few black artists on the radio now, and practically none on MTV, the new video channel. Was this all still part of the disco backlash? Sib once almost caused a riot at Whelan's when she filled in for her friend Larry, the D.J., during a bathroom/weed break and played one Earth, Wind & Fire and two Michael Jackson songs in a row. "What's with this nigger shit?" one of the locals, whose name was Tuke, shouted across the foosball table that abutted the D.J. booth. So when Larry came back he threw on the Who's "Eminence Front" and a couple of Zeppelin tunes, hard-rock sedatives, savage soothers. Sib had heard there would be a new Michael Jackson album at the end of the year, but she couldn't imagine he'd be able to top his last one, *Off the Wall,* most of which she thought was brilliant. And in spite of its success only a couple of years ago, there was now enforced apartheid on the radio, at clubs, even in crappy bars like Whelan's. She was skeptical about the new album's messianic potential.

If the job hunt went well that day, Sib thought, she would stop at one of her favorite record stores in Manhattan, Downstairs, on 43rd Street, and pick up "Forget Me Nots." As she headed out the door in her one interview outfit — a green top, black denim skirt, sneakers that she would change out of when she got close to the employment agency — she saw that her father had left her a $20 bill on the kitchen counter. She thought, I can't keep sponging off Dad, and started down the stairs and out the back door. But then she took a glance back at the 20. "Well, in case of an emergency," she said to herself, and went back into the kitchen and scooped it up like one of those hot grounders to short.

5. New York City, Summer 1982

She didn't really miss food. At least not the way she did when she was a teenager or in the early years of their career when she was on a forever diet. Back then it seemed as if she were surveilled by it. She'd have her Tabs and salads with low-fat dressing and dry turkey sandwiches on "lite" bread but could still always feel the presence of pepperoni pizza or cheeseburgers lurking around the corner. Every comma and quotation mark she saw in a book or magazine curled into a pop-top from a Coke can. She couldn't even look at the stars without thinking of food — the Big Dipper was the name of a sundae at an ice-cream shoppe when she was a kid back east.

But now it — eating — was just another phase she had passed through, and that was why relearning it was so hard. She couldn't, she figured, be the eater she had been any more than she could be the teenager she had been or the amateur musician she had been, or the married woman that she would stop being very soon. It was only when her doctors in L.A. told her she'd be dead by the time she was 40 that she finally agreed to seek treatment. And even then she only half believed them. Six months of therapy had passed, and while she had mostly kicked the laxatives — she'd gotten up to 40 a day at one point — she could still only nibble and pick at meals. Food was still as far behind her as jumpers and bangs and acne and training bras and the Best New Artist award and white lace and promises. But she'd try to relearn. She always was a good team player.

While her nose was still the best early warning for the proximity of food, the canary in the canary's coal mine, there were some smells of the city that she loved, especially the unexpected ones. Once while she was wandering the theater district, she discovered a lumberyard and was shocked to find the same piney scent of wood shavings and freshly cut 2-by-4s and feel, smack in the urban canyon, that same edge-of-town thrill of the lumberyards of her youth. In Greenwich Village she discovered a barbershop with a bench and small garden out front, but it wasn't the scent of the blooming hyacinths in cement planters that held her; it was the limey, musky aroma of lathers and tonics and pomades, the bracing, uncomplicated power of maleness, so unlike the prissy, sudsy smell of beauty parlors. It was the smell of the bathroom early in the morning after the father had finished — he was always the first in, before the women and the late-rising brother. It was the smell that often welcomed the day for her when she was young. Once or twice she got into Carnegie Hall off-hours, late morning or early afternoon, and there it was: the smell of emptiness that she liked best as she sat in one of the upper boxes, the direct path of the blunt varnish to her nose, that took her back to the couple of times she was actually on that stage, about a decade ago, at the peak of her and the brother's career. Their manager had advised against the booking, suggesting that they stick to venues in the suburbs, that New York City had no use for them and they had no use for New York City. But they voted him down — hadn't they had five Top 5 singles in a row on WABC, New York's big Top 40 radio station? Didn't New York have a Republican mayor, even if he was a turncoat? (She often thought of the brother and herself as rock 'n' roll wolves in easy-listening clothing anyway.) They sold out two nights.

But the smell she loved most came from record stores. Not the Disc-o-mats and Record Explosions whose inventory and clerks' knowledge were only a few months' deep, redolent of shrink-wrap and fluorescence. She preferred the oldies shops, like Golden Disc on Bleecker or Downstairs Records on 43rd, dim and deep wood-lined hulks. These stores sold mostly used records, and so their stock was smoked with the cedar of countless closets, infused with the fumes of countless garages, soaked with the mildew of countless basements, just like her own, where they kept the suitcases that they'd unzip once a year and then become revived by the fresh mustiness of the shore, the smelling salts of imminent vacation.

She usually went at lunchtime, which took her mind off the fact that she was supposed to be eating, and in fact she'd arrange her visits like a meal. For an appetizer she'd have a plateful of Manny, the muscular Puerto Rican dance-music expert at Downstairs, who was always stationed at his turntables in front of the store, like a carny barker in a tight black T and tattoos and a large, loud gold crucifix, trying to entice her into a calliope of rap or electronica. She never paid him much mind, until one day he caught her tapping on her leg the rhythm of Afrika Bambaataa's "Planet Rock" — *bop bop ba-da-da dop* — which he was spinning at the time, and locked his eyes on hers.

"Hey, Slim," he said, all 20-year-old brio, "turn that cap around and scuff up those shoes and you can come to one of my house parties."

She smiled, but offered no reply. Sure, she had mastered the rhythm. But she missed the melody.

She would next step down into the main room, as big as a small banquet hall, with records filling the carrels and bins on the floor and crates piled up in columns. Her next course was always the current-45s wall, where she admired the orderly, alphabetical slots, labeled and dated, like bread wrappers or milk cartons, showing when a record entered the store and suggesting when it might expire into oldies status. Then she would move to the bins on the floor, also partitioned into neat, farmlike rows by artist. That was the real status in this store: dated, vintage.

She didn't really recognize many of the new songs; most of her life she usually just liked whatever the brother did. Now she was trying to cultivate her own taste, and so she pulled out records by people she knew — the latest of her friend L., which was ending its Top 10 run and continuing her recent sexy makeover, and then something called "Tainted Love," because it had been on the charts for months. She took the latter song over to the public turntable in the corner and put it on; more bleepy piddling, another dronish vocal. She had a particular distaste for the programmed drums.

But the new songs, too, were a pre-course. It was the oldies bins she was interested in, one section in particular. But just as she would have to clean her plate before she could get to dessert when she was a kid, she flipped through hundreds of 45s before she got to the section she wanted, rubbing shoulders with the suited men, usually in their late 20s and early 30s, who were there for 45s to fill their basement jukeboxes with songs from their glory days, before marriage and kids and commuter tickets, Beach Boys and Stones and the occasional Motown reissue; gawky older men in severe specs who looked like Steve Allen and forlornly pawed the pre-rock vo-

calist section, the Bing Crosbys and June Christys and Louis Pri-
mas, from the era before everything went "off the cliff"; the tubby
savants with hairless faces and stained T-shirts and instant recall of
every Lesley Gore and Orlons B-side, down to the playing times
and the catalog numbers and musicians and recording-session dates
and catering menus. ("Brenda of the Exciters ate jerk chicken before the session for 'Tell Him.' That's why it sizzles so.") And then
there were the ponytailed, cowboy-booted customers with tobac-
co-stained fingernails and short stacks of Merle Haggard and Er-
nest Tubb and the Statler Brothers records at their sides.

But she always kept one eye on the '70s-groups section, to see
if anybody else lingered to finger the green sleeves whose heavy-
weight paper seemed to convey status on the records they encased,
offering a layer of protection that the flimsy sleeves on the new releases couldn't provide, much as her bulky sweaters did for her. The
few times she'd been in the store before, she'd never seen anybody
spending much time in that section and made her way to it unim-
peded. Even before she got there, she could tell generally from a
distance if the section she always checked looked smaller, and when
it didn't, she still flipped through one by one, like an accountant
poring over rows of numbers. The tallies in her head — someone
must have bought one — and the tallies that the section yielded just
never did reconcile.

There weren't many rarities in that section: an odd side effect
of all the group's records being hits, or at least big enough to get
through one or two pressings. And enough time hadn't passed for
them to be nostalgia or camp. Still, she counted them hopefully
each time, slowing down when she got into the 20s, hoping her
fingers would surprise her and there'd be one less than 27, the total
she counted the last time. She'd even rearrange them, like rotating
stock or crops anywhere else: first chronologically, then in order of
their peak chart positions, and then in order of her own preference,
which meant that the huskier vocals on the earlier songs (which

were also the group's biggest hits) were shunted to the back ("they just sound so lumpy," she once told the brother), while the more recent, lighter vocals, eminently preferable to her ears (but also their smallest hits), were pushed up front. No matter how she arranged them, the count was always the same: 27.

Today the store was crowded, so much so that, as she feigned her usual interest in the new 45s and stared at that week's *Billboard* chart, posted on the wall, as if it were hieroglyphics, she didn't notice that someone else was at her station. As she made her way around the island on the floor and toward the section, she finally saw the young woman in the sneakers and the denim skirt and figured she must be looking for something else: Canned Heat, maybe? The Captain & Tennille? Eric Carmen? But with each pass the young woman hadn't budged, and so she became a little bolder, and looked a little closer, and realized that the woman was stalled in her very own section. Who was she? She took inventory: The girl's shoulders were as broad and solid as a harness, with that backpack slung over her almost as big as a guitar. Her calves popped through her pantyhose, and one time around, she saw the thick fingers flipping through every one of the 45s, lingering, considering, holding them up to the light of her standards. From the opposite side of the table she stole quick glances at the girl's face, but with the girl's eyes suddenly downcast and set on the records, she could see only the smudged daubs of rouge and the runny mascara. Her third time around she noticed the girl was clutching one 45, massaging it almost, and when she craned her neck to see which one it was she didn't notice her charm bracelet getting caught on the woman's backpack.

6. Queens, N.Y., Summer, 1982

"Chiffon Kelly!"

Sib was sitting at the end of the bar at Whelan's, cradling a Michelob, her change from her dad's $20 sitting on the bar, still in her interview get-up, a bit wrinkled and wilted from a long day on subways and city streets, a stressed wall in need of shoring up, "Forget Me Nots" in her backpack, when she heard the voice emerging from the glare of the open door at the front of the bar and, as the door closed, the silhouette filling in as it moved closer and the bar got dark again.

"Timmy Sweeney, where'd you slither in from?" He was a year younger than Sib, home from Bates, working in a bank for the summer but knowing that he still had another year to delay real life, maybe more if he went to grad school. Though they'd grown apart a bit since Timmy went away to college, Sib never minded hanging with him or the fact that he always called her "Chiffon." It was one of the few intentional manglings of her name that she could stand, unlike "Chevron," "Chevy Van," "Shiver," "Sit On." And that was because she loved the old '60s group the Chiffons. Their big No. 1 hit "He's So Fine" was one of the first 45s she could remember being downstairs in the rec room, Kieran's record, signified by his perfectly stenciled "KK" on the back label. The song's "doo-lang" refrain was an essential part of her early language, among her second tier of learned words, once she got past "Daddy" and "Mommy" and "Keen," her toddlerhood name for Kieran.

But three years had transfigured Timmy: Once the neighborhood's chubby, nerdy outcast, he was thin and scythelike now, the pointy ears no longer a deformity but the final touch on a budding artist's tableau that also included vintage sport coats and fuchsia Chuck Taylors, the occasional beret with a well-placed sine wave of red flowing out from the front. He had figured something out after all, had stopped trying to define himself by what he wasn't. Whelan's for him was usually just a way station for him to the Crop, a club that played Romeo Void and Yaz and other cool-kid music. Timmy Sweeney, a cool kid. Go figure. Every now and then one of the meatheads at Whelan's, a few beers into the night, would mutter, "Look at this freak," whenever Timmy came in on his way to or from the Crop, older versions of the taunters from the school hallways and playgrounds. But those kinds of comments just rolled off cool Timmy, who moved now with a wiry-springy grace. And best of all, Sib thought, he did it without turning his back on where he came from, without becoming a dick.

Another thing Sib liked about Timmy was that after the accident, he was one of her few friends not to ladle on the pity, not to treat her like the girl with the dead brother and mother. He seemed to realize that the sad smiles and the hands-off treatment and the awkward avoidances in the halls were really just a more polite, and therefore crueler, kind of ostracism, just a different way of rendering you the ultimate freak. He even signed with her a few times, though, during the years when she couldn't hear, Sib "functioned as a hearing person," as her doctors called it, because she could read lips and imagine, from the years before the accident, what voices sounded like and so she never signed that much.

"Please, today I am Duncan," Timmy said as he pulled up the stool next to Sib's.

"Diva, doomed king or yo-yo?" Sib said.

"Buyer's choice," Timmy replied, eyeing the three fives and two singles sitting next to Sib's coaster. "I'll be whoever you want me to be for a quaff."

"Forget it, Sweeney," Sib said, clamping her hand on the cash and drawing it closer to her. "That's gotta last me all week. You're the one with the job. You should be buying me another round."

"Fair enough," Timmy said. "Barkeep, another round for the lady and your finest mead for me."

"Yes, sire," said the bartender, Dom, a short, handsome Italian in his early 20s, who had good hands and an officious smile, and was quick over the bar when anyone got a little too friendly. He'd been the regular Friday-night bartender since before he got out of college, had his eye on the Fire Department test but wasn't in any hurry. The money, the hours, the girls were just too good for now. A lot of the other guys he graduated with, regular patrons of Whelan's, already had jobs driving for UPS or Frito-Lay or hauling something or other with their fathers' construction companies, but they weren't married yet, so they had plenty of beer money and the beginnings of spare tires, foreshadowings of the next 50 years. But Dom ran and lifted and played flag football on Sunday nights in Queens and Long Island, had held onto his senior-year body. The seed could wait. Sib sometimes went to see him play. He, too, still had time to figure real life out. "Another one, Sib?"

"What, oh, no, Dom, I'm good," she said. Sib had barely drunk half of her beer, and a lot of what was left was backwash. She didn't really like beer; it was one of the few guy things she didn't take to, or maybe she was just remembering all the glasses of Schaefer her mother and her aunts used to down at the kitchen tables. So she would order one and then nurse it most of the night. She knew Dom would let her sit there as long as she wanted; it was in between happy hour and the night crowd anyway, and she was just killing time before going home to catch the Mets game with her dad.

"When are you gonna let me play flag football with your team?" Sib said.

"Ha, you'd be better than a lot of those All-Stars," he said and moved down toward one of them waving a bill around at the other end of the bar. "Come on out some Sunday and we'll see if we can get you in."

"I'd like to pull out one of your flags," Timmy said, not quite so out of Dom's earshot.

"*Shh*," Sib warned Timmy, though she knew Dom, decent guy that he was, didn't mind. It was just a general warning for Timmy to remember where he was, to not drive through Bethpage. Yet Sib also couldn't help admiring him for having figured that out, too.

"So, Chiff, what's the sitch?" Timmy said.

"I was pretending to be an adult finally, in the city looking for a job," Sib said, recalling the crowded airless employment offices she'd been in and out of all day, being reviewed by corpulent, emphysemic women in pastel-colored pantsuits whose main qualification seemed to be the ability to make people wait, fill out forms, take tests. One woman told her she was a good proofreader but a poor typist, another told her she was a good typist but a poor proofreader.

"Any luck?" Timmy asked. "Any prospects for the next great music critic, sportswriter, muse?"

Sib laughed. "Nah, not much out there. Thank you, Ronnie R. One woman even said to me, 'Oh, and before I can even consider forwarding your résumé to a potential employer, you've *got* to do something about your attire. Sneakers'" — Sib had forgotten to put on the flats in her backpack and so still had on her running shoes — "'and a denim skirt? That will never fly in an office.'" A small window had been open next to the woman's cluttered desk, and Sib could hear some salsa music floating up through the heat. She had felt like saying, "Is that Carmen Miranda?" but instead she just thanked the woman and moved on to the next employment office, with an occasional assurance that she'd get a call if something opened up. Finally, after three or four of these agencies, she headed to Downstairs.

"Well, I, for one, love the look," Timmy said, drawing a cigarette from a pack of Salems with two tinelike fingers, almost beckoning it toward him. "Celery and chocolate" — he waved toward Sib's top and hair, now out of its ponytail and falling over her shoulder. "There's a lot of summer in that look."

Summer. Here it was, the first summer of her official adult life, and she'd been trying to draw a bead on it all day: Would it be like 1969, the last summer they were all together on vacation and man was on the moon and the Mets were practically as ascendant and they got caught in the Woodstock traffic on their way back from the mountain resort they went to every year; or would it be like 1974, the first summer after her hearing had come back but after all the hoopla of her recovery had died down, when she and her father could finally try to start their lives over again; or worse, would it be like that summer of the accident, or any of the silent summers that followed? "Geez," Sib thought. "I've turned into a nostalgist. I shouldn't live like I'm an oldies station." The state of music, so often a barometer of her emotions, wasn't helping matters. And the Mets, rebuilding now for the fifth or sixth year in a row after the disaster of letting Seaver go right before the brutal summer of '77, weren't, either.

And yet, she entered Downstairs Records that day with some small filament of hope. As desultory as pop music was these days, there was still the occasional gem like "Forget Me Nots." Sib also really loved Squeeze's "Black Coffee in Bed," which she knew would be far too literate to get Top 40 play, and there was a new Melissa Manchester song, "You Should Hear How She Talks About You," that was hitting her ears the right way. Though even that was just a good girl-group pastiche by a B-plus singer (she laughed when she heard that Toto played on it; she liked them much better as a studio backup band). Just where had all the great female singers gone? No wonder Top 40 was in the doldrums. Female singers usually got the best songs, and now there weren't that many good ones around to sing them anymore, so they weren't being written. Sib and Larry, the D.J. at Whelan's who also wanted to be a record producer, had decided that whoever found the next great female voice could basically print his or her own money.

Sib had been wandering around the store and as usual found herself in front of the same section, thumbing again through the 30 or so singles there. Why was she still so drawn to that group's section every time? That was really the nostalgist in her that she couldn't bear the most. She looked at the arrangement of the singles: chronological order again, with the droopy Beatles' cover in front and then, in spot No. 2, the song that started everything. It was the song that she had disagreed with Kieran about, the song that was No. 1 that day, the last song they heard together.

Sib yanked the 45 out of its place, as if calling it into account. She rubbed her index finger around the center hole over and over until she almost cut herself and then picked it up with two hands and squeezed and pressed her palms so hard against the sides that the record almost shattered. Then she forwarded to that other song, the one that was No. 1 and playing on the radio on the day her hearing came back. The joy of sound, so suddenly returned to her after more than three years, was undercut by the bitterness of that voice, still so sweet and sickly to her ears. The group had other hits in between, and to Sib those two songs were like bookends of misery from those years. She gathered up all of those other hits and poked her fingers through them and shook them and squeezed them tight into the bottoms of their heavy green wrappers, until one of the store clerks started giving her looks. But one thing she never did was play them on the public turntable. Not one. In fact, she'd never heard all those in-between big hits. She hadn't been able to when they were first popular, and later when she got her hearing back she simply changed the radio station if one of them came on. Good thing most of her friends were boys, who wouldn't be caught dead with one of those records anyway. And then the group disappeared after a few years, and their songs weren't played so much. But she still couldn't bring herself to listen to them.

Sib was getting ready to pull herself away from the section and go to the register to pay for "Forget Me Nots" when she had a vague notion that someone was walking in circles around the carrel, a slight figure who seemed to be a woman. But with a baseball cap covering the hair and the Ray-Bans and no discernible cleavage, Sib couldn't tell at first, until the person passed and had her back to Sib, and she could see the wide hips that seemed to have been assembled onto the wrong chassis, a Buick trunk on a Datsun. Even so, Sib had her city-girl elbows ready to jab, just in case the woman tried something. You couldn't trust anyone these days.

The last time the woman passed, something got caught on Sib's backpack. It was the woman's bracelet, which seemed to have little gold records on it. As the woman tried to untangle herself, she kept her head down and seemed to mumble something that sounded like, "Are you going to buy that record?"

"*Buy* it?" Sib said as she turned back toward the carrel to pull herself free from the bracelet. "I'd rather burn it." As she turned back toward the woman, she said, "Here, you can have it," but by then the woman was scurrying out of the store. "Weird," Sib thought. "Even the record store isn't safe." But then, Sib had known that for years.

"Where'd you go, Chiff?"

"What, oh, just thinking about some strange woman I saw in the record store. And generally practicing this whole grown-up thing called stress." Sib looked at the clock behind the bar. It was game time. "Gotta go, Sweeney. Don't take any wooden Duran Durans."

"*Please*," Timmy said. "I should be so lucky."

7. Brooklyn, N.Y., Early 1950s

Genie loved the basement. The burner, the toolboxes, the paint cans, the overalls on a hook. Some man, she thought, must have installed that hulk of a burner, with its pipes and cranks and sliding toggles and tightened-for-life nuts and bolts, its wheezing roar. Some man must have swung the hammer in that toolbox, screwed the screws, turned the wrenches, worn the overalls, slapped that paint on walls somewhere. On top of one paint can there was a pair of tattered boxing gloves, with loose, threadbare laces; somebody, some *man*, must have worn them while sparring, boxing with *another* man, his hands and face and body absorbing and inflicting blows and bloodying *some other man's* face.

But Genie never knew who. Maybe her father, whom she'd never seen. "He's with the angels," was all her mother or sisters would say whenever she'd ask. Some relative or other occasionally chimed in: "Oh, a safe dropped out of a window and landed right next to him, and he went crazy and was never seen again. They put him away somewhere." Somebody else said he had gambled all the family money away or ran whiskey during Prohibition and was exiled to some flophouse. Genie got to the point where she didn't know what to believe, and just stopped asking. There were never any photographs of him.

There was also a brother, much older, who had gone into World War II when Genie was in grammar school. When he came back, Genie went to embrace him, and he pushed her away, saying, "I don't know who you are." For a few weeks he just sat in a corner strumming a guitar. He was supposed to give her sister Bern away at her wedding, but never showed up. "Oh, he was a guard at the Nuremberg trials and went crazy hearing all that horrible stuff," her sister Maddy's husband, a cigar-smoking, braces-wearing soda salesman named Charlie, said. After that, he, too, disappeared from the family photo albums, had his name erased from the family Bible.

It was a Sunday afternoon, and Genie, still in her church clothes, was taking deep inhales of all this phantom maleness in the basement, a few shards of sun poking through the window wells, the air dank and boozy, like some gin mill out on the avenue during St. Patrick's Day season, which in her neighborhood started around Valentine's Day and practically lasted till Easter, itself a male thing. She walked over to one of the walls, stepped out of her dress and good shoes and, in her bra, girdle and stockings, pulled the overalls off the hook and put them on. She was top-heavy, the most buxom of the sisters, with a rounder, less stately frame than the straight-spined Maddy or Con or especially the spindly, wiry Bern, and in the overalls, she felt less self-conscious about her breasts, which almost seemed to get lost in the roomy flaps, the way she would when she hid behind the winter drapes as a child. She kept her crucifix, given to her by Maddy for her confirmation, on. Jesus, after all, was a man. She dug her hands into the bottomless pockets. Pockets everywhere! You could fit a couple of hammers in them, maybe even an entire drill.

Genie then grabbed some dumbbells off a shelf and a spring contraption called a chest pull, in a box with a drawing of a shirtless bodybuilder who looked like Jack LaLanne. She did a few biceps curls with the dumbbells, then pulled the spring contraption across her chest five or six times. Her breasts snapped to attention with each stretch, and her crucifix followed in a bouncy, syncopated rhythm. Together the sound of the expanding springs and the clinking chain almost made some kind of musical tone, a melody of male-femaleness. Genie didn't have any goal in mind, any number of reps, any new body she was trying to shape. She was just doing what felt good. What felt easy.

After the third or fourth pull, Genie became aware of a small pair of eyes peering at her through the slats on the stairs.

"Who's there?" she said on an exhale, with the springs at full extension.

"It's just me, Aunt Genie," came the peepish voice from the stairs. It was Colleen, Bern's oldest girl, 6 or 7 now, in her Sunday dress, saddle shoes and ringlets, already a skinny glam bean like her mother.

"Colleen, come over here," Genie said, without breaking her motion. The girl went all the way down the stairs and skipped over across the concrete floor, but as she got closer and beheld her aunt in overalls and crucifix, pulling apart the contraption, her skip became tentative, slightly stumbling. Genie could smell the fear, the way she could when she used to wield her stickball bat during the neighborhood games or barreled around a corner on her roller skates years ago. "Don't mess with Genie," everyone said. The businessmen who parked near Ebbets Field during Dodgers games were always happy to hire young Genie to keep vandals away from their cars.

As Colleen got closer, Genie knelt down on the floor next to her. "What can I do for you?" she said, locking her eyes with Colleen's while continuing to pull the spring thing across her chest.

"Grandma wants you to come upstairs and sing," the girl said. Then, with a slight stutter, "Aunt Genie, are you . . . are you a boy?"

Genie smiled and put down the chest pull. She picked up the boxing gloves, near her on the floor, one in each hand, and gathered the girl's face between them. She pressed against the girl's temples just hard enough to elicit a shudder. "No, honey, I'm a girl just like you," she said. "Only not as pretty." Then she fluffed up Colleen's ringlets with the gloves and said, "Now you scoot back upstairs and tell them I'll be right there."

Colleen skipped to the staircase and up to the first floor, while Genie changed out of the overalls and back into her dress. She had slipped away into the basement while the others were clearing the dishes from dinner. But now they must have been ready to move on to the last part of the Sunday-afternoon tradition, singing in the lacy front parlor. The sisters' mother, Lillian, played the piano, and though her fingers, and her memory, were a little creaky, she could still knock out 10 or so songs from memory, early Tin Pan Alley ditties like "Let Me Call You Sweetheart" and "Sidewalks of New York." Genie liked singing with her sisters almost as much as she liked being in the basement.

She rinsed her face at a large basin where they usually wrung out clothes — unlike her sisters, she never wore makeup, so there was no need to reapply — and headed upstairs. On the way she saw her old stickball bat in a corner. Another thing that always felt easy to her.

Upstairs, Maddy, Con, Bern, Colleen and Mrs. Rooney had already gathered in the front room. Genie took her place with them as

Mrs. Rooney spread her fingers into "Sidewalks of New York," and the sisters burst into, "East Side, West Side, all around the town." Then another Irish drinking song, "Harrigan." They all sang in unison, with verve and solidarity. Then "Let Me Call You Sweetheart," during which the girls joined hands and swayed together, sisters in tune musically and epistemologically.

Genie wouldn't have minded if their mother, who sat stone-faced at the piano and bumped into a few wrong notes here and there but still kept up with the girls, had learned something a little more current or jazzy, like "Come On-A My House" or a tune from the score of *Guys and Dolls*. But she knew that wasn't likely to happen. Genie owned these records, but whenever she played them, or songs by Billie Holiday or Nat King Cole, her mother called them "jump numbers." Yet she still looked forward to singing with her sisters every week because they all doted on her, baby of the family that she was, the only one to have graduated from high school, and now attending Brooklyn College, paid for by Maddy and Con. (Bern, after running away from home at 16 and becoming a Broadway gypsy — all the Rooney girls were great dancers — had met and married Uncle Billy and moved into the house next to their mother's.) Genie was something of the family's last chance for redemption now; the same kind of hopes were being invested in her that most families in the neighborhood invested in their sons. Maybe, they thought not so secretly, she'd become a doctor or a lawyer.

And she also had the best voice, a silvery alto that, like everything else she did well, seemed effortlessly tuneful.

After four or five songs, Mrs. Rooney's fingers started plunking out a few upper-level chords: Here was the most current song she knew, and the sisters all sat up in their chairs. It was Cole Porter's "I Get a Kick Out of You," almost 20 years old now but still being recorded by popular singers of the day like Frank Sinatra and Ella Fitzgerald. Maddy said, just out of habit, "Genie, you take the lead."

Genie touched the crucifix at her throat, her chest and lungs fully expanded now after a brief session with the chest pull, and as her mother continued to play arpeggios, sang of a sad story. But her voice was anything but sad. It was calm and assured, a natural buoy bobbing on a calm sea, with a slight surge every time she sang the hard ending *k* in "kick." Maddy and Con each took a line of the bridge, but Genie was back soloing for the final verse. The line had no desperation or need, the way it did when most other singers sang it. It was an affirmation, almost as if she were singing the song to herself. It was all lilt.

"Oh, Genie, that was wonderful," Maddy said, with her usual slightly ditzy, slightly regal effusiveness. Bern and Colleen did an exaggerated box step across the room. Her mother just closed the piano lid. No more singing today, she barked, nothing could be better than that. Only Constance, the usual killjoy, was qualified. "Very nice, Genie, but shouldn't you get to studying? You have school tomorrow."

Genie did have a sociology class at Brooklyn College the next day, and her books sat on the stairs waiting for her. She smiled and nodded. "Yes, Con, you're right." What she didn't say was that she was planning to quit college at the end of the semester. She'd never had trouble in high school. Making the honor roll was a given. But college was hard. All those papers. All those god-awful footnotes. All those other smart kids. And now most of her friends — who were men — were being shipped off to the Korean War, and school started to look like a bigger version of her house full of women.

Genie thought she might enlist herself. But that would probably be too hard, too, and she'd just be in the ranks of more women.

Before they broke, though, Maddy's husband, Charlie, appeared, a few drafts on his breath, and said he wanted to take a picture. The girls gathered in front of the fireplace, glamorous Bern with her hair in a shiny pile and Colleen on her lap looking right at the lens. Maddy and Con looked vaguely at Mrs. Rooney with some kind of admiration, while Mrs. Rooney herself, the stately center of the frame, turned in profile away from them all. Genie was in the bottom corner of the shot, looking into it, seemingly perched on a starting block, ready to break out across it.

A man might have been taking the picture, but as was so often the case with the Rooneys, men were out of it.

8. New York City, Summer 1982

"Did I tell you about the girl I saw carrying a backpack the other day? It looked really odd."

"What was so odd about it?" asked the doctor, seated in the bigger of two leather chairs in his East Side office, across from the wall of books in the dark-paneled room. Most of them, she thought, were the imposing, embossed, stiff psychology texts that never seemed to have been opened, but one, slightly off center in the middle shelf of the middle section, was his own, which had been a best seller and the first widely read book about her "problem." Of course she had the best therapist in the business. Once, that is, she admitted there was "a problem." He was older, kind of avuncular, looked like family and money.

The last therapy session had been particularly dismal, devoted as it was to her "homework assignment" — she was to think of meals she would serve when she returned to L.A. Ever the mathematical patient, she had broken them down into three groups: a birthday party for her godchildren, F.'s twins, with croque-monsieurs and frites and individual cakes for 32, the face of each attendee lovingly spackled in double-chocolate frosting ("Lindsay, I just ate my nose") and Tiffany goblets overflowing with M&Ms; a Thanksgiving dinner with galantine of turkey and oyster dressing and yams stuffed with orange marmalade (to cut down on the butter) and fresh cranberries from Cape Cod (she got the recipes from a New England magazine in the library) and, because she knew she'd be eating with her family, the mother's inevitable greasy green beans and bacon; and finally a Champagne brunch for her friends in the business, singers and costumers and caterers, the ones the mother referred to as "the Uptown crowd." The misery of the experience was relieved only for a moment, when she thought of how her hairdresser had once shown up for a luncheon in crepe de Chine and pumps and she said conspiratorially to F., What would the mother think if she saw this?

The assignment was discussed down to the place settings and the palate cleansers, and then the weekly weigh-in was held. The make-believe menus, intended as an imaging device, didn't quite have the desired effect, as she was down a pound.

"I don't know, you just don't see that kind of thing in L.A. She may as well have been carrying a guitar on her shoulders. You know, we never had a female guitar player on any of our albums." As usual, it was a half-truth, the answer she thought he wanted. While they had never had a female guitar player on any of their sessions, she'd certainly seen them around the studios. And not just folkies like Joni Mitchell. Real Stratocaster slingers.

She also didn't bother to tell him that when she encountered the young woman in the record store, she had a brief exchange with her — she'd seen the record the girl was holding and asked her if she was going to buy it. When the girl turned away and said she'd rather burn it, it was time to go. Why would she say that? That record sold millions of copies. It was still being sung in subway stations in New York City! She had hurried out of the store but then waited a few doors down for the girl to leave and followed her for a few blocks. It wasn't so much the fact that the girl had a backpack that amazed her now, but how freely the girl walked, the sidewalk panels rising up to greet her, it seemed, always a measure ahead of the other pedestrians, the traffic lights, the changes in the wind. Once or twice she thought her footfall was too heavy and the girl might know she was being tailed, but the girl didn't seem to hear her. A native New Yorker, she figured. Why couldn't she just go talk to the girl? Why was it *always* so hard for her to talk to other women?

"Still, what's so unusual about that?" the doctor asked. "You played the drums for all those years. Why did you stop playing by the way?"

"That's a cracker," she said. "Cracker" to her meant joke, as in something that's cracked. Most people usually asked her why she started. No one ever wanted to know why she stopped.

"I never stopped," she said. "I just don't play them on the records or in the shows anymore. The guys who play for us on the records now are much stronger." Another self-deprecating answer she gave to throw him off, give her time to ruminate over the real reason. She thought of the team coming to her when they started to become successful and saying, it's time for you to stop hiding behind the drums and to stand out front. In a magazine article one of their label bosses said her coming out from behind the drums coincided with her "becoming a woman." For a while they kept a short spot in their shows where she'd run from drum to block to cowbell and do a lot of high-energy rudimentary stickwork, tongue-pressed-to-the-corner-of-her-mouth kind of stuff, but that got dropped, and then the shows stopped, too.

"So where do you play now?"

"Oh, EV-ry-where," she said. "That's a great tie, by the way."

Deflecting. It was what she did best. She'd spend the next five to eight minutes thinking about what to buy him for Christmas. She'd already purchased her cards and had spent that morning making out her Christmas-card list.

"What do you mean, everywhere?" he said, interrupting her as she was mentally browsing the tie section in Brooks Brothers.

"Oh, my knees, the handle on the shower door, the bedpost. Anything I can get my hands on."

"Do you miss it?" he asked, making notes.

"I don't have time to miss it. Today I made out my Christmas-card list."

"But it's only the middle of summer, why so soon?"

"Because I won't have time when I get back. There will be sessions to do and plans to make for next year's schedule. I WILL be home for Thanksgiving, won't I?"

"That's up to you. What's the count this week?"

The count, meaning, how many laxatives had she taken. She was up to four boxes when she first started seeing him, almost 40 a day. The plastic crackled when she opened them, just as she remembered it did on a sleeve of Oreos, and she would down them almost as quickly as she once did the cookies, not stopping long enough even to taste them. The faster she could bite and swallow, the faster she could have another.

"Three," she said.

"The same as last week."

"I know, I guess I'm being nostalgic. Next week two for sure."

She could tell that she wasn't putting anything over on him; if she really was close to kicking the laxatives, it didn't show. If anything, she looked gaunter and frailer, older than she had four months ago, when she started therapy. One concerned fan had written after their last TV special, a couple of years ago, and said she looked about 55 years old. She had actually been 30. "I thought one of those awful dancers was going to snap you in half," the fan wrote. "You are turning into human dissipate."

Her therapist asked, "Did you talk to your mother this week?"

"No. Where's the best place in New York for lamps, I need . . ."

"Not so fast. You were going to ask your mother if the family would come here for a group session."

She had in fact asked the mother, who replied simply that their family did not believe in such things and told her again that if she'd just come home for a few months for three squares a day, she'd be cured in no time.

"I kept missing her," she said. "I'll try again this week."

She was changing the channels again in her mind, searching for something to get them away from the mother and through the last 10 minutes of the session. She looked up at the books and remembered a word she'd seen while thumbing through the leather-bound classics the mother had given her after she moved into her high-rise condo, with a guard at the gate and a baseball team of people to tip at Christmas. And a professional jumbo refrigerator that was always empty but looked nice anyway. She hadn't had time to actually read one of the books cover to cover. She just liked having them around, like the laxatives she hid all over her hotel room, like the jumbo refrigerator.

"Do you know the word *logy*?" she asked. It wasn't the kind of word she'd find in a song, though because it had a long vowel, it would be a hard word to sing flat. Not that she ever had a problem there.

He nodded, questioningly.

"Do you know what it means?" she asked.

"It describes a state of sluggishness, as from overeating. Why?"

"Oh, never mind," she said. "Same time tomorrow?"

9. Queens, N.Y., Summer 1982

Sib checked her watch as she tried to tiptoe up the stairs at the back of the house — 2:45. Even in her stocking feet, all five steps from the side door to the kitchen seemed thunderous, as if every one were being dropped inside an echo chamber. All these years later, even the smallest sounds could be amplified, rediscovered, celebrated, thanked-over-grace-at-the-dinner-table. Usually the feeling this elicited was residual elation from the first days and weeks that her hearing returned. Now, though, she could use a little silence.

She was trying not to wake her dad, whom she'd stood up for

dinner and the Mets game. Just as she had been leaving Whelan's, Larry, the D.J., called to say he was going to be late, and Dom asked if she wanted to spin for a couple of hours. With her funds and confidence running low after her long, smudged day of looking for a real job, she could use some time in the booth. Larry was going to be delayed only an hour anyway, so she'd probably get home by the seventh inning. She called her dad, who told her he'd keep the pizza warm. One Friday out of every month they still "splurged" for pizza from Morelli's, a neighborhood joint that was holding steady even as so many of the stores and restaurants of Sib's youth were shuttering their doors, because the pizza tasted exactly the same, just as good, as when all four of them ate there years ago. Owning a pizza parlor in New York City seemed to be the surest defense against a bad economy. Sib kept wanting to tell her father that it was O.K. if they maybe had it more than once a month, or on a different day of the week, or if he invited Mrs. Donovan over and told Sib to get lost altogether for the night. But routine was what had saved their minds, probably their lives, since the accident, and she was not going to begrudge him that.

But then Larry kept calling to say he'd be even later, was having car trouble, couldn't find something or other — Sib figured it was more like girl trouble, or he was waiting to connect with his dope dealer — and so suddenly 7:30 became 9 became 11:30. The last call she made to her dad was that she didn't know when she'd be home. The Mets were in extra innings, which she knew already because the game was on at the bar. "Be careful, have someone walk you home, call if you want me to come get you," he said. Sib could hear him tamping down the deflation in his voice. She hated to disappoint him, but she really needed the money, and a reason to not be in the house one more night, a good reason to be awake at all hours of the morning.

It had been a decent Friday night at the bar, packed but not over-stuffed with the usual locals with full pockets and big thirsts from their week out on landscape crews, truck routes, nursing shifts. Saturday the bar wouldn't get crowded till late as the regulars returned from date nights or some other event that involved better clothes, more money, more decorum, more hope of sex. But by 9:00 on Fridays, the bar was two or three deep, all the tables were filled and Patrick the owner had to jump behind the bar to help Dom. "Keep the blood flowing," Patrick said as Sib headed to the D.J. booth.

Larry must have had some of his records with him because the booth, a plank-board tower between the bar and the bathroom, was roomy, not crammed with the crates that usually left just enough space between them and the turntables. The tables were cheap things that Patrick bought at Crazy Eddie, not the really good Technics models with the strong motors, more like something you'd find in the bedroom of the average music fan, and you couldn't mix on them, because the belts weren't powerful enough. But that didn't really matter, because even though Whelan's had a small dance floor and a strobe, it was rare for anyone to dance, and even then it would usually be just the girls, or occasionally the punkettes, or Sib and Timmy Sweeney when Larry took a break from the white-boy rock he usually played.

Still, Sib thought she had enough to keep things going until Larry showed up. She started with the Dazz Band's "Let It Whip." It was an "up" song (keep the blood flowing, Sib), and she knew she could go anywhere from there, rock, new wave, even, God forbid, something funkier. In the first hour, before the bar got really crowded, she played mostly Top 40 hits, Survivor and John Cougar, every fourth or fifth song mixing in something she really liked, like Cheri's "Murphy's Law." And as the locals filed in, she picked it up with "Don't You Want Me" and "Tainted Love." She kept the hounds at bay with Judas Priest's "You've Got Another Thing Comin'."

The D.J. booth was next to the foosball table, with just enough room between them for someone to pass through. But when the bar was crowded and a game was being played, and there was a group around the table, it got dodgier, and any hard shot could make a record skip. And no one could get to her to make requests, so skinny Timmy Sweeney, who also decided to stay at the bar for a while, would have customers write them on little slips of paper, and he'd ferry them to Sib, threading his svelte self through the foosball players and their groupies. He'd look at the request first and say something like, "Ah, brilliant," or "That would have been my choice, too." And then when he reached inside the booth to give them to Sib, he'd flick the inside of her hand if he thought the choice was ridiculous, like King Crimson or some long Zebra track. Occasionally there'd be a dollar bill inside, and Timmy would nod twice when he gave those to Sib. The night was making her feel both giddy and focused, in her element, and she was only too happy to fulfill a request if she had it. But then she opened one of the slips — Timmy had given it to her with a shrug — and saw that someone had asked for "Are You Ready?" an oldie by a one-hit wonder called Pacific Gas & Electric. Sib blinked. It wasn't so much that the song was so obscure now. It's that it was another song from that awful summer. Sib thought about tossing the request, but instead she dutifully dug through the few crates in the booth, which were all arranged alphabetically, not even expecting that Larry would have it. But then there it was, a 45 in decent shape, on the original Columbia label. She was holding it when a shot from the foosball table made the needle skip over the climax of the Who's "Baba O'Riley."

"*Hell*, yeah!"

Sib turned her head toward the table and groaned. It was that clod "Tuke" Tewksbury, still in his green oil-company uniform, stains on the knees from whatever basement he'd been in that afternoon, throwing off a vague smell of oil from the burner he'd cleaned or serviced, already half in the bag and talking twice as loudly as he should have been. He'd scored a goal with a hard shot that made his hand roll off the handle on the table. Sib took a few deep breaths. First "Are You Ready?" and now this jackass? Couldn't just one part of the day not be spoiled with bad old memories or bad new ones?

But she was determined not to let them ruin her night. She dropped the record on the turntable and kept her eyes on the Plexiglas window in front of her, which looked out to the dance floor. Tuke would probably lose soon enough and have to give up the table and then disappear back into the crowd. And the record would be over in three minutes' time.

But Tuke and his partner kept winning, and there would be exaggerated shots and whoops that kept making the records skip, to the point where people at the bar were looking over at the booth. Sib knew this was an occupational hazard considering the geography of the bar, but after the fifth or sixth time, she glared at Tuke, whose real name was Harold (but no one dared call him that). Sib took in the stupid grin, the leering, first at the foosball table, then at the player across from him, then at the girls who were watching the game. Suddenly he turned and they locked eyes; he nodded his head and said something into the ears of the guy he was playing with.

What Tuke didn't know was that, because of her superhearing — and her ability to read lips — Sib knew what he said: "I hate that bitch, watch me make her records skip." And so he kept making showboat shots, some raising the table off the floor and at one point causing the needle on the turntable to skip across the entire length of Haircut One Hundred's "Love Plus One."

There were five or six people between Sib and Tuke, including Timmy Sweeney, who'd arrived with another request but when he saw trouble brewing tried to get between it and Sib. Tuke took another wild twirl of the handle and the ball went in the goal, just as Sib was cuing up her new copy of "Forget Me Nots," practically as a silent dare to him. The tremor made her drop the needle, and it skidded across the record. Sib had had it.

"Hey, Harold, you know what they call it when you let go of the handle to make a shot?" Sib shouted across the heads between her and Tuke. "*Dolly* foos."

The leer drained from Tuke's face. He lifted up the table by two handles and let it slam back down on the bar's floor. A full beer bottle in the nearest booth fell and shattered.

"Shut the fuck up, you stupid bull dyke," Tuke yelled, starting to push through the people between him and the booth. Timmy was the last one standing between him and Sib, who, a step and a half above the floor, was still barely looking down on Tuke. "And play some goddamn decent music."

"Now, now, sir," Timmy said. "Let's not be uncivil. Remember that we're living in the year of our Lord, nineteen hundred and eighty-two."

"Get out of my face, you three-dollar bill."

"Sir, you overestimate my value," Timmy said.

Sib had grabbed the nearest thing — her headphones — and was ready to clock Tuke if he got any closer. But just as Tuke's arm started to swing behind him, it was caught by Patrick. Tuke was a brute, had always been a bully, a terrorizer, a rabid dog you didn't want to cross, but he was no match for Patrick, who towered over him by a few inches and who, unlike Tuke, had seen the inside of a gym recently.

"That's enough, Tuke. Calm down," Patrick said, as he now had Tuke's arm pinned behind him. "You're cut off. Go home and sleep it off."

"I'm not drunk," he said, trying to wriggle free as Patrick nudged him around and toward the front door. "I spend half my fucking paycheck here every week. Isn't that good enough?"

"You've spent enough for tonight," Patrick said, letting Tuke go as they reached the door. "Go home."

"All right, all right, lemme go," Tuke said, shaking himself free of

Patrick's grip. "I'll take my money someplace else. Someplace that plays better music." Under his breath, he muttered. "Stupid cunt. She should have died with her goody-two-shoes brother." Sib was too far away to hear that.

Larry showed up a few minutes later, and by then the glass had been swept up and the beer mopped and the music was playing skip-free again, and it looked like another typical Friday night at Whelan's.

"Dude, you always miss the drama," Sib said as Larry, curly-haired, wiry, stoner-sanguine Larry, changed places with her in the booth.

"Ha, ha, and you always seem to *not* miss it," Larry said. He had a crate with him that included a promo copy of a single called "Everybody," by a singer Sib had never heard of called Madonna. Larry threw it on. Fake British accent, too canned, Sib thought, but still, it had a good beat and the semblance of a melody. The woman's voice had no special resonance, no otherworldly vocalese, but there was something, a neediness, Sib thought. And it was a catchy thing.

Sib and Timmy stayed at the bar another hour or so. Suddenly she remembered the Mets game and her dad, and looked up at the screen, which was showing some Nascar rerun.

"Time to go," Sib said, and Timmy followed, half bored and half concerned that maybe Tuke was waiting for them. Once or twice on the way home he thought someone might be trailing, thought he caught a shadow in a streetlight. But no one emerged. Timmy mentioned it to Sib, who brushed it off. "Tuke's an idiot," she said. "But he's not that stupid."

Sib was running all of this through her mind in the kitchen, and she considered going up to bed but was still too jazzed from the night's events. No way she'd be falling asleep much before dawn. She pulled a cold slice of pizza from the refrigerator and was just starting to cut it into smaller pieces when she realized she had meant to tell Larry about the bizarre woman who seemed to be stalking her at Downstairs Records that day, who followed her out even, a woman who was both overdressed and underpresent. Then she heard the door handle jiggle at the bottom of the kitchen steps. She knew she'd locked it, but now the door was opening. Had Tuke followed her home after all? There was no time to scream for her dad. She grabbed the knife she had been using to cut the pizza and crouched behind her chair while she listened to the footfalls on the stairs, which even more than her own a few minutes before sounded like horse clomps.

"Put the knife down, honey, it's just your old man." There was her dad, with a flashlight in his hand, Mets cap on his head, in his drawstring shorts and a gray U.S.P.S. sweatshirt.

"Dad, you scared the hell out of me! Were you waiting up?"

"No, I was just . . . I was just sitting out in the garage."

The bicycle hooks again. Had the Mets' latest loss driven him to that? Or the fact that she'd stood him up?

"Dad, why do you torture yourself like that? The Mets aren't worth. . . ."

Her dad cut her off. "I got a call tonight, Siobhan," he said, looking out the window into the dark yard. "Rose Birnbaum died."

Now it made sense. It wasn't the Mets, or Sib, who had driven her dad back into the garage, had made him want to stare it all in the face again. It was Rose Birnbaum. Fat Rose. Maybe the last person to speak to Kieran.

10. New York City, Summer 1982

She was on her daily trek up Madison Avenue. She didn't have much shopping to do today — all the birthdays and anniversaries within three months had been checked off in her planners. So she headed toward Central Park, and she knew she was getting close from the smell. She didn't mind the horseshit; it was the hot dogs that bothered her. Around the point where she was thinking about turning toward Fifth Avenue, the bumper-to-bumper traffic reminded her of the little scene she had with the brother on the eve of the release of their third album, when she was quickly learning that success came with its share of inconveniences.

"So let me get this straight," she'd said to him. "They want us to play in a parking lot?" She'd understood, kind of, when they weren't allowed to sing their big hit movie song at the Academy Awards because they weren't movie stars. Never mind that their version of the song was still in the Top 10 the week of the show. At least the producers did get one of their favorites, Petula Clark (Petula Clark!) to sing it. And one of the songwriters had the class to thank them when the song actually won the Oscar.

That song became their third consecutive million seller, and the next single was well on its way to becoming their fourth. Their third album — the one with just their name on the front, in a big new swirly logo against a tan background — had to be held back from release because the second was still selling big, after the bump it got when they were surprise winners of a couple of Grammy Awards the month before. They'd beaten the Beatles, for chrissakes. At that televised ceremony she let him do all the talking when they accepted the awards, while she basically just tugged on his sleeve. They even talked to John Wayne (John Wayne!) backstage. He'd seen them playing somewhere a few years earlier, when he was getting ready to film *True Grit,* and contacted them, told her she should come to audition for the part of the tomboy frontier girl. She went to the screen test but didn't get the part. That night at dinner she tried to tell the parents how exciting it had been, the screen test, reading the lines, how the casting director told her to keep at it, she really had something. But the brother started talking about some new arrangement he had written, and that was that.

It was right after the awards show when he told her about the parking-lot gig, which they had to play because it was a request from the wife of one of their bosses, for some shopping center or hotel dedication or rich-ladies social club or something. This was the kind of gig they were supposed to have left behind, the minor leagues from which they were supposed to have been permanently promoted: the high-school assembly, or the seedy, smoky club set where they'd follow or precede some hippie trippers and then be shorted of their take, when they'd load their gear and instruments into the wagon and hope the twine keeping everything together would hold.

"You have *got* to be kidding," she said. *"A parking lot?"*

"Put a sock in it," he said. "He's our boss." And so she did what he said, as usual. He always said her opinions were too blunt, just like their mother's, and he rarely listened to her anyway. When he brought her that song he'd heard on the *Tonight* show, the song about the groupie, she balked. She knew the song already and told him she thought it was kind of dopey and just tossed off her vocal, reading the lyrics off a napkin. He changed one word, "sleep," to "be." Wouldn't the mother have blown her top if they'd come home with the line "sleep with you" in one of their songs.

After she finished the take, there was silence in the studio, and then the engineer, the second engineer and the bass player and the oboist and, yes, the drummer, broke out into a round of applause. She snickered. Oh, they're making fun, she thought. I'll definitely have to do a more serious take.

But they weren't kidding. The brother kept that first take, and it went on the album. Ah, well, she thought, *that* song will never be a hit. O.K., so she ended up being wrong about that one.

She remembered eventually looking forward to the parking-lot gig, once she was resigned to doing it. If it was a nice day, then maybe her drums wouldn't get too banged up from being outside. Even though she wasn't playing drums much on their records now, she did still play during the concerts. It got a little tricky, maneuvering the sticks and the kick pedal in a maxidress. But she managed to hold the beat, to keep time.

In their new single, she sang about the weather, and after the session, the label presidents themselves had come into the studio to tell them how much they liked it. She'd be singing the song live for one of the first times that day. But the other reason she was excited about the gig was that F. would be in the audience. F. was the wife of one of their managers and had been assigned to "mentor" her once it became clear that their success was no fluke. She didn't have many girlfriends. There were her childhood gal pals back east, but once the family moved to L.A., when she was 13, it seemed all her friends at school and then in the band were guys. She'd tried a few times to find some new girlfriends, but there just wasn't much time between classes and rehearsals. The summer after she graduated from high school, she found herself in a studio where one of those mixed vocal groups — men and women — was recording. She tried to strike up a conversation with the husky girl who sang lead, but all she could think of the whole time was that the girl had been off-key for most of the session.

She preferred hanging out with the guys, anyway. Girls were just too concerned with perfume and gossip and boyfriends. You never found a girl who wanted to go bowling or talk time signatures.

At first she didn't like F. much. She seemed too glamorous, too magaziney, too showy with her sapphire earrings and that ridiculous gold watch (it turned out her father was a jeweler), just a grown-up version of the obnoxious girlie girls from school. Silk scarves. Not her style at all. F. had probably never owned a pair of sneakers in her life. But she had to admit that F. was shapely and pretty and had a handsome husband and money. And really seemed to like her. F. had taken her shopping on Rodeo Drive and introduced her to a hairstylist in Beverly Hills. "Did you ever think about growing out your bangs?" F. asked her soon after they met. The mother, who usually picked out or made her clothes and did her hair, hit the roof when she heard this. "What do you need with that Uptown crowd?" the mother had said. "Uptown" was the mother's way of saying she didn't approve of F.'s Jewishness.

So she was particularly on at that gig. When she got to the crescendo of the new song, the one about the weather, she let it rip, her voice in that last phrase completely cascading over his, then crashing over the audience, which itself seemed to snap to rapt attention, in awe and just a little bit of fear at such a force of nature. Odd that she was singing words about being down when she had in fact been soaring. Even the brother seemed surprised, as he turned to her from behind his keyboard, his eyes so enlarged that his brows practically touched the rim of his pageboy cut.

She was elated. After the show they made the obligatory rounds with the greeters, paid their respects to the label boss and his wife and the members of whatever society club they were being shown off to, and then while the guys broke down the stage, she went to find F. It took her a few minutes to wade through all the autograph hounds, more and more of them hanging around now at every show. Grandmothers and kindergartners and everyone in between. One older woman came up to her and said: "Thank you for saving music. There hasn't been much on the radio since Elvis that I could stand, but you kids give me hope." When she didn't see F. right away, her tiptoe mood sagged a bit. But then the crowd parted, and there was F., in a smart blazer and a miniskirt that matched her sapphire earrings, with spiky boots and an unspiky smile.

"Oh, honey, you were wonderful," F. said.

She blushed and dipped her chin down. "Well, slightly sharp sometimes, and the guitarist missed a couple of entrances" — they'd be sure to talk to him tomorrow about that — "but not bad." She spoke metronomically, practically cutting off every word early because she was in a hurry to get to the next thought.

"You're way too hard on yourself," F. said, now locking their arms. "What are you doing tonight? Want to go eat? I found a good new sushi place."

Sushi, yuck, she thought. She'd much rather go for pizza with the guys. But maybe it would be O.K., with F. Maybe she'd try it.

As they were walking, the smog dissipated and the late-afternoon

L.A. sun broke through in a way she had rarely seen. It bounced off
the Crayola palette that lay in the field ahead of them: crimson
Darts and goldenrod Novas and periwinkle Dusters, the occasional
onyx Lincoln or Cadillac. They fell in step a few feet behind an
unwitting young couple about midway between her age and F.'s,
he in sideburns and shades and green bell-bottoms, she in culottes
and flats. "That girl has a marvelous voice," the woman said. "It's
so distinctive. She's so strong and low, almost like a man, and yet so
tender and expressive."

"Yeah, I'll give you the voice," the man said, "but now after seeing
them live, I think there's just something strange about them. He
looks like a Sears mannequin. And what's the deal with her playing
the drums?"

"What's the matter with that?" she said. "Do you have something
against a girl playing the drums?"

"Eh, I don't know. She just looks weird. Those bangs, those severe brows. I mean, Mama Cass may be fat, but at least she's kind of
pretty. That girl just looks like a linebacker in a prom dress."

She'd read a few reviews that called her "pudgy," but she'd never
heard anything like this before. She suddenly didn't feel much like
sushi, or pizza. The smog rolled back in.

F. just squeezed her hand.

Back on Madison Avenue, a horn suddenly honked her out of
her memory.

When she got back to the hotel that night, she made her usual pass at the dinner tray from room service. She'd heard somewhere that carbohydrates after 6 p.m. were like double the calories, so she always ordered a salad and iced tea, her old meal from
the days when they were touring 200 nights a year. A few bites of
wedge, half a dip into the low-cal dressing, lots of lemon. Then
she changed into her nightgown — a Mickey Mouse T-shirt that
drooped off her like a collapsed sail, catching only slightly on her
hips, which, though drained of every bit of body mass, still jutted

out a bit. Those damned big bones.

She was swimming in the king-size bed as she fired up all the video equipment she'd had brought in. There were stacks of *Dallas* episodes she hadn't seen, and after she got through a couple of those, she watched a taping of the *Tonight* show, and one of the guests was a great songwriting friend of theirs. They were the ones who made him famous. They had been all set to release that moon-dust song when the brother saw a bank commercial — and recognized the songwriter's voice in the background, singing something about white lace and promises. The brother called the songwriter and found out that there was a full song, worked up an arrangement, and from the first minutes they started to record, there was something magic about it, some cosmic confluence going on unlike any of their previous sessions, even the one for the moon-dust song. The ace studio drummer said, "This is it, this is the one." They almost halted the release of the moon-dust song, but as it was already set to ship to radio and was written by legends (who were also tight with their record-company bosses), they decided to hold the bank-commercial song for the next release.

Many of the musicians praised her lead vocal, but she just let those comments slide off her in a slick of denim and self-denial. This song, she knew, worked because of *his* genius: in hearing the song in a commercial and recognizing it as a hit, in working up the great arrangement with the raised 7th opening, the dynamic build, the tambourine that shook like a lead instrument, setting her voice in the right range. He was the one who, years ago, realized that she even had that amazing low voice. "The money's in the basement," they often said.

The drummer, though, persisted in his praise for her. The drummer who was the top session guy in L.A. The drummer who wasn't she. She'd played drums on every cut of their first album, but the company decided it wanted a "stronger" sound now. The mother flipped out. But she wasn't going to win a battle with the men who signed the royalty checks.

She felt behind the small mound of goose-down pillows. Then in between. Still there. Her stash of laxatives. She kept them around even though she wasn't ingesting them as much. She hid them behind the pillows, in drawers, in the pockets of sweaters and blazers. She even slipped them into every one of her new running shoes, which lined the perimeter of the suite. Even if she wasn't taking them, she just liked knowing they were around, like those crazy dolls and figurines and amulets that bingo ladies framed their cards with to bring them luck.

The songwriter — who was short and chubby but, she always thought, cute in a cuddly, teddy-bear way — was yukking it up with Joan Rivers, who was the guest host that night. Look at him, she thought, such a big star. He'd had a better second half of the '70s than she'd had; he scored movies, he even starred in a few, he won an Oscar writing a song with the Greatest Singer of All Time. When the GSOAT had her other blockbuster movie-song hit, earlier in the decade, the one about memories, a few journalists were sharp enough to point out that it was basically a slowed-down version of their second big hit, and one writer even suggested that by listening to them (to her!), the GSOAT had finally learned to stop singing in all caps. There were a few years when she would get fan letters that compared her to the GSOAT, telling her that she had a future in movies and Broadway, too. She shrugged them off. The GSOAT just "fractures me," she said in an interview.

They'd met, almost, a few years ago at a fund-raiser in L.A. This was during her midchart years, when nothing she and the brother put out could get much higher than No. 35. The kooky one about the extraterrestrials *almost* got them back to the Top 20, and then there was the perky country ditty, the only song they recorded that she actually found herself and brought to the studio. These were good records. But they couldn't break through to that upper tier of radio anymore, the stations that just a few years ago would have played anything they put out — how many times in the early years had she heard the old line that she could sing the first 10 pages of the phone book and it would be a hit? One nutty fan even wrote to say that the brother should "strap a microphone to her so that you can record whatever she sings around the house or in the car." She'd get maybe five to ten marriage proposals a week. The cops were often called to clear stalkers from their house.

Nowadays, though, they weren't getting many letters like that. After their chart fortunes started to falter, she said to a reporter, "If somebody would just let us know what the problem is." But no one ever really did.

The GSOAT looked all permy at that fund-raiser and was wearing some glittery white get-up, out to promote a new movie and a big new disco hit. She herself had her own perm and was making her own disco-y album, with P., who had also worked with the GSOAT. It was her first solo project, and it was taking a long time, all the sifting of material, the flights back and forth to New York, learning to work with a new producer, new arrangers, a new band, trying out a higher range in her voice. Well, she had thought, I've got time. Disco will be around for a while.

Their eyes met across the room, and there was a flash of recognition from the GSOAT, but then she quickly turned away as she was driven inside by the mini-swarm of fans. Oh, well, she thought, don't consider it a slight. The GSOAT, she figured, probably didn't recognize her without the bangs and the old curtainy dress. She then stepped into the press ring herself, but in spite of her oversize name tag, only a few stragglers, from the back of the GSOAT's train, bothered to say hello.

Joan Rivers and the songwriter broke for commercial, and she lunged for the remote. She hated commercials like everyone else, but for her they weren't just interruptions to a program; they were more ways for food to find her. She didn't want to know about having it her way, or the break she deserved, or the piles of grease-free chicken that could be made with Mrs. Brady's cooking oil. Commercials for her these days held no lace or promises.

She must have dozed off then, because the next thing she knew she was watching another talk show, a new one, hosted by someone she didn't recognize. She was feeling herself nodding off again when she thought she heard him say . . . *their name.* She bolted up in bed. Had the host just said that they were going to be on his show? No, it wasn't possible. Had their manager booked them without telling her? They hadn't rehearsed in months. They didn't even have a record out. True, she was eager to get back to her career — too eager, her therapist suggested — but even she knew that she was in no shape to sing on national TV. Her pulse quickened, almost doubled in rate, the way it used to when she downed a triple dose of thyroid medication. The medication that was confiscated from her at her first therapy session, when she, once the premier singer of love songs, got her first dose of tough love from her doctors. You won't live to see the end of this bottle if you keep it up, they said.

Suddenly she heard the talk-show audience laughing. And she realized she had heard correctly. The host *had* said that they were going to be on his show. But he was just making a joke, playing up his nerdiness by ridiculing theirs. And that's when she felt the familiar flutter, a low hum, like feedback spilling out of another musician's monitor across the stage. It would soon be a rustle, which would soon be a gurgle, which would soon be a rumble. She knew the routine. As she had done many times in a recording studio, at a restaurant, in her own dining room, she got up and calmly walked into the bathroom. She looked up at the wall of mirrors, pulled back her hair in one hand — it was starting to grow long again — and gripped the counter, made of Chilean granite, with the other. As she leaned over the chrome basin, all she had to do now was wait.

Her breathing got heavier, made little clouds on the mirror. Seven or eight hyperventilations, the full-body tremor, then finally the expulsion: "What an asshole!"

A few saliva projectiles dotted the breath clouds on the mirror. As with her other egestions, when the offensive material was eliminated, she covered her face with a cold cloth, then calmly wiped her mouth and took a swig of Scope.

She looked over at her preparations for her morning ablutions, which she had laid out in clusters in the vaguely trapezoidal configuration of a drum kit. One circle of lotions and gels and unguents up to the left, another to the right, slanting down the way the toms would. A center cluster for her atomizers and sprays and roll-ons. And over to the left, assuming the high-hat position, was what she thought of as "the happy pad." It was a fresh tampon. She hadn't menstruated in a few years, but she could always hope that tomorrow would be the day she'd start again. It was part of the four-item checklist she needed to fill before she could pronounce herself well, which she'd written out on the plane to New York:

1. Gain 30 pounds (so far she could only manage seven or eight and then would drop them again; her current weight: 83). 2. Kick the laxatives, thyroid medicine, diuretics and emetics; she was almost there. 3. Get her period back. 4. Eat in front of her family, and hold the meal.

Thanksgiving dinner was the target for all of this. She still had a few months. And then she went back to bed. There were so many postcards to write in the morning. As she drifted off, she found herself thinking about that girl from the record store.

11. Queens, N.Y., Spring 1965

"Come behind the counter and say hello to your Aunt Rose."

Sib was both scared and thrilled as she beheld the largest person she'd ever seen. She hadn't even turned 5 yet, but she had already been asking her father to take her to Rose's Record Room ("Where the Music Will Bloom"), on Liberty Avenue, the place where Kieran and her mother bought all their records. It was wedged between a cloudy-windowed luncheonette and a hardware store on a stretch of the bustling street that Kieran had only just recently been allowed to travel to alone on his bicycle, and Sib's fear of the cars flying by, of

the Don't Walk signs that seemed to always be flashing, of the hurried pedestrians, of the rumbling el above were more than shouted
down by her anticipation of visiting the mysterious place.

Sib already loved candy stores, playgrounds, her basement (where
the family record player lived) and an amusement park on Long
Island called Adventure's Inn, where they would go about once a
month in the summer. But as she gripped her father's pinkie she
beheld a different kind of wonderland: records everywhere, aisles
of them, thickets of records hanging from the walls, what seemed
itself like a giant playground of music and youth and color. The
glass counter behind which the big woman sat was off to their left,
and it was filled with record cleaners, spindles, guitar picks, har-
monicas. On the wall behind the woman, there were black, wooden
slots, with cloth tape that announced the occupants on each one
in slurvy Magic Marker, every 45 ever made. Or at least that's the
way it seemed to Sib. This was better than the rows of Charms and
Tootsie Pops at their corner stationery.

But now, as Sib walked around the counter, all she could see was
Rose, the many folds of her, sitting on a throne-like swivel chair, a
whole menu of Chinese food cartons arrayed before her on a desk
that was otherwise cluttered with order forms, magazines, more records — a messy, spattered business, but a thriving business never-
theless. Rose was big, almost circus-lady big, and Sib felt that same
kind of thrill-fright that she did the one time her parents had taken
her to see the Ringling Bros. at Madison Square Garden.

"So this is the famous little sister I've been hearing so much
about," Rose said as she stabbed her fork in another carton and into
her mouth. "Tell me your name, sweetheart," the words coming out
in some kind of garbled pidgin of English and Mandarin chicken.

"Siobhan," Sib said, and because she was already in the habit
of having to say her name more than once because of the look of
incomprehension or unfamiliarity she would get, the nose crinkle,
the narrowed eyes that conveyed — what kind of name is that? —

she said it again, drawing out the words defiantly: "Shi-vawn," then grabbing onto the counter to steady herself from the wafts of food and Rose's baby-powder-and-body-odor smell. Rose was wearing a tentlike smock with so many flaps that Sib wasn't sure where the clothes stopped and Rose started. But the closer she got to Rose, the less scared she was. Her face, underneath a slick, towering finger-paint-black beehive, was cheeky and sparkly, the face of a birthday cake with lit candles, of Christmas lights, of still-wrapped presents.

"Siobhan, Siobhan, a beautiful name," Rose said as she reached out her arms, slender up to the elbow but then exploding into islands of jiggly flesh hanging down off her triceps. Sib looked around to her father, who was now watching from the side of the counter, and he nodded, and so Sib let Rose pick her up and hoist her onto the counter. She was dizzy, but not because Rose had picked her up too fast or too high but because now she could see all the 45s.

"Siobhan. A Hebrew name originally, the grace of God, but I think I'll call you . . . let's see . . . Sipper . . . Little Chip . . . Chipper. Yes, that's it, Chipper. If that's O.K."

Sib hated the name but she nodded shyly, still focusing on the wall of wonder in front of her.

Rose looked down the length of the counter to where Roy was standing, watchful, strong, quiet Roy. "So what brings you here today, Mr. Postman, you and your pretty young daughter? Picking up something for Kieran or the Mrs.? He was looking for that 'Concrete and Clay' the last time he was in, but I didn't have it. Got it now."

"No, actually, Siobhan wants to buy something," Roy said.

"Chipper wants some music? Well, what can Aunt Rose get for you? We have a whole kids' section. Do you like the *Mary Poppins* soundtrack?"

Sib didn't want any of that kiddie stuff. She had heard on the radio that morning a new song by Gary Lewis and the Playboys. Kieran had their last big hit, "This Diamond Ring." Sib really liked the new song, "Count Me In," and she knew Kieran didn't have it yet, so he'd be impressed if she got it first.

"I want a record that I bet you don't have," Sib said. "It's called 'Count Me In.'"

"Oh, a sharpie like her brother. O.K., Chipper, let me see what I can do."

Rose swiveled around. Sib felt the counter shake as Rose got up from her chair, wiped some orange sauce off her hands onto her smock and lumbered over to a pile of 45s on her desk, a new shipment that hadn't yet gone up on the wall. Sib watched as Rose's meaty fingers flipped slowly through five, 10, 20, maybe 30 singles, and still hadn't come up with "Count Me In." Rose was almost near the end of the pile now, and Sib's hopes were starting to sink, the beginnings of a pout were starting to form on her face, when suddenly Rose latched onto a 45 at the bottom of the pile, stretched out her boat of an arm and placed it in Sib's hands.

"Is that what you were looking for?" Rose asked, plopping back down in her chair and scooping up her fork.

Sib was thrilled. Not just because she had the record, but because it was *her* record. Because she'd been on Kieran's turf and made an impression all by herself. Roy started to take a dollar out of his wallet, but before he could give it to Rose, Sib hopped off the counter, marched over to him, took it from his hand and walked back to Rose to pay for the record herself.

"Oh, I see we have a do-it-yourselfer, here, Mr. Postman," Rose said to Roy as she took the dollar from Sib. "O.K., Chipper, that will be 79 cents." As Rose went over to the crank register and rang up the sale, Sib was taking in her dazzling prize: The label was called Liberty, the same name as the very street they were on, black with orange and blue, the lettering of the title and artist in silver. It was so beautiful. She'd almost forgotten what the song sounded like. Then she caught a glimpse of something coiled near the end where the counter stopped and the rest of the store opened up onto the floor with albums and older 45s. Sib did a quick step back in her

Keds, thinking it was alive.

Then she remembered Kieran telling her about "the whip." Rose used it to scare off shoplifters who might think that, just because she was a big woman, she'd be too slow for them, that her inventory was easy pickings. The Rose Whip was legendary on Liberty Avenue. Kieran said that the word was that Rose had snapped it only once, at the feet of some junior-high kid who was trying to lift a copy of *Meet the Beatles*. But it was in plain sight every day, lying in wait like a crocodile ready to snap on fingers that carelessly lingered where they shouldn't.

Rose caught Sib's little stutter step. "Don't you worry 'bout that, honey, that's not for good girls and boys like you and your brother. That's for anyone who thinks he can just waltz in to Rose's house and help himself to what isn't his."

Sib had already fallen in love with the place and with Rose for having it. Loved her for being so kind. By the time they left the store she didn't even mind the name "Chipper" so much. And the feeling was mutual. From that day on, Sib was in the store every week, either with Kieran or just with her dad, and Rose gave her free run, because Sib could read the labels and pick out her own 45.

When Sib and her father got home from Rose's that day, Kieran and her mother were playing basketball in the driveway. Her father had just installed the hoop and backboard, and it seemed Kieran and her mom were out there every night after dinner and weekend afternoon like this one, now that the weather was getting warmer. The basketball was too big for Sib to handle, it practically swallowed up her hands, and she was too small to shoot it, so some of those nights she would sit on the steps or stand inside the screen door and watch. Kieran would flash her a smile or say her name as he made a shot — he was only 8 in those first days, but already his shots had height and accuracy. And their mother, in a crouch or her own graceful arc to the hoop, was always putting on a show, seemingly without any effort. "Isn't Kieran great, Siobhan?" she would say after Kieran made a few shots in a row. "I could stay out here forever." She never seemed to notice when Sib had already gone inside.

That day, though, when Sib came home with "Count Me In," she didn't stop to watch Kieran and her mother, who had her back to Sib and was trying to teach Kieran how to transfer the ball from hand to hand and then dribble between his legs. Sib waved the bag toward Kieran, who recognized the logo from Rose's, a long-stem poking through the hole of a 45, and his eyes widened so much that he missed a pass from his mother. "Keep your eye on the ball, son," she said. Sib went downstairs and put the record on the small hi-fi; she may not have been able to handle a basketball yet, but the buttons of a record player were already second nature to her. She knew the speeds, the knobs, knew to put the record on the platter first before she turned it on.

The first time through, Sib loved watching it as much as hearing it. Her 4 1/2-year-old eyes were mesmerized by the blurring words and colors of the label, even as her skin was tingling from the sound. When the record finished, she lifted the needle and played the song again, this time remembering the chorus and singing along, though still transfixed in front of the record player. The third time around, she started to dance too, causing a slight skip in the record and a momentary shudder as she thought she'd broken it. When it resumed playing, though, the tears that were about to flood her eyes ebbed, and she started dancing again, this time a little farther away from the record player. She'd nudged the volume up a little more each time, hoping Kieran would hear it outside.

Sib was about to play the song a fourth time when she heard the side door slam. Kieran was coming in! She couldn't wait to play her new record, her first record, for him. But when she turned and looked up the stairs, she saw it was not Kieran but her mother, holding the basketball under her arm, looking down at her. And then heading toward her. Whenever she was with her mother, Sib was filled with a sense of familiarity once removed, as if her mother were someone she'd seen on TV.

"Mommy, I got a record!" Sib said.

"I heard," Genie said. "And heard. And heard."

Sib almost started to cry again, because she thought her mother was going to yell at her for playing the song over and over. When Genie moved toward the record player, still with the basketball in one hand, Sib almost ran in front of it to protect it from her. Genie reached down to pull the needle off. But then Genie turned and said, "Can we hear it again?"

"Yes, Mommy, put it on again!"

Sib was almost as happy now as she was behind the counter at Rose's. Her mother liked her record! Genie put the needle down and, 16 bars into the song was humming along. And then her mother's voice started to take over from the friendly but nasal lead singer on the record. By the end her mother was singing real words, and soon all Sib could do was gaze at her mother, sweaty and bobbing, spin out music. "It's a nice song, Siobhan," Genie said. "Did you pick it out yourself?"

"Yes, Mommy, Daddy took me to Rose's shop. She let me behind the counter and everything!"

"Oh, Rose," Genie said, turning her head slightly away. "The big Jewish woman. She's very nice."

"What's Jewish, Mommy?"

"That means she goes to a different church from the one we do," Genie said.

Just then Kieran bounded down the stairs, his face a red ripe tomato, the spaces between the freckles filled in with the blood-rush of the basketball playing and the promise of record playing. "There he is," Genie said. "There's my boy. Where is that record you got the other day?"

Kieran reached up to the shelf next to the record player and pulled out Petula Clark's "I Know a Place." He took "Count Me In" off the hi-fi and put it carefully back in the sleeve. Sib snatched it from him when he handed it to her and held it close.

"That's the one," Genie said. Soon Genie was smoothly skating above the voice on this one too; next to Genie, even a singer as good as Petula Clark had as much fidelity as the telephone game Sib and Kieran played with two cans and a piece of string. She put the basketball down and soon was twisting across the room with one child on each arm. Sib wished they'd still been listening to *her* record, but she was thrilled now that, even with wobbly legs, she could do this with her mother and Kieran. And when her mother sang, suddenly she wasn't so strange to Sib anymore. Her voice seemed bigger than them and yet available exclusively to them. It was warm, roomy, authoritative, like the blankets their grandmother crocheted for them when they were babies, and suggested a secret life beyond their little plot of space in this crook of Queens, N.Y., in the shadow of an international airport; the voice said that their mother was this thrilling creature who did more than open boxes of frozen peas and jars of peanut butter or put up jump shots in the driveway. When she sang for them, it meant that they were part of her overworld, too. She had more than enough voice for both of them.

Near the end of "I Know a Place," Genie was twirling both of them around, and Sib got so lost in the spin that she broke loose from Genie's grip. She sat down on the floor and put her head down. When she looked up, she found herself alone. The music had ended, the gentle thrum of the song's bass line replaced by the resumed thump of a basketball on the driveway above. The joy of the morning, of the record store and of her mother's voice, of her mother's attention, was starting to drain out, and though she was in her own basement, with the beloved record player only steps away, she suddenly felt alone and 4, as if she'd been plopped in the middle of a strange park or a supermarket. She sat down on the floor and started to cry.

After a few minutes, there was a noise on the stairs and then a figure shadowing over her. She suddenly felt herself being lifted up by a strong pair of arms, heard the hi-fi being turned off as the two of them moved toward the stairs. "C'mon, honey," her dad said, as Sib sobbed and sniffled into his shoulder. "Let's go have some lunch."

12. Queens, N.Y., Summer 1982

Andy hadn't been able to get the woman he followed to the subway
out of his mind. Her potential identity. The more time that passed,
though, the less he believed it was she, that musical hero from his
teenage years, from that one perfect summer day in 1970. There was
some odd contradiction about the woman he'd observed: the desire to
disappear, which Andy knew all too well — the sunglasses, the quick
step, the slipping away from him in the subway station — and yet still
the need to be noticed — the big wad of bills, the virgin white sneakers, the weird California get-up. The look-at-me-don't-look-at-me

vibe. One thing he knew about celebrities: They always wanted attention, long after it stopped being offered. Maybe especially after it stopped being offered.

And besides, the only vision of her on file in his memory — if it was she — was more than 10 years old. He needed to update. He went to the library and took out all the albums that he'd missed while he was in college or only knew from the radio hits. Made copies of newspaper and magazine articles he found indexed in the *Readers' Guide to Periodical Literature.* He had a routine for when he'd examine the material. It would be on his day off; he'd shower, brew some coffee and slip into his soccer shorts and a fresh NYPD T-shirt, vacuum the clean floor and reorganize the kitchen cupboards and bedroom closet and medicine cabinet and linen shelf. He needed the coffee smell and his body smell to be fresh, the clothes clean and soft against his skin, the house to be in undistracting order, unlike days when he was going out on duty on the street and needed to carry the stink with him. The surrounding space needed to be as tidy as the duo's music. He would then spread the album covers and articles out on his kitchen table chronologically like evidence in one of the precinct rooms, looking for some clue the totality might yield that each would not individually. He did notice that in later pictures and clips she had become thinner and thinner — to the point where, by the time of the group's TV specials in the late '70s, she was a frame denuded of its flesh, that she seemed to have aged 20 years instead of 10, that chunks of her seemed to have fallen off like snowcaps during a sudden spike in the temperature, or the marble of an overzealous sculptor. And yet the face was always so made up and airbrushed that he still couldn't tell if that was the face he'd looked into a few weeks earlier. He'd heard a word in the hospitals where, when he was still in the squad car, he and his partner had to bring some accident victims, some cut-up perps: "anorexia." The starvation disease.

But Andy was more interested in the *sound* of her. After the "Tan

Album," there had been seven albums altogether, and while they were all solid musically, the woman's voice seemed to become less present with each one, seemed to leach away a little more, which Andy found odd, because at the end of the '70s, she was still only in her late 20s; her voice should have been getting stronger, riper. At first it wasn't that noticeable; her phrasing was still confident and deliciously low and fluid. But by the time the group's Christmas album came out, late in the decade, the transition was complete. Her voice had hollowed out; she'd become an impersonator of her former self. Not that she was ever a belter, but on those later albums, she'd often bail on her phrases at the big moment, the ones she used to knock out of the park. The voice essentially had all the fat trimmed out of it, which is to say, it could still be nourishing — even in its diminished state. But it was decidedly less tasty. And on the Christmas album (and the one before it, with the silly songs about the South American kingpin and the extraterrestrials), there wasn't even a picture of her. The Christmas album did have an artist's sketch in which of course she looked perfectly chipmunk-cheeked and healthy.

Andy came upon a series of articles from 1979 that said the singer was making a solo album with a hotshot New York producer. There would be mentions of it through the year in the "trades": "Seen in _____ studio, _____ with _____." Or "laying down overdubs at _____, _____ with the producer _____." But exactly a year after the news was first reported, a short piece in *Billboard* said that the solo album had been shelved, and that she would return to the duo. Then a couple of months after that, a boldface item in the gossip columns said that she'd become engaged. The woman he saw a few months back wasn't wearing a wedding ring. And if she was making music in New York in 1979, no surprise that it wasn't deemed worthy of release. The city was such a wreck then; how could she have possibly been inspired?

So Andy still wasn't sure. And now there were more questions:

Why had this singer, who was at the top of her game in her early and middle 20s, who seemed to be set up for a career for life, become intent on throwing it away? She was no flash in the pan; her kind of voice was ageless, and she seemed to have more talent and career sense than the various geniuses whose careers and lives were curtailed by some addiction or other. If he ever did track down that woman from the street, and verified she was the singer, that might be the first thing he asked her. His second question might be, what were she and the brother thinking when they cut that song about the extraterrestrials?

13. Queens, N.Y., Late 1960s

Sib asked her father to take her to Rose's every Saturday, and over the years Sib's and Rose's roles were almost reversed: Sib became Rose's own circus or freak-show attraction, the little girl who "from the time she was 2 years old could read all the labels and knew every song on the charts." Well, Sib knew that she was 4 when she started going to Rose's shop, and she didn't know everything on the charts, just the songs that she or Kieran liked. That made Rose almost childlike in Sib's eyes, and she didn't try to punch any holes in Rose's fantasy. And Rose's counter became a kind of pedestal for her; she spent

almost all her allowance and birthday money there, except for the
weeks when she was getting a new Spalding ball or box of crayons,
and Rose always made sure to give her an extra 45 on her birthday
or at Christmas. On Sib's First Communion day, when she tugged
and straightened and fussed and squirmed in her dress over and over,
almost tripped on it when she ascended the step of the altar at Immaculate Conception and received the Host for the first time, the
only thing that got her through the ceremony was knowing that after
they all went to breakfast, Sib would be in Rose's shop, where Rose
told her to pick any album off the wall. She chose Aretha Franklin's *I
Never Loved a Man the Way I Love You*, mostly because she loved "Respect." "Now that's a pretty smart pick, Chipper," Rose said. "You're
going to run this place someday."

By this time, in the later '60s, Rose's shop was diversifying into
posters, candles, incense, rolling papers, and was suddenly being
frequented not just by listeners of big radio stations like WABC
and WMCA but by all kinds of what her mother called "colorful
characters" and the rest of the world called hippies. They flocked to
the store because Rose had become both everyone's Jewish mother and the oldest teenager in town — some of the Kellys' neighbors called her "an overaged beatnik running a head shop." When
she was about 7 and in the store, Sib heard one young woman,
with straight red hair almost to the floor and sunglasses and a mole
on her ghost-white face that, rather than trying to cover up with
makeup, she'd drawn a starburst around, to call attention to it, ask
Rose if she could get her "penicillin." Sib asked her dad what that
was, and he said it was a kind of medicine. Sib wanted to know why
the girl was asking Rose for it and what it was for — did she have
a bad cold? Why didn't she go to the drugstore? Roy said he didn't
know and then changed the subject to Sib's new record, Friend &
Lover's "Reach Out of the Darkness," and Sib was off on how it
sounded just like the Mamas and the Papas but wasn't, and soon the
snappy bass line was putting all thoughts of hippie chicks asking for

medicine out of her mind.

And so Sib's and Kieran's record collections grew week by week, month by month, year by year, his stack always a little higher, so neat and sleeved and cared for, with the carefully stenciled KK on every one, and Sib's, acquired with precocious ears, left otherwise to the mercy of a preadolescent — sometimes in their covers, sometimes not; sometimes left on the hi-fi; carefully removed from its cover on the first play but by the 10th fingerprinted and scratched, her name in a wobbly scrawl on the back, in competition, as Sib grew, with her nascent athletic pursuits. On that linoleum floor in their paneled basement, with their dad's baseball and their mom's basketball and bowling trophies and the extra bathroom and refrigerator, the bar where their parents sometimes entertained on Saturday nights or holidays, it was where not much of anything in life went wrong.

* * *

July 1970

In the front of the house, the breakfast-time sun was still only just breaking through the fleshy maple leaves in small apertures and keyholes, but in the back, it was splattering through the kitchen window, blurring the colors of Sib's Trix. Sib was enrolled in a morning rec program at the local public school that summer, while Kieran, just past his 14th birthday, had already finished his paper route and would be off soon to P.A.L. baseball practice. But what was really putting the spring in their cereal spoons was that it was new-survey day on WABC, and they knew that at 2 p.m., the crazy D.J. Dan Ingram would unveil the new Top 14. Sib was hoping that her current favorite, Freda Payne's "Band of Gold," would hold down the No. 1 position for a fourth week. Sib loved everything about the song — the insistent beat, the tradeoffs between the bass and the electric guitar, alternating twin musical lassos that pulled you in tighter with each wraparound; the shimmering tambourine; and that piercing, pleading lead vocal. It was almost as good as any Supremes record. And of course Sib loved the Supremes, even their new incarnation without Diana Ross. It was hard to go wrong with a girl group, even a second or third version of it. Sib was planning to get the record that weekend at Rose's.

Just then the song came on the radio, stationed next to the toaster on the counter. Kieran started tapping out the beat with his spoon, then his knuckles, and then the side of his hands, balled into percussive fists, were hammering out the 4/4 beat as he wiggled in rhythm in his seat. Sib started to sing. Her 9-year-old voice was mostly in tune, but all plaint and wail, still a child's voice. Sib didn't understand the lines about something that went wrong on a wedding night, but it didn't matter. The record was just so exciting. And it was going to be No. 1 again, she was sure of it. "Lovely Freda Payne," said the WABC morning man, Harry Harrison, "will she still be No. 1 on the new survey today?" Sib whooped a "Yes" that lifted her off the padded chair and back down so hard that the vibration caused Kieran's orange juice to slosh around in its glass and spill over. Harry Harrison then said, "Or will it be this fast riser?"

Sib heard the tinkly opening piano riff and almost spit out the last of her cereal. In her five-plus years of being a music fan and record buyer, she had amassed a collection of big hits and cool misses (all those Reparata and the Delrons singles that no one outside New York ever seemed to hear). She either liked a song or just ignored it. But this new song just made her gag. It was so soft, so . . . old-sounding. Sib didn't know too much about the group, who had seemingly come from nowhere. A girl sang lead; Sib loved girl singers, but this girl sounded too light, *too* grown-up. She didn't sound fun or thrilling like Aretha Franklin or the girls in the Supremes or the Shangri-Las. And the song itself was like something they'd sing in chorus class. No way this stupid song was going to knock "Band of Gold" out of the No. 1 spot.

Sib got up from her chair to change the radio station, but just then their mother came into the kitchen and said, "Wait, I like that song."

Sib sat back down and shot Kieran a conspiratorial look, the us-against-them code shared by sister and brother, but though Kieran looked right back at her, his eyes didn't return the ridicule. He seemed to be staring through her to the radio, as their mother started to sing along. The aural thrill that their mother's voice usually provided was diluted for Sib by her distaste for the song. But why was Kieran ignoring Sib's contempt?

She got her answer when the bridge of the song arrived and Kieran started to sing with their mother the line, "Sprinkled moon dust in your hair." The same words anyway, but not the same notes. They were doing what Sib had just learned about in music class — harmonizing — singing different notes to blend in a chord. In her head Sib tried to latch onto one of the parts, but every time she thought she had one down, she'd teeter onto the edge of the other and soon get caught somewhere in between, while Kieran and her mother held onto theirs solidly. Boy, did Sib ever hate this song.

Sib looked up at the clock above the sink. 8:40. She bolted up. Time to go, time to be released from that icky tune. Before she could get down the side stairs, though, her mother said, "Aunt Maddy is coming for lunch, so don't dawdle on the way home."

Aunt Maddy! The favorite aunt. The nice aunt. The rich aunt. Sib wouldn't have to wait for the weekend and her allowance after all. She might have "Band of Gold" before the end of the day. Soon all memory of that other, stupid song had flown from her ears.

14. New York City, August 1982

She sat at the Queen Anne desk in her dressing gown, going over her checkbook and the latest royalty statement. Even though there had been business managers and lawyers to handle their finances for more than a decade, she kept an eye on her money, almost as closely as she watched the scale. There was still some of it drib- bling in from their catalog, especially overseas. Their Christmas album sold every year. While they were recording it, she went to the brother and said she wanted to recut her vocal on their famous Christmas song, which they'd put out as a single the first year of their success. She wanted to tone down the huskiness. "I used to oversing on the earlier albums," she told a writer from *Billboard*.

But the money was nothing like it was only a few years ago. She thought about when the royalties started getting really ridiculous, in 1974. Their Hits album had reached No. 1 in the States; that had always been the plan. But it also broke sales records in Britain, in Japan, in Australia. When *those* checks started to come in, she had to keep staring at the zeroes and counting them, to make sure she was seeing right. Not that they had much time to spend all this money. Between the world tour they did that summer and the fact that they still lived at home, it just got salted away. The brother had a big car collection, one that filled up a few garages — he got that from the father, the cars, the collecting, the tidy curating gene. You could eat off the floor of the father's garage. But in those days she had only one, a sweet '72 Mercedes that she just kept upgrading. The touring kept them out of the studio for much of that year, but she figured the Hits LP and the concerts would sustain them until the brother found enough good songs for a new album. "Every minute of every hour," somebody on their team said around then, "somebody somewhere in the world is playing one of your records. Listening to *you*." There was something invincible-feeling about it all. They even talked about confronting the mother when they got back to the States and telling her that they were moving out.

But there was one number she couldn't abide in those heady days of success: the one the scale kept reporting. She would have traded a few of those royalty zeroes to once, just once, see the first two digits of her weight be 1-0. She'd tried all kinds of diets and work-out regimes. There was one that had her doing bicycle pedaling before bed. It made her butt firmer but no smaller. And there was another, recommended by Cass Elliot, who'd become their friend (and dropped the "Mama" from her name). They first had dinner with her in the early '70s in L.A., and back at Cass's place, she tried to get them high. She'd taken a few tokes of a joint over the years, but it never did much for her. And she swore it off altogether when she realized it just made her hungry. They ended up having coffee.

Cass had lately found what she said was a foolproof diet, with one simple rule: Avoid all white foods. She tried it. What a kick, she thought. The critics call me white bread, and I'm not even eating it now. But when she saw some footage of them on a Bob Hope special, she thought she still looked heavy, and asked the brother what he thought. Maybe you have put on a few pounds, he said.

She was whisked back to the present by the breakfast tray. These days she always ordered big. There were pancakes smeared with mascarpone, scrambled eggs, bacon, oatmeal. She had her usual revulsion when she lifted the silver domes on the room-service trays, but she could always hope. And anyway she wanted to make sure there was plenty for her friend, I., who sometimes stayed with her at the hotel. I. was a glamorous singer and the wife of P., who produced her solo album. During those sessions three years ago, I. was the sister she never had and the one who had basically navigated New York for her. I. made the dinner reservations, told her what to wear when they went out to clubs, even tried to set her up with one of P.'s superstar acts, a recent Grammy winner. Didn't work out, but then she never had much luck with guys in the music business. Nowadays when I. stayed with her, they'd have breakfast together in the suite, and she'd try to get it down, she really would, even though the food in front of her still always seemed like a mirror that spit back the same assessment: "chubby," "pudgy," "tomboy," "Mack truck." She would have a forkful of eggs, a sliver of banana, sips of tea, a bite of pancakes. And then try to stay at the table long enough for it to take. Then record the numbers in the other ledger she kept, her calorie journal. For every 50 calories or so from half a piece of toast, she'd make sure to walk enough to burn, say, 45 of them. As long as she was in the calorie black, she figured she was making progress.

She was essentially trying to reverse the process that began during that long world tour in 1974, when she finally figured out that the only way to lose weight was to gradually just eat less and less of everything, until she was essentially not eating anything at all. Cass died in London that summer, everyone said from choking on a ham sandwich, though it was really a heart attack. Their Hits album had recently finished its long run at No. 1 on the British album charts. And the fact that they were away from the mother for so long helped, because she wasn't being force-fed fat on a daily basis.

They returned to the States late that summer, and everyone marveled at her new look. She was around 110 pounds then. That was enough, for them anyway, even though she kept thinking, *just five more*. The publicists and art directors at the record company, who'd always struggled with how to package their look, thought they finally had something to work with now. Something almost glamorous. The photo for the ad in the trades for their next single, a remake of a Motown oldie, showed her head thrown back in a musical rapture. She's almost sexy, one of the publicity assistants wrote in an office memo. Of course when the ad ran in the trades, it was cut in with a picture of the brother.

The president had just resigned around the time they got back. She felt sad. He had been kind to her when they played the White House, just a few months before. "You're a talented girl," he said. She wore a white maxi and still had her bangs. The first lady, she remembered, was tall and friendly and smelled clean and perfumed, like laundry soap. The only downside of that day was when she remembered something a nasty critic had written in a review of their last album, that her trying to sing a rock tune reminded him of the first lady's "eating an ice-cream cone with a spoon." Why did everything always come back to food?

Back home after the tour, they confronted the mother. "We're moving out," they said. The mother flew into a rage, and said if they did, they could take the father with them. They compromised,

offering to move to the same house together, just a few blocks away
in the same suburb, not up to one of the "Uptown" parts of L.A. like
Brentwood or Santa Monica. The mother accepted this deal.

She perused the entries in her check ledger. The hotel, the doctor, New York, those were all her choices, much to the chagrin of
the brother and the mother, who wanted her close to home in L.A.
But it was the cost of the husband that was mostly on her mind. For
the year or so of their marriage, he treated her like his personal cash
register. Twenty thousand here, 30 thousand there. A house, land,
a $500 bottle of dusty wine to stick in the face of the guard at the
gate of her condo complex, who always called him by *her* last name.
The one thing he gave her, a car, turned out to be leased, and she
was home when the company came to repossess it. That was the last
night she saw him. He was her lawyer's problem now.

Why had she married him? So fast? Well, he was good-looking.
He was blond. ("His hair is a little too perfect," P. had said.) He
claimed to have money ("His own yacht!"). And to have no idea
who she was. The family liked him. She'd just had a big letdown
when the solo album was shelved. Maybe this would kick-start
things again. When he proposed, two months after they met, she
said yes by playing a song for him in her car. Their courtship and
engagement took less time than it had for her to make the solo album. And while they were dating, no one told her she was too thin.

But even before the wedding, she knew it was all wrong. Among
other things, he'd come to her a few days before the ceremony and
said he'd had a vasectomy. She went to the mother, told her she
wanted to stop the whole thing, but the mother said: "The invi-
tations have been sent, *People* magazine is coming, your brother
has written a new song for the occasion. Deal with the problems
later." A few times she thought that maybe the mother wanted her
out of the way, that once she was married the brother could finally
take center stage. On her wedding day, she stood at the back of the
room in the Beverly Hills Hotel with F., her matron of honor, and

said, "O.K., let's get the worst day of my life over with." She must be a good actress, she thought later, because one of her friends told the reporter from *People* that she'd never seen her looking so happy. The wedding made the cover, but only an inset at the top. The main picture was of Angie Dickinson, who had a big comeback movie that year. Well, she thought, if Angie can do it. . . .

That day I. was back with P. in Westchester. (She'd forgotten to change the breakfast order.) I. had recently delivered some big news: She was pregnant, due in early February.

"Wow, was that in the plan?" she asked. "What about your career? Are you sure you want to do this?"

Of course she was happy for I. and P., though. She wanted children, too. Someday. But for now she couldn't imagine any other priority in her life than being a singer. She'd seen a news report recently about a janitor in a New York high school who was a famous doo-wopper in the '50s. How does anybody stop being a singer? she thought. She had as much trouble wrapping her brain around that thought as she did around the fact that their song about the extraterrestrials hadn't been a bigger hit, or when she heard that one of their fan-club members had died. Or that one of their fan-club secretaries had drowned while on vacation. How can somebody who bought one of our records not be alive anymore? she thought. Or somebody who worked for us?

She figured she still had a good 10 years of fertility, though, and there were all those other things ahead of it on her list: the career resurrection, dumping the husband and finding a new one. Of course she also had to get her period back. No such luck there today.

15. Queens, N.Y., July 1970

The three-hour rec session that morning couldn't go fast enough for Sib. She tore through arts and crafts, could have made maybe 20 lanyards. She was a holy terror in dodgeball, catching anything that was thrown remotely near her and nailing her going-into-fifth classmates with boom-boom precision. In the game room, she banked shots off the sides of the knock-hockey table and into the slot goal with such accuracy that a crowd gathered, and even took her mind off Aunt Maddy and "Band of Gold" for a quick minute.

But by 11:45, when the classes were lining up for dismissal, she was practically shimmying in place to the rhythm of the song, and half-sprinted all the way home, taking the sidewalk squares two at a time. She bounded up the steps by the side door, and there they were, her mother and Aunt Maddy, setting places at the kitchen table.

"Siobhan," Aunt Maddy said, bending down for a kiss, and suddenly Sib was aware of her sweatiness, her lack of girliness, in the presence of her still-pretty aunt with her Shirley Temple copse of gray curls and her straight spine and bright colored-in-the-lines lips and print dress and heels. Late-night-movie glamour. Old-lady glamour, especially in comparison with her younger, no-nonsense mother, in her plain white blouse, black slacks, tennis shoes and barbershop cut. Over Maddy's shoulder, Sib could see the platter of cold cuts laid out from the deli, rare roast beef and turkey and Virginia ham (not like the packaged Oscar Mayer stuff they usually ate), paper containers of coleslaw and macaroni salad, a whole dill, a bag of freshly sliced bakery rye bread, an Entenmann's chocolate cake for dessert. And four place settings with cloth napkins. Sib knew all of this was Maddy's doing. Maddy always traveled fancy, even with deli.

And, Sib knew, with a heavy purse. At some point Maddy was sure to slip Sib some cash. Her mother would object, and Maddy would find some excuse for it. Sib could practically see "Band of Gold" spinning now on the downstairs hi-fi. But how would she get to Rose's store to buy it? She still wasn't allowed to go there by herself; it was too far down Liberty Avenue. She'd have to get Kieran to take her. But even though there was a place set for him at the table, he was nowhere in sight. Sib hadn't seen his bike outside.

"Is Kieran coming home for lunch?" Sib asked her mother as she gently extracted herself from Aunt Maddy's embrace. Despite Sib's sweatiness, Maddy had offered no whiff of disapproval.

"He called to say that baseball practice was running late but that he'd be home soon," her mother said, as Maddy now emptied the paper carton of macaroni salad, which she called "elbow," into a proper dish. "Now go wash up."

Sib used the basement bathroom — it was closer — and passed the record player on the way. "Gimme Dat Ding," by the Pipkins was still on the turntable; Sib picked it off and put it back in its sleeve and ran a dust cloth over the hi-fi. She wanted the machine ready for "Band of Gold." Where was Kieran? She had to have the record that day.

Back at the kitchen table, Sib reached for a piece of rye bread.

"Just a minute, young lady," Aunt Maddy said. "You know you're supposed to spread your napkin on your lap first."

Sib was stung by this comment. Usually it was Aunt Constance who set conditions, who made them say grace or wash a second time because they'd missed a spot under a fingernail (or at least made *her* wash again; Kieran never seemed to miss a spot), who insisted on the proscription before the pleasure. Sib picked up her napkin and unfolded it, but before she could put it on her lap, two crisp dollar bills fluttered out and got there first. *Aunt Maddy!*

"Well, look at that," Aunt Maddy said. "Someone must have been a good girl."

Sib scooped up the bills and put them on the table, one on each side of her plate. Suddenly she had forgotten about lunch.

"Really, Maddy, you shouldn't have," Genie said, only halfheartedly, because she'd probably reap some of Maddy's generosity herself before the afternoon was over.

"Oh, now, Genie, I haven't seen her since the school year ended, and I heard she had a good report card, so she deserves a belated reward." Aunt Maddy glanced over at Kieran's place setting. "Just don't ruin the surprise for your brother, all right, sweetheart?" she said, winking at Sib.

Sib could barely contain her joy. *Kieran, where are you?* she was thinking. *There's money from Maddy and an extra trip to Rose's.* She was practically trying to will him home.

The lunch conversation buzzed and flitted all around Sib but never quite landed; maybe her mother or aunt intoned the usual line about the roast beef being sliced thin, something about a sale at Lord & Taylor or A&S. Maybe a cameo by Carmen Miranda. All Sib could think about was spending that two dollars at Rose's shop. She gobbled down her sandwich and dessert and kept listening for the bike in the driveway, but still there was no Kieran, no way for her to get to Rose's. Aunt Maddy and her mother left his silverware while they cleared the rest, then sat back down at the table and poured themselves tall, cone-shaped glasses of Schaefer.

Sib couldn't wait for Kieran anymore. She was going to look for him.

"Mom, I'm going to ride my bicycle," she said.

"O.K., but don't go too far or stay out too long. Come back in time to say goodbye to your aunt. If you see your brother, tell him to come in for lunch."

"Have fun, sweetheart," Maddy said, a beer-foam mustache bleeding into her lipstick.

Sib had the two dollars buried in her shorts as she pulled her green Sting-Ray bike with the banana seat out of the garage and set off looking for Kieran; if she found him on his way home she could let him know that Maddy was at the house and beg him to take her to Rose's after his lunch. She knew he wouldn't say no. But after riding around a few blocks, she still hadn't seen him. She rode down to the ball field at the school where baseball practice was that day, but it was deserted. Where was he?

Finally Sib found herself at the intersection of Liberty and Rockaway, near the cemetery, where Sib was not to go by herself. Beyond, the crossings were too wide, the traffic too heavy and coming from all directions, the neighborhood a little sketchier. Even someone as confident on her bike as Sib might have trouble negotiating all of that by herself. Rose's shop — and "Band of Gold" — were waiting several blocks beyond, but she didn't dare try the trip on her own.

Sib turned around, back to the safe confines of her neighborhood, and took another pass by the house to check for Kieran's bike in the driveway. Still not there. She rode around some more as the sun got higher and hotter and eventually got back to the corner of Liberty and Rockaway. By this time she knew that even if Kieran got home soon it would be too late for him to take her to Rose's; he'd be too tired or would need to practice piano. It was now or now.

The minute the front wheel of her bicycle rolled over the curb at Rockaway, Sib's whole landscape changed. Everything seemed clouded over, tinted dark. The intersections became like Olympic-size long-jump pits, or Evel Knievel canyons for her to ford, with the scary snouts and jaws of the cars and taxis and trucks all around ready just to crush her or swallow her up. The rumble of the overhead el, which Sib had known her whole life and which had become almost as familiar and comforting as her mother's singing voice, was now like an upside-down earthquake. Her legs and feet, usually so steady on the bike, at any physical pursuit, became jelly globs, her feet slipping on the pedals as she tried to steel herself, the bike sometimes as wobbly as when her dad taught her to ride years ago. She kept her mind on "Band of Gold" the whole time, singing it to herself, using the song's frequent vocal and percussive accents to pump her legs, restore their power. Every horn honk, every shout, every dog bark in the distance seemed directed at her. Just keep going, she thought.

She got across nine of the blocks — dodging pedestrians, an old lady with a pushcart of groceries, a city bus that seemed so close Sib could almost feel it on the skin of her arms — until she was finally one block away from Rose's store. While she was waiting at a light, she looked around and saw a man on the corner — scraggly, graying beard, tie-dyed T-shirt, army boots with detached flaps — turning around in backward circles, drinking something out of a paper bag. Suddenly he stopped circling and said, facing Sib, "That's an awful purty bike you got there, baby girl."

Sib didn't respond. She turned back to the light, idling her bike, and just kept staring at the walk signal. For a few seconds the lyrics of "Band of Gold" gave way to an Our Father, a Hail Mary and a Glory Be.

The light changed, and Sib shot out. She could see Rose's shop now, and the fear started to leave her as she got across and pulled up on the sidewalk, the cloud cover suddenly being drawn back. Other than her own house, there was nowhere as comforting to Sib as this dusty, cluttered, magical place. She'd made it. But when she got closer to the shop, her attention was diverted to the curb. There was Kieran's bike, a three-speed English racer, locked to a No Parking sign.

So he was here already! Suddenly Sib's competitive fires were lit, and she hurriedly fit her bike into his as she had hundreds of times in their garage — her pedal sliding neatly into his frame, her handlebars draping over his seat, car and sidecar, hero and sidekick, note and top note, body and limb. She clicked her lock and bolted into the store. She not only had to have "Band of Gold" now; she had to have it *before* Kieran. As she rushed toward the counter, she took a quick survey of the store: She didn't see him, so maybe he was in the back looking at the albums. Maybe he hadn't bought anything yet. Maybe Sib would get to "Band of Gold" first.

Rose was behind the counter twirling some spaghetti on a fork, a tin of eggplant parmigiana, half a loaf of garlic bread, a green salad and a coffee milkshake arrayed in front of her. Sib marched behind the counter. "Chipper!" Rose said. "Here by yourself? Your brother's in the back. . . ."

Sib slid a copy of "Band of Gold" out of its slot on the wall, put a dollar on the register and headed toward the back of the store. Rose had a booth tucked in a corner where customers could listen to their purchases or play a few seconds of the store copy of a record, and when Sib didn't see Kieran in the aisles, she figured that's where he had to be. As she got closer to the booth she could see the shadow of someone about Kieran's height behind the frosted pane on the top of the booth's door. And she could hear something coming from the booth. It was . . . that song they'd heard at the table that morning, that song that Kieran had sung, in harmony, with their mother.

Well, if Kieran was going to waste his time with that stupid song, Sib thought, she would show him that she had the real prize. She yanked open the door to the listening booth and had "Band of Gold" at the ready to shove in his face, as if to say, "I got it first!"

When she opened the door, in the split second of her gaze, she could see Kieran, his back to her, still in his baseball jersey and cap. She could smell the outfield grass and mud still wedged in his cleats. But then that sickly song, softer when the door was closed, assaulted her ears in full force. And she noticed that there was someone else in the booth with Kieran. And the two of them were swaying, at least as far as the cramped space in the booth would allow. And they were . . . holding hands. It was only after a few more seconds that Sib realized that the person in the booth with Kieran was another boy.

16. Queens, N.Y., July 1970

Sib froze. Until a few minutes ago the scariest experience of her life had been the solo trip on her bike down Liberty Avenue. But now it had been replaced by that vision in the listening booth, by the sound coming from it. Why was Kieran at Rose's without her? Who was that boy? What were they doing in the booth? She'd felt as if she wanted to scream, not just to get Kieran's attention but to break the spell. Maybe it would all go away. That other boy. That dumb song. It was all that dumb song's fault.

Instead she just turned around and ran. Through the album

aisles, past Rose, now slurping the last of her milkshake. "Chipper," she yelled as Sib dashed by, "you forgot your change." Sib heard her but didn't care. All she wanted now was to get back home, back into the kitchen with her Aunt Maddy and her mother, back to that moment at the end of lunch when this was looking like the most perfect day ever.

Sib was still clutching her copy of "Band of Gold" when she got outside to her bike. She threaded it through the handlebars and fumbled with her lock. She didn't know if Kieran had seen her, but she didn't want to wait around to find out. She spun the dial on the lock and overshot the combination numbers a few times until she finally steadied her hand and it clicked open. She uncoupled her bike from Kieran's and hopped on the banana seat and was suddenly shooting back over those same treacherous roads she'd traveled on her way to Rose's. But while on the outlaw trip there she had been aware of every pebble, every bit of graffiti, every hot-dog wrapper in the street, every whiff of exhaust and White Castle grease and malt liquor, the way back was all a blur, as if somebody else were making sure all the lights had changed, that the cars and pedestrians weren't too close. She didn't even hear the el. Once or twice she checked to see if "Band of Gold" was secure on the handlebars, but otherwise she was on autopilot, her bike wheels traveling smoothly in the same groove they'd struggled to carve out of Liberty Avenue just a half-hour earlier, the city streets blending into one another in a kind of reverse loop.

About four or five long blocks before the turn off Liberty, Sib was stopped at a light and spun around to see if Kieran had followed her out of Rose's. She could make out a far-off figure in a baseball cap on an English Racer. She couldn't tell yet if it was Kieran, but she started pumping the pedals harder, riding out alongside the curb when the sidewalk got too crowded, taking the intersections even after the Don't Walk lights started to flash, riding through traffic with the abandon she had earlier that day in dodgeball, at the knock-hockey table, whizzing by pedestrians and weaving in and out of stopped cars that barely knew she was there before she was gone. But no matter how fast she went, she felt something, someone was gaining on her. At 88th Street, she finally had to stop because the light was red, and she turned around and saw that it *was* Kieran behind her, about three blocks away, the Mets insignia on the cap, now facing forward, unmistakable. He was alone, and charging.

While she waited out the light, Sib kept turning around, trying to make out the figure on the bike behind her. The light was stuck, and she was trapped. She could see now that Kieran's mouth was moving, but in the traffic and clatter of the city, she couldn't hear what he was saying.

After what seemed like hundreds of cars had passed, she looked to her left and felt a break in the traffic. Maybe she could make it across while the light was still red. Then she'd be sure to get green lights all the way home. She darted out into the street.

There was a gold Chevy Impala gunning toward the intersection. Sib's legs were like pistons now pumping on the bike, a warrior's battle. She kept turning to look at the car almost in a game of chicken. She could take it. The car seemed to slow, to be cowed by her glare. She got to the curb and lifted the front of the bike in triumph, almost into a miniwheelie, and was ready to keep going. But as the bike rose and jerked in front of her, the copy of "Band of Gold" was jostled off the handlebars and went flying. When Sib turned around to see her prize fly out of its sleeve and shatter in the gutter behind her, she also saw that Kieran was now in the middle of the intersection.

"Sib, wait!" he yelled.

The Chevy was now just a few feet away, but Kieran was going to make it. When he got to the curb, though, a woman in a housedress and slippers walking her pug appeared from around a telephone pole, and he swerved to miss the dog. A shard of the record lying in the gutter sliced through his thin front tire, and it blew. He'd been going so fast that the momentum sent him flying headfirst over the handlebars and close to Sib's bike a few feet away. His natural athleticism should have saved him, but the graceful arc he flew in once he was in the air actually made the crown of his head, the center button of the baseball cap, hit the pavement first. His legs then swung into Sib's bike and sent her and it down.

Soon a crowd was gathering. High above, a piano riff drizzled out of an apartment window, as the WABC D.J. Dan Ingram was announcing a new No. 1 song.

17. Queens, N.Y., July 1970

Mrs. Logan lifted the sheer curtain in the front room and looked out the window at her son pushing a mower across the lawn, swiping the back of his hand on his forehead at the end of every row. "I'm worried about the boy," she said.

"What is it now?" Mr. Logan, in a wing chair, said, looking up from his pipe and a biography of Grover Cleveland.

"He just seems especially preoccupied today," Mrs. Logan said. "He barely said a word at lunch."

"He's 14, not a guest on the *Tonight* show," Mr. Logan said. "He's not supposed to keep us entertained. Or at this point in his life even like us very much."

"I know, I know," she said. "He's just always by himself. He doesn't seem to have many friends. It can't be good for him, this isolation. Even his room . . ."

"What about his room?"

"It always looks a little too clean. You should see his drawers. Everything in neat, folded piles."

"You looked in his drawers?"

"Only one."

"Would you have been happier if you found dope or some girlie magazine?"

"No, maybe, I don't know, I just, just. . . ."

"Dear, how many parents would complain about having a son who keeps his room clean and gets good grades and generally doesn't have to be told twice to do something? He's honoring his word to read for at least an hour in the morning during the summer vacation. He must have gotten through 50 pages of *Moby-Dick* today. He has his soccer and his music. Not everyone was born to be the life of the party. I'd say he's coming along just fine."

"I guess. But have you ever noticed how a room is always a little tidier after he leaves it, even though you never really see him doing anything? The other day I couldn't find my glasses, and then he came into the room for a few minutes, and when he left, they were right on the table next to me."

"Dear," Mr. Logan said, even as he was remembering the night that he was having trouble balancing his checkbook, and then Andy appeared, asked his father to sign a paper he needed for school and how after he left suddenly the checkbook was balancing. "Shouldn't we . . . ?"

"What?"

"Shouldn't we just feel lucky to have him at all?" Mrs. Logan pulled a strand or two from her gray ponytail behind her ear, let down the curtain and said, "Yes, darling, of course you're right." Mrs. Logan knew that Andy was a good kid, and he'd always been a bit of a mystery. He arrived after she and Mr. Logan had tried for years to have children and given up. She was almost six months along before she even knew she was pregnant, figuring she was going through the change. She didn't really think she and her husband had brought some socio-sorcerer into the world. Still, as it turned out, her maternal intuition wasn't so far off today.

Andy had been especially bothered the last few weeks, ever since the day he discovered that girl's voice on the radio. It was unlike any other he'd heard. Low, almost mannish, yet unmistakably coming from a girl. A hawk's precision with the vulnerability of a baby sparrow. A world-weary naïf. The song itself was a throwaway — there was some bit about moon dust and hair — and Andy didn't really care for all the choral waves the song rode out on. But the rest of the arrangement was so clean, so spiffy, every piano and drum fill efficient, every note of the flügelhorn leaving space around it, the sauntering beat giving the girl the perfect leverage she needed over the song, giving her room for her slightly halting cadences, for her tongue to poke gently in her cheek. It was like a break in the humidity after a summer storm, a clearing, a cleanse.

Andy was ever-discerning about the records he'd admit to his collection. He wasn't a sloppy music profligate, like Cousin Tom, a five-spin-and-out kind of guy. When he decided to make space in his collection, in his life, for a record, he was going to take care of it, honor it, commit to it. Not consign it to some half-attended aisle next to his bed. It had to be special. The first time he heard this record, he knew he had to own it.

And the song was also the source of his funk. He'd been to half a dozen record stores, and everywhere he went, there was an empty slot. Everywhere a clerk saying they were out of it. One pit-stained, cigar-chomping, Ralph-Kramden-type store owner said, "Every teenage girl in town wants that record. And not a few teenage boys, either." He gave Andy a smirky look. "Only *they* ask for it quietly."

He thought about going back to his neighborhood music shop again the next day, but then he remembered a store he'd heard about down in Jamaica or Ozone Park, owned by a fat woman who used a whip to ward off shoplifters. After he finished mowing the lawn, he got out the Yellow Pages. *Rose's Record Room,* on Liberty Avenue. That was it. He'd have to take a bus and a train to get there, but if the store had the record in stock . . .

He phoned the shop a few times, but the line was busy, busy, busy. What a wasted trip, a wasted summer afternoon it would be if he went all the way down to Jamaica and that store was out of it, too. Still, he had to have it, to play it when he needed it, not when the radio decided that for him, even if lately the song seemed to be on every five minutes.

After he bagged the grass clippings and cleaned up, he told his parents, who were both now reading in the backyard, that he was going out to look for a record.

"Be home in time for dinner," one or the other said from their twin chaises, looking up from their plastic-sleeved library books. "Keep your wallet in your front pocket," the other one said. "And don't get recruited for anything." Mrs. Logan thought to herself, at least he's getting out of the house.

Andy didn't like public transportation very much, the crowds, the close proximity, the tight clusters, but it might not be so bad getting to the store at midday. He caught the bus on the corner and found a seat with empty ones on either side. So far, so good. Space.

The subway was a different story, though. Not a seat to be had, even at a non-rush-hour time. Baby strollers, women with large, swinging pocketbooks and big hair, smelly men in polyester, bumping, staring, barely enough room to stand near a pole, the el rickety and listy as it rolled into the southern part of Queens, the train just getting more crowded, stuffier, hotter. Andy cooled himself with the thought of the song, itself a thermostat adjuster, a course corrector; it would be worth a mini-odyssey, navigating these urban Scyllas, he kept telling himself. If the store had the record, that is.

When he finally got out on Liberty Avenue, the city hit him full blast. Car traffic, foot traffic, air traffic, everything congested, noisy, fettered, fast yet tethered. People desperate to get somewhere they weren't. A kind of stagnant urgency. After a few blocks of the crush, he began to wonder if the record was worth the trip, if maybe he could have waited a couple of days.

His first sight of Rose's Record Room didn't give him much hope, either. The store's window looked as if it hadn't been washed in weeks, the record covers inside the display years old and yellowed, the sign for the store missing half its letters. And when he walked in, his sinuses were stung by the smell of sandalwood and jasmine and patchouli, his eyes by the sight of hanging beads and psychedelic posters. So the store didn't sell just music. It was a den for hippies, a few of whom were wandering around the place. Maybe Cousin Tom bought his records here, Andy thought.

Andy approached the counter, and behind it, there was the woman he'd heard about, maybe 400 pounds of her, mounted on a huge swivel chair, swinging a forkful of spaghetti in the air like a conductor's baton, small splotches of tomato sauce either side of her mouth. The 45s were behind her on the wall; Andy couldn't make out the titles from where he was, so haphazardly and lurchingly were they scrawled on cloth tape. And there was the whip, an arm's length away from the woman, coiled loosely, lying in wait.

As Andy kept squinting at the 45 wall, the woman suddenly spoke.

"Can I help you, honey?" she said as she pulled a napkin from somewhere in the tent of a frock she was wearing. It must take her an hour to get dressed every morning, Andy thought. Yet there was something about her he liked. He heard a sweetness in her voice, a lack of hucksterism, a matronly balm that put him at ease, made him think that maybe he was right to come all the way down here after all. It might have just been part of the sales pitch, but it was effective. He asked for the record.

"Oh, I'm sorry," she said. "I just sold my last copy a few minutes ago. Something else, that record, isn't it? There's always one every year that I can't seem to keep in stock. Last year it was 'Sugar, Sugar.' The year before it was 'Hey Jude.' Now it's this song. I must have sold 100 pieces already. Girl has some voice, doesn't she? Clear and sparkling as crystal. Like the singers of my day. If you like, I can put one aside for you when it comes back in."

Andy had no idea when the woman's "day" might have been; her face was so made up, her swirled hair so shiny, slickly black, her body so big, that you couldn't really tell how old she was. And now he'd come all the way down to this smelly place with nothing to show for it. "Oh, thanks, but I don't live around here, so I'm not sure when I could get back," he said.

"Came out of your way, did you? I can tell how special that record must be to you," she said. "And let me tell you, it is a special record. You know what, the young man I sold the last copy to, he's one of my regular customers and a very nice kid. In fact, he's still here. He just took the record in the back to the listening booth. Maybe if you asked him, he might let you buy his copy, and then he can come back for another one tomorrow when the new shipment arrives."

Andy's first impulse was to get out of there. He wasn't about to go asking some kid he didn't know if he could buy his record. If the kid was playing it in the booth now, the record would be used anyway. For a song this important, Andy wanted the first listen to the pristine copy to be his, to be able to drop the needle on the shiny, unspoiled wax, inhale those first perfect, unsullied notes. But he had to have that record, and before he could leave the store, the idea of asking the kid started kicking around in his head — gently at first, as he found himself drifting toward the album aisles, and then the idea like a soccer ball that he got more and more comfortable with as he handled it downfield, warding off thoughts of turning back the way he would a closing defender. He found himself standing in front of the frosted door to the booth, a red light above indicating that it was occupied, and through the glass, he could see the silhouette of the boy, who was wearing a backward baseball cap. He'd just started to listen to the record, as the girl's voice, even muffled by the closed door, was coming through indelibly, softly-firmly encircling Andy as she sang the song's first few phrases.

Andy knocked.

He could see the kid take the needle off the record and then reach his arm behind him. The door handle clicked. The light above the booth changed to green. The boy opened the door and turned around.

In the back of his mind, Andy was photographing the details of the boy, which he'd be able to call up years later whenever he thought about this day: the perfect half lock of strawberry-blond hair that peeked out of his baseball cap, the freckles and dots of baby fat on his Irishy face that were the last traces of childhood in a boy who, though he was about Andy's age, was already seven-eighths a man. The forearms that widened just below the elbows, the chest that was pushing against the front of his baseball jersey, the coat of reddish fur on the boy's calves, the baseball cleats.

They caught each other's eyes: the boy's wide and kind, mini-lighthouse beams of blue, Andy's rounder, darker, absorbent, his brows fuller, maybe the only thing about him that was more filled in. But what really locked were their ears: the girl's voice, still so fresh and hanging in the air, connecting them, making speaking unnecessary. That voice told them everything they needed to know, who they were, what they shared.

The boy pushed the door open and beckoned with a slight side nod of his head for Andy to join him. There was barely enough room in the booth for both of them, but suddenly Andy wasn't aware of space, or the lack of it. The boy pulled the door closed behind them. They stood shoulder to shoulder, and both just looked down at the record in front of them, still shiny and spinning, the almost-virgin vinyl. The kid lifted the needle and put it down on the record. The four-bar intro gave them a few seconds to prepare, to take a deep breath, to clear whatever else about their day, about their lives might have been a distraction: What they'd done before that minute, what they planned to do after the song was over, who needed them, where they had to be. None of it mattered. In the last two beats, in that pitch of anticipation just before the girl started to sing, their hands clasped.

As the girl took over the song, Andy felt something transferring out of him into the boy and felt himself drawing something back, and felt both of them drawing something from the girl's voice, its velvety spike, its lambency and gentle exasperation. It was like a current suddenly switched on. It made Andy almost sick with happiness. The jolt made his knees buckle slightly. In that girl's low tones, Andy was hearing his better self, or a payback for every good deed he'd ever done. And feeling the grip of someone, which as they held onto each other and the song continued, just grew stronger, someone who understood, who felt the same way, who got him.

They were almost near the end of the second bridge when suddenly the door opened behind them. Before them stood a girl — younger than they were, not a teenager yet — with a record in her hand. The look of shock on the girl's face stunned Andy and, it seemed, unnerved the boy, breaking the spell. The girl bolted away, and the boy, just as the singer finished her lead vocal, unlocked his hand from Andy's and ran out of the booth. He left behind his record, by now into the fade of the choral wahs.

Andy stood still in the booth. He still wasn't sure what had happened in the last five minutes of his life, why he was shaking, why something had suddenly, wonderfully swirled out of his control, why everything was very different now. The boy was gone but the record was still there, and when it was over, he carefully lifted the needle, replaced it in its stand, took the record off the turntable and slid it gently back into its sleeve. He brought it up to the front of the store, where the woman was now slurping up the dregs of a milkshake.

"That boy left his record," Andy said, with a slight quiver, offering it over the counter to the woman. Maybe the boy hadn't gone far. Maybe Andy could find him and return it himself.

"Did he?" she said. "Well, he's already taken off. Why don't you keep it, then? He'll be back in soon enough for another copy."

Normally Andy would do no such thing. But that record now meant something more to him than he'd even imagined it could when he set out to buy it. He fished out his wallet from his front pocket and offered the woman a dollar. He would have paid $10 or more if she'd asked. But she waved it back at him.

"This one's on Rose, honey. I've made a nice piece of change on that record already, and I'm bound to make a bit more. I'm telling you, that girl's a keeper, she's probably going to be bringing customers into Rose's store for years. You seem like a nice boy, and Rose likes your taste in music. It's my present to you. Just come back and see me again, all right?"

"Yes, ma'am, thank you," Andy said. "I will."

Andy walked out of the store and stepped out into the hot asphalt, and as he held the record in the same hand that had held the boy's, his middle fingers threaded through the center hole, suddenly the city didn't seem so smoggy, so sweaty, so crowded, so exposed. The graffiti bombs and peeling handbills he could see on a storefront on the other side of the street looked like the botanical gardens in full bloom now. The feeling, if he had to describe it, was like being refilled, refueled, restored, reset, but even those words didn't do it justice. He floated to the subway station, holding the record close to him, keeping the girl's voice and the feeling of the boy's strong, capable hand in his head. As he entered the stairs to the el, he barely realized that he was helping a woman in front of him with a large cart filled with groceries on her ascent, lifting up the back side of the cart to make her going easier.

He got home and raced up to his room and his record player. His mother noticed the change in him instantly. The lightening. "Everything O.K., son?" she called up after him. "Find what you were looking for?"

"I sure did, Mom," Andy said. He couldn't even begin to explain to her how happy he felt. He must have played the record a dozen times in a row. The girl's voice alone made the experience almost as good as if that boy from the listening booth had been there with him. Almost as good.

Andy did go back to Rose's Record Room several weeks later, when the singer, who turned out to be part of a duo with her older brother, had a new song on the radio, one that Andy, much to his surprise, liked even more than the first one. It was a stronger song, had a leaner, more active arrangement, and the girl just sounded even more . . . vital. Another necessity, another requirement for his collection. And in the back of his mind Andy was hoping that maybe he'd run into that boy again, or at least gin up the courage to ask the woman who owned the store where he might find him. He was sure the boy liked this second hit as much as he did.

But when Andy went to the shop again, on a crisp October Saturday, it was closed, its doors shuttered "by the authority of the I.R.S. for nonpayment of taxes." "We'll be back soon," the woman or someone had written on a sign on the door. Andy felt sad for the woman, for the hippies, for the boy who had to find another regular record store, even oddly felt sad for the whip, with no perpetrators now to snap into line. He was getting ready to leave when, in the back corner of the window display, he saw a faded Polaroid of the boy's face. The scribbling underneath it was too blurry; Andy could only make out the word "Farewell." So the kid had moved away, Andy thought. He said a prayer for the kid: Be safe.

He ended up buying the duo's new album, which had both hits on it, at another store. And he never saw that boy in the baseball cap again, though he would think of him often, especially when he heard that girl sing. And he kept that single, the one that the boy's hands had touched first, in an honored place, curled his fingers through the center hole every now and then to bring back, to maintain, the muscle memory of that other hand. "Not a few teenage boys" want this record, that one clerk had said. But no boy like that boy.

18. Queens, N.Y., Fall 1970

They brought her the boy's cap and baseball glove, in their pressed uniforms and shiny stripes and badges, the way military honor guards present American flags to the parents or spouses of their fallen comrades. Her sisters all showed up in their Sunday dresses and veils. They told her he'd gone away. Well, of course he had. That morning he seemed to have a mission on his mind. A special mission for a special boy. A boy who had been an answered prayer.

She'd just wanted him so much. It would be easy to say that it was because she grew up in a house filled with women, where for whatever reason there was no room for men, the father she never knew, the brother who disappeared off the grid. The men who always went missing, maybe driven away themselves by the number of women in the house. In the orbit of the Rooneys, it seemed to be a liability to be a male.

Until Roy came along. It was after Korea, right after she'd dropped out of college and was working for a business-machine company, that she met Roy down by the Red Hook ball fields, big, kind, strong, capable, incombustible Roy. He'd done his time in the service and had a good job with the Post Office. He never asked too many questions. He knew that just because he could hit a ball, he didn't have to be Willie Mays, or even *want* to be Willie Mays. (His name even rhymed with "boy"!) Their courtship was spent mostly at football and hockey games, Ebbets Field and the old Madison Square Garden. Her sisters wondered if maybe she could do better than a mailman. No, Genie thought. He's a mailman. He was an infantryman. He was a first baseman. Her own man. A *man* who wasn't going away.

Early on she was curious about sex, and on the way home from a Rangers game one night she asked if they could get a hotel room, if maybe they could try it before they were married. But he said no, let's wait, let's do it right, let's do what the church says. Genie almost broke it off with him over that, but after a couple of weeks, when he kept calling, and when not many other suitors did, she finally said yes, she would go out with him again, then yes, she would marry him, then yes, they could wait, and they did. Sturdy, undisappearing Roy.

The first year of their marriage, Genie went to Mass not just on Sundays but at least once during the week, and prayed for a boy. God rewarded her, she knew, almost immediately, when she conceived the night the Brooklyn Dodgers won the Series for the first and only time. Nine months later, she almost couldn't believe her ears when the nurse said, "Mrs. Kelly, you have a son."

And the boy, from the first minute he was put in her arms, was everything she wanted. Yes he cried and shat and ate a ton, but it never felt like work raising him. Every second they were together, he seemed to be telling her that all those years of waiting were really over now. He was handsome, he could throw a ball, he started to read early, he had a sweet nature. He was worth it all, this boy.

Genie thought she finally had everything she wanted: a good son, and a good husband, their own home. A home with men. She didn't really love to cook or clean. She did most everything out of a box or a can or something prewrapped, so her meals were never as sumptuous as her sister Maddy's, who could make even a main course taste like a confection, or Constance's, whose dinners were more basic but still tasty. (Ever the spinster scold, Constance told Genie once she got engaged to Roy that maybe she should spend a little more time in the kitchen and a little less time sticking her nose under hoods, and start getting her hair cut in salons instead of barbershops.) Maybe the mops and the dusters in their house never got all the way into the corners. But once a month or so she'd make a cake from a mix. She took care of the boy. They were happy, the three of them.

She always knew he was destined for something special. She just didn't think it would be this soon. He was only going to start high school in the fall, that big Catholic one on Long Island. Every morning and afternoon and into the night she would wear his cap and mitt and sit in the backyard or at the top of the driveway and watch the planes soaring into the sky from J.F.K. Was he on one of them? Maybe the White House was calling him to consult on all the youth unrest in the country. Or he was being called to the Paris Peace talks to help end the Vietnam War. A very special boy.

She'd been spotting for a while, but she thought nothing of it. She'd always been strong and healthy. And she never liked going to the doctor. Maybe she might even be pregnant again. It was a long shot, but not impossible. She hadn't gone through the change yet. A third child, to go with the boy and the girl. She'd know soon enough.

Oh, yes, the girl. She'd never really thought about another child then, so perfect, so finally complete was her life, but about four years after the boy was born, she found out she was expecting again. Could she get lucky one more time? Have another boy? Handsome Jack Kennedy was on TV campaigning for the presidency. She was due around the time of the election. Just as she conceived the boy when the Dodgers won the Series, her new due date seemed to augur something good. Kennedy won the presidency in a squeaker. A Catholic was going to the White House! She went into labor two days after the election.

But then, a girl. Constance told her she should have some girls' names ready just in case, but Genie never thought about not having a boy. She let Roy name her, after his grandmother. That was fine. She liked Roy's family, his mother cooked and baked hearty fare like pot roast and corned beef and cupcakes (always left unfrosted) and sewed and scrubbed and always made Genie feel warm and welcome in her home. She was an Irish nanny or rectory cook right out of central casting. Ample, uncomplicated, unquestioning, like her son.

The girl, though, was colicky. And always gave Genie trouble about food, wouldn't eat anything but cereal until she was almost 4. Then was picky about everything else, clothes, getting ready for school, where she'd sit in the car, asking them to stop every hour on a long ride so she could go to the bathroom. And the girl always got in her face. While the boy would say, "Mommy, that's coffee," or pick out something on the piano on his own, the girl would say, "Mommy, what's this, what's that?" "Mommy, how do you make pudding?" "Mommy, what's a 9-iron?" "Mommy, what's a period?" "Mommy, Mommy, Mommy." With the girl it seemed that every day Genie's love had to be declared, reaffirmed, annotated. God, when Genie was in college, how she hated footnotes. So fussy. So tedious. So much effort. "Yes, yes,

Mommy loves you. Ibid."

The boy knew how his mother felt about the girl. And so he took care of his sister, watched out for her, got her out of the house, out of Genie's face, included her in his very special life. The girl was athletic, too, if not as graceful as the boy. And she was musical, if not as tuneful as the boy. She overdid everything. Oversang, overcharged the basketball hoop. Still, the boy didn't seem to mind. And when the three of them had their dance parties in the basement, Genie would swing both of them around, and suddenly the girl got in step. Those dance parties were their best times together.

A very special boy. And a girl who wasn't as special but still had her moments.

The girl was away now, too, at a sleepover somewhere.

They just seemed to understand each other, she and the boy. Once he could talk, he never wasted his words. They laughed at the same jokes. The girl would say, "Mommy, why is that funny?" at something or other on TV, while Genie and the boy would look at each other and not say a word. They just knew.

And they liked the same foods. Broccoli and blueberries. How could you not love a kid who loved broccoli? Sometimes she'd stay out in the yard until 10 or 11, into Indian summer now, not caring about the night chill, the leaves starting to gather and crunch around her feet, the stars popping out earlier and earlier, and Roy would plead with her to come in, but she'd say no, she still wanted to listen for his bicycle at the bottom of the driveway. "This is the night he's coming home, Roy," she would say. One night she actually thought she heard him coming and ran into the house, figuring he'd be hungry. She didn't even bother to turn on the kitchen light. She went right to the freezer and yanked out a box of broccoli. She threw the frozen chunk of it into a pot and just let it cook, till the water boiled out and it started to smoke. He'd smell it and want to come in, she thought. She just stood there in the dark over the pot and inhaled and waited for him. When after about half an hour Roy turned off the burner, she went up to the boy's room. She'd kept it clean — she knew he'd like that — but she also knew he'd want it to *smell* clean. So she got out the bottle of Clorox, opened it and left it in the middle of the room. As she did every night since he left, she slept in his bed that night. When she woke up, the bottle was gone. Maybe he'd been there. Maybe he'd known.

Every night he didn't come home, there were a few more drops of blood.

The boy had a secret. She knew this. But he kept it to himself, and she never pressed him on it. He seemed to have it on his mind that morning. Maybe it was his mission. Maybe that was the secret. Maybe he already knew that that was the day he was going to leave.

Didn't everybody have secrets? She certainly did. Years ago she laughed when that surf group from California had the big hit with the lyric about the bad guys leaving them alone. She laughed because some young connected guy from the old 'hood in Flatbush had said that about *her* when she was about 15 or 16. The bad guys know Genie and they leave her alone. Because they knew what was good for them. And no boy wanted to get his ass kicked by a girl.

Whatever was on her boy's mind, everything seemed perfect that morning. They were singing along with a song from the radio, by a new young singer — lovely voice, light and heavy at the same time. Genie and her boy sang in unison, then harmonized, then unison, then they'd split, she'd go up, he'd go down, he'd go up, she'd go down. The daughter was at the table, too. She tried to join them. She almost had it a couple of times but couldn't quite hold her part. But the boy, he had it. They'd probably be able to pick it out on the piano.

On the last night, when she couldn't cover or clean up the blood anymore, she crawled into the boy's bed. She left the window open to listen for his bicycle, and she thought she could hear that girl on the radio again, somewhere in the distance, but singing a different song now. She'd close her eyes and listen. Such a pretty voice, that girl.

19. New York City, September 1982

Summer was nearing its end, and three things were weighing on her mind, the first and foremost being, of course, her weight. She still hadn't gained much, despite the therapy and the fact that she was actually starting to keep some food down. Second, there was the family's imminent arrival from the coast, for a group therapy session. And third, oddly enough, there was I.'s pregnancy. After her initial joy for I. and P., and the mental gymnastics that told her she still had time to have children of her own, she got to thinking of the child she did have. The "baby" she had with P. They made the decision to have it, conceived after several weeks, helped it gestate for months. I. was even the midwife who coached her through the pre-delivery classes. The baby got to full term. And then . . .

How happy she was in those first weeks in 1979, thinking that she was going to bring something like this into the world: an album of her very own. She loved those days when she and P. would drive down to the city and the studio, reviewing songs, making an A list and a B list, going over tempos and keys. This project, this album, *her* album: She was calling the shots. Not the brother. He was brilliant, and she owed him everything, but now she wanted to try some different songs, some different styles, a different vocal register, a sexier lyrical approach. She liked how D.S. sang. Well, who didn't in those heady days of Studio 54? (She was invited to go but declined, reported the fan club dispatches, because of her work schedule.) She didn't think she was D.S., but hey, she had a voice, too. The day she signed on, she drove down Sunset with her windows open and "Hot Stuff" blasting from the speakers.

Don't do disco.

Oh, he wasn't too happy about the album, the brother. He was taking time off — he had a little problem with pills — and he wanted her to do the same. You're not well, either, he kept saying. Let's both take a long break and get some rest and get healthy and then hit the new decade running. But she wasn't interested in not working; and wasn't work always the best therapy, for her anyway? He pouted, acted hurt, betrayed. Gave her the silent treatment for a while. But she knew he knew how stubborn she could be, and he finally relented and gave his blessing. He warned her about being too trendy, too dancey, too cheap. Don't drag our good name through the disco mud, he said. Just when he was getting out of his treatment and driving all over the country, she was getting on a plane to New York.

They put out a call for material, she and P., and naturally got back lots of disco songs, including a couple of rough tracks from a hot songwriter that she liked but that even she thought sounded a little too funky for her. She told the songwriter to come up with something else. And she and P. kept going through the piles of tunes. Every day more demos. Stacks of them. People who wanted *her* to sing their songs. Some were too similar to what she'd already done, too lovey-dovey, she could hear P. thinking. Some were too different, too "out there," she could hear *herself* thinking. And finally there were two dozen or so that gave her that tingle, that "chill factor," the brother called it, only he would never consider these songs. It was all so thrilling.

So sue her, she picked one disco tune, written by a woman. It had those swirly *Saturday Night Fever* strings and a dope bass line played, strangely enough, by one-half of the other sibling act on her label, who had a few pop/funk hits of their own by that time. Would critics call her album pop/funk? Well, she wasn't sure, but they certainly wouldn't call it "easy listening." The settings were leaner. She was singing higher than usual. Her low voice, yes, it had been their bread and butter, but music had changed since their early days, so why couldn't she change with it, even for just one record? Their last few albums hadn't sold in huge numbers anyway, so why not try something different? Their legacy was already solid. This could only benefit them. And sometimes she couldn't help feeling that that low voice was the property of the brother anyway.

It took a while for her to get used to a new band, a new producer, a new city, the rock/R. & B. inflections. To work things out with the guys sitting around, instead of just having everything done for her already when she got to the studio. To find a different voice. To her, a sexier voice. To winnow down the two dozen or so songs to a perfect 11 or 12. To, as P. said, "grow up" with her audience. By the end of summer, there were four or five tracks in the can. A couple of label guys from New York came over to check on the progress. The Champagne flowed.

She flew home, elated, with a tape of those early tracks. Took them over to the parents' house. They had dinner first. "You're not eating," the mother said. "I'm too excited," she said, pushing the food around her plate. Then she played the tape. "So what do you think?" she asked. They pushed the songs around on their plates. "Well, that's different," one or the other of them said, head down. "Now let's clear the table." While she went to collect the tape, the mother said: "You should see your brother. He's looking really refreshed, says he'll be ready to go back into the studio soon. He's put on some weight. . . . "

By the sixth month, they were still only about halfway done. There were delays. P. was busy with other artists. She worried about her parents' reaction. While she was recording one of the more challenging songs, which required a lot of vocal calisthenics, she was soaked in sweat and had to excuse herself; this time the trip to the bathroom wasn't pre-planned. And there was that fainting spell she'd had at P. and I.'s house. When the paramedics came, she was already awake. P. begged them not to tell anyone who she was or what had happened. Disco was still around but seemed to be peaking, maybe starting to fade. Something called new wave was all the rage. Dizzying. Spinning. A turbocharged turntable platter.

The hot songwriter came through with a few new songs. Meanwhile, the songs of his that she turned down when the sessions for her album started months ago were completed and sent to the grown-up Motown wunderkind. His version of one of them was starting to climb the charts. She heard it on the radio and loved it. "You couldn't have done that for me?" she said to the songwriter.

They finished almost nine months to the day after they started. P. recommended a photographer from Vogue to shoot the album cover. When she saw the glam proofs, she felt as if she were looking at someone else. "Look at me, I.," she said. "I'm pretty. I'm really pretty." She'd never been so excited about an impending release. The album already had a catalog number. The record company was chatting it up; even though not many of the staffers had heard any of it. They were banking on her name and P.'s name to guarantee a smash. All that was left now was the delivery.

She and P. gathered the label bosses. And she requested that the brother be in the delivery room, too. Oh, they were going to love this.

Except, they didn't. After every track the label chiefs just sat there, bone silent. Or said something like, "Why would you do a song like that?" H., handsome H., did like a couple of the tracks. But over all this was not the reaction she was expecting. What was wrong with it? she said to P. later. They wouldn't tell her outright, only that it didn't give them the same good feeling they had about the records she made with the brother. P. told her the more overtly sexual songs must have made them think he was despoiling their daughter.

And the brother? He couldn't find enough bad things to say about it. The songs are crap, he said. Your voice is too high, he said. Nobody at the label likes it, he said. It's utterly unworthy of us, he said. At one point he said she was "stealing their sound." How could she be stealing something that she helped create?

She wanted to kill him. Or at least tell him off. What do you know? she wanted to say. You haven't exactly been producing many hits for us lately. You could never make a record this cool. Maybe you don't know everything. If the record is a hit, it will only help us. If it bombs, it will only prove you were right. It's a win-win situation for you, she wanted to say.

She actually said none of this. Maybe she *was* stealing their sound. Maybe in a way she was stealing his life. He was supposed to be the star. At least when they were a "duo," when he was adding his voice, his arrangements, his production, when they were out on the road together, he still had a version of that life. On this album, he had nothing.

She and P. did try to save it. They worked up some different mixes. They changed the sequence of songs, burying that disco tune in the middle of Side 2. P.'s close friend Q., a legendary producer in his own right, who had overseen the Motown wunderkind's big album, invited everyone to his home for a second listen. But to no avail. Her baby was stillborn.

The spin on the dead album was that the brother was healthy now and she wanted to go back to their career. The solo project was just "something to keep me busy," she was quoted as saying. The more she kept telling friends and reporters this story, the more she started to believe it herself. Half a million and almost a year of her life spent on "something to keep me busy."

Now, though, more than two years after the official burial, she had a mad craving to hear the album again. She didn't have a copy of the tape with her in New York. She knew P. would have it at the studio, though. He was in there today. She had planned to go shopping for I. and P.'s baby — even though it wasn't due for months yet, she wanted to have all the presents bought and scheduled to be sent before she went back to Los Angeles — but instead of heading up Madison Avenue, when she got outside the hotel, she found herself wandering west. The guy with the shopping cart was at his usual post on Sixth Avenue; he was shirtless again but wearing a chef's hat marked with grease stains, and a cardboard sign was planted atop the pile of junk, which included a discarded Easy-Bake Oven in his cart: "A Taste of Nam Honey," it said, written in lipstick, with a "menu" underneath that offered Agent Orange Chicken, Napalm Spring Rolls, My Lai Mai-Tais and Sub-Cuticle Bamboo Shoots. "Stick to stick," he was saying. *Stick*, she thought? *Drumstick?*

The back "plate" 45 on the cart was Jefferson Airplane's "White Rabbit." The front "plate" 45 was the T-Bones' "No Matter What Shape (Your Stomach's In)." Drumstick, she thought, something you play with, not something you eat. *Music, not food. Music, not food.* She decided to skip the donation.

As she waited for the light, the vet suddenly rolled the cart in front of her. And just as suddenly his cheek was next to hers; she could feel the stubble brushing against her face and smell the stench of him as if it were coming from within her. "Play to your ugly," he said, then spit on her.

"What?" she said, wiping her face with her sleeve and trying to move away but blocked by the cart. "Play till I'm ugly?"

"YOUR ugly," he croaked. "YOUR ugly. OWN your ugly."

By now a few people had started to look over at them. The vet let out a hoarse cackle, jerked away and started back up Sixth Avenue, the chef's hat slipping down the side of his head and the Easy-Bake Oven rattling on top of the cart. The light had changed to red again, and she was stuck on the corner. A young man in a jogging suit asked if she was all right. She took a Kleenex from her jacket pocket and wiped the rest of the cart guy's saliva off her face. "I'm fine," she said, "thank you. Crazies everywhere in New York." And then when the light turned green, she hurried across Sixth Avenue.

I am not ugly, I am not ugly, I am pretty, she whispered to herself as she crossed Sixth Avenue. Now she not only needed to hear the solo album, she needed to see the cover again. *Vogue photographers don't take pictures of ugly girls,* she thought.

P.'s studio was on Seventh Avenue, and as she got near it, she started to remember how nice everyone had been in those first months of the solo sessions, the receptionist who always brought her tea, the guys in the band who treated her like, well, like one of the guys. "What do you think of that take?" she would ask the band, who always stuck around to hear her lay down her vocals, and they would say, "What's important is what *you* think." I. would cheer her on from the control room. And there was that silly but wonderful phallus-shaped cake. Maybe she should have taken a bite after all.

She was a block away when she abruptly turned and circled back around a side street. She wasn't quite ready to go in yet. Even two years later, the wound was still too fresh.

She'd lost track of the block she was on when she passed a church with a line snaking around the corner. The line comprised mostly sad-looking men in unseasonal clothes, oversize sweat pants, tweed jackets, tattered work boots. Smudgy faces and, as she got closer, body odor like spoiled fruit, like the cart man's, so fresh in her nose. One old guy was shadowboxing in the gutter. It looked like a Depression bread line, the kind she'd seen in history books and old black-and-white movies. Tramps on freight trains. But this was 1982. Who was hungry in America in 1982?

Then she saw someone emerge from a side door with a huge block of cheese in a cardboard box. It wasn't the strange geometry of the cheese that surprised her but rather the woman holding it. She was wearing high heels and had long polished nails and hair climbing high in a beauty-parlor do. A blue, slightly wrinkled silk dress that might have come from Saks. She blinked to look; yes, it had to be a food line. Then around the corner, at the back, she saw a man in a seersucker suit reading *The Times*.

Maybe it was a movie shoot, she thought, except she didn't see any cameras. As an oniony aroma hit her nose, she instinctively looked for the nearest tree or planter, the way she did when she passed a roach coach or a hot-dog cart; she knew that the leaves absorbed the smell.

People in line for food. In 1982. She thought of what she'd left on her breakfast tray in the hotel, food that had probably ended up in some trash bin. If she'd known, she might have brought it with her.

She turned back toward the studio. This time she got as far as the door. Would the receptionist be the same one and recognize her? she wondered. Would the tape be there? She hadn't listened to it in a couple of years. How would it sound? How would it feel?

In the end, she couldn't go in. It would be like entering a nursery that was fully appointed — crib, layettes, stuffed animals — but had never been occupied.

She thought about heading back toward her subway platform, but it was too soon for the finale. So she went to the record store.

When she got to the back room, there was that girl again, the one with the broad shoulders and the backpack. She was in front of the same section. Only this time the girl was with a man about her age. And they were talking about a song she didn't know.

20. Queens, N.Y., Summer 1982

The service for Rose was held on an almost unbearably bright, hot morning at a Jewish funeral home in Belle Harbor. Sib had heard it was going to be open casket, and she wondered where they'd find one big enough to hold all of Rose's body. But when she got there, the coffin was in front of the room and looked to be normal size, and Rose was comfortably nestled into the pillowed, upholstered box, looking almost svelte, her bouffant now deflated, like the rest of her, and her hair hanging down in prim obsidian strands around her pancaked face and just reaching her pink chiffon dress. *Chiffon.* Sib smiled. Rose looked beautiful. Sib thought about how she herself was still in a coma when Kieran and her mother were waked and buried.

At some Catholic wakes things like sports pennants or military medals or family pictures were allowed inside the coffins with the deceased, and especially with women, rosary beads were often threaded through the fingers. Jewish burial rituals didn't allow this. But in the front row of seats, on a chair by itself, was Rose's beloved whip, as if it were one of the deceased's immediate family receiving mourners, its handle shiny, its thong in the middle of the circle brushing up against a black-and-white photo of Tony Martin, Rose's favorite singer. The funeral home was filled with all manner of customers from the store: jazz cats and elementary-school teachers, former hippies now in suits and oxford shirts and neutral-colored pantsuits, aging still-hippies with unwashed frizz and paunches sticking out of their tie-dyes, other regulars of the store like Sib and Timmy Sweeney and Larry the D.J. and her father. Over the years Rose had gone out of her way to find some treasure for all of them, musical or nonmusical. Her husband — yes, there was a husband, a pomaded and Old Spiced and spit-shined man named Horace, who owned a nightclub — greeted and thanked them for coming. Sib was moved to see all the men wearing yarmulkes out of respect for Rose and her faith. The record store had actually closed for good in 1974, just after the first energy crisis, when Rose said she couldn't bring herself to charge "a whole dollar for a 45." But all these years later, the mourners who remembered her kindnesses came out in droves. "My beautiful Rose," Horace said. "The perennial bloom."

There was a shiva and a spread back at Horace and Rose's apartment, but Sib, Timmy and Larry decided that a better tribute would be for them to go to the closest thing to Rose's store now. So they got on the subway and headed into Manhattan to Downstairs, without bothering to go home and change. Sib as always had her running shoes in her backpack anyway. They arrived around lunchtime, and the far room, with all the good stuff, was crowded. Sib couldn't help herself. She was soon in front of the same section again.

"Why do you do this?" Timmy said. "Do you really need to keep reliving it?"

As Sib thumbed through and considered those 45s, especially that first big hit, the memory assaulted her senses once more. She could smell the deli on the kitchen table, and the Schaefer on Aunt Maddy's breath, and the patchouli in Rose's store, and the exhaust on Liberty Avenue in those last minutes before the crash, and then the antiseptic of the hospital room, and she could feel, everywhere, the strangeness again. The guilt. How she woke up the first time, in a different bed from her own and attached to monitors and IVs, and looked at her dad, standing over her, and how the thing she was aware of most was Kieran's absence. Then when she woke up the second time, it was not the hospital room that surprised her but another absence. She looked at her dad, again near her bedside, and just mouthed the words. "Where's Mom?" The sudden squint in his eyes told her everything. Then she woke up a third time, for good now, but again with a sense that something *else* was missing. Her father was sitting by her bedside this time, looking at the sports pages of *The Daily News*. "Dad," she said. And she realized that she couldn't hear.

So it wasn't just an emptier house she went home to after weeks in the hospital, a house without Kieran, without her mother. Now it was a house without sound. No voices. No el. No footfalls on the stairs. No TV. No creaking of her bed when she rolled over. No water splashing into the sinks or tub. *No music.* She kept thinking it would come back any second, that something just got caught in her ears and would shake itself loose. She'd turn the radio on or play a record, certain that sound would return if only she tried to hear hard enough, turned the volume dial far enough, if she willed it back.

Her father took her to ear-nose-and-throat docs, to audiologists, to psychologists, even to an acupuncturist. She was asked the same questions over and over: Do you have any ringing? *No.* Do you hear crickets? *No.* Can you hear this? *No.* The pressure in her ears was tested again and again. Normal every time. Every specialist told them the same thing: There was nothing physically or anatomical-ly wrong with Sib's ears. She had a condition known as hysterical deafness. It's usually caused, Sib learned, by some kind of psycho-logical trauma. The hearing could come back at any time, or the loss could last indefinitely.

She didn't want to go to a school for the deaf or learn sign lan-guage (though she and Timmy Sweeney did invent a kind of sign shorthand, mainly to sum up their moods, up, down, sideways, the number of fingers designating the degree). She became a quick study at lip reading, paying close attention to actors on TV and in real life positioning herself in front of faces, deliberately speak-ing slowly so that whomever she was talking to would go at her speed. Her dad got small blackboards and sheaves of notepaper to write messages to her, but she never wrote back. She always spoke. She went down to the basement and put on a record every day. Watched it spin. Pressed one ear and then the other to a speaker so that she could at least feel the vibrations. Sometimes Timmy would come over with some latest hit or other and sing along with it, and she sat near him and felt his breath and watched his lips. She liked, so far as she could tell from the words and rhythm of Timmy's lips, Carole King, Carly Simon, the Spinners, Roberta Flack, the O'Jays.

She insisted she could stay in regular school, but that's where her father and school officials drew the line. In the end she had a tutor.

The hearing loss did have one upside, in that it helped both Sib and her father take their minds off their other losses. For Sib, some-times she felt that if her hearing came back, maybe they would, too. Not really, but dealing with deafness generally helped keep her mind off missing half her family. She kept Kieran's record collection in immaculate condition.

Every Saturday Roy would still take her to Rose's shop. Rose would place her hands over Sib's head, tap them 18 times (18 was a special spiritual number in Hebrew, Rose started to scribble in a note; Sib grabbed the pen out of Rose's hand and made her say the words instead), and Sib would just bow, not expecting that anything would really happen but figuring that if anyone had magical powers, it would be Rose. Sib would scan the *Billboard* or *Cash Box* or WABC charts, look up and down the 45 wall. But she always averted her eyes when she saw a song by them. One hit after another. Four, five, six, eight, 10 big hits in a row. This was almost more torture than not being able to hear or losing Kieran and her mom. She blamed them for everything, almost as a way of not blaming herself.

So it went for more than three years. Sib turned 11, then 12, and then 13, and still every day she was sure that it was going to be the one when her hearing returned. Neighbors came over with covered dishes, especially kindly Mrs. O'Keeffe, who lived next door and from whose kitchen there were always warm, sweet and yeasty smells, who never complained when Sib was pounding the basketball on the driveway early in the morning or after dark. Sib loved her chocolate-chip bars and homemade iced tea. The aunts from both sides were always popping by. (Constance: "Make sure to keep your ears clean, dear. That will help the sound get through." Sib didn't even have to read her lips to know what she was saying.) No team would let her play sports, no hearing team anyway, so she would play catch with her dad or shoot foul shots for hours in the driveway, or they'd go play golf on a pitch-and-putt course and she would scream "Fore" at the top of her lungs. In the reflection from their clubs she could see that her face was busting red. But no matter how loud she screamed, she still couldn't hear a sound.

Her father had discovered a new countdown radio show, something called *American Top 40*, which was broadcast on Sunday mornings, and he put it on every week. Maybe some part of her was hearing it, he thought, absorbing it, archiving it in her brain for later recall. The host was a friendly, if slightly smarmy, guy called Casey Kasem. And Roy would write down the songs every week for Sib to cross-check with the local lists at Rose's store, and so that Sib could have a record of what to catch up on when her hearing did return. Except he left the slots blank that were occupied by the act that Sib hated. She couldn't even bear to see their name, much less in her father's handwriting.

About a month after Sib turned 13, a couple of Sundays before Christmas, the show was on the radio. Sib and her father had been to Mass that morning — Sib knew the liturgy by heart and so never had trouble following it; she never really asked her dad about the homilies — and now he was making lunch in the kitchen while Sib sat in the front room, lazily dragging her fingers over the piano keys, out of habit now more than hope, Sunday-afternoon adolescent ennui for the unhearing. She planned on turning off the radio near the end of the show because she knew that that hateful duo's latest smash hit would be played. It had been No. 1 the week before. She wanted to actively choose not to "hear" it.

Such a feeling came over her.

With about five minutes left in the program, she got up from the piano bench to turn off the radio, and suddenly felt unsteady, tingling, a little flush. She felt something warm on her leg — she'd changed out of her church clothes and into her sweats, and rolled them up to see a trickle of blood, then a steadier stream. First she thought she'd bumped her leg on something, maybe on the edge of the piano bench.

But then she realized what was happening. Her first period. She knew it would be coming soon — her breasts were filling out, her body hair was filling in — but didn't make the connection between that and the mild cramps she'd been having the past few days. (The aunts tried to prepare her. Maddy: "You'll feel so grown-up, like a young woman." Bern: "Midol and Chanel No. 5 will get you through it." Constance: "God's way of making sure you bathe.")

"Dad!" she yelled out.

"What is it?" Roy said, reflexively, craning his head around the doorway of the kitchen, pancake batter dripping from the spatula in his hand.

"I'm bleeding down my leg. I think my period started."

Roy grabbed the paper towels and some hydrogen peroxide they kept in a kitchen cabinet and started to head to the front room. Then he suddenly realized what had really occurred.

So had Sib. Their faces met across the dining room. He'd been too far away for her to read his lips, and anyway she was looking at her leg when she replied to him. She'd heard him. She screamed. He yelled. They ran to each other and Roy picked her up, his 13-year-old daughter, and kissed her ears. Then she ran around the dining room, the kitchen, the living room, still dripping a little blood, banging on everything, pinging, dropping things on the floor. Shouting. Whispering. She could hear it all. She forgot about the period. The countdown show was over. She flipped off the radio, because she didn't want it to decide what the first music she heard would be, especially any residue from that duo's group's current hit.

After an hour, which also included running outside with her basketball just to hear the bounce-thump of it on the asphalt, and after showering and changing her clothes, she went down to the basement, stopping short in front of the phonograph. She was almost afraid to try it. She wasn't entirely sure it wasn't all an auditory illusion. And what record should she pick? It had to be the perfect one. The first song she'd play after more than three years. Her dad stood at the top of the stairs. "Are you O.K., Siobhan? Sure you want to do that now? Maybe you should wait a little while."

"No, Dad. I've waited long enough."

She looked over at Kieran's collection on the shelf under the window well, those records still in near-mint condition since that horrible day. She started to pull a few out, but every time she'd look at a title, her eyes would go to the stenciled KK on the label. The first one she saw was "He's So Fine." God, how they loved that one. She put it back. Too obvious, and so was the Supremes' "You Can't Hurry Love." Then the Beatles' "Yesterday." Too sad. She took out the Jackson Five's "The Love You Save," the last record that all three of them had danced to in the basement. Too painful. Marvin and Tammi's "Ain't No Mountain High Enough." Getting closer. Finally she found one of those Reparata singles, "Captain of Your Ship." It was so joyous, and because it wasn't much of a hit beyond Queens, Brooklyn and Long Island, it was a song that really seemed to belong just to them. She put the record on. She'd never heard anything sweeter than the sound of the ship's horn and bells at the beginning of the song. By the end of it she was singing and jigging and punching her hands in the air with joy, snapping, clapping, intentionally bumping into anything that made noise.

"Say what you will," Timmy intoned, drawing Sib back. "They had quite a streak with those first 12 or 15 singles. They were bulletproof."

Sib looked through those first 12 again — they were back in chronological order — and when she got to the last one, its almost sickeningly cheery sound came flooding back, just as it did the first time she heard it. But the song was soon drowned out by her recollection of the joy she felt in those couple of weeks before Christmas in 1973, when everything sounded like music, when everything sounded like Christmas: cars screeching, pots clanging, teeth chattering, chalk on a blackboard, even the sound of her own breath. She'd wake up in the middle of the night and rustle the covers or snap her fingers just to make sure her ears still worked. She'd listen for her own heartbeat. She'd bang the trash-can lids. She played practically every record in her and Kieran's collection, in the basement late so many nights that her dad had to keep reminding her to go to bed. Once he found her asleep on the floor in front of the stereo, wrapped in a blanket, 45s piled around like vinyl parapets.

Sib waited a few days before she went to Rose's store. She'd wanted to surprise Rose, pretend she still couldn't hear, then have Rose lay hands on her and tap 18 times and then Sib would spring the news. But Rose, even with her attention on a holiday-shopping Saturday crowd, the syrup from her tall stack of waffles dribbling down her chin, knew the minute Sib appeared behind the counter.

"Chipper!" Rose said, at the top of her lungs. Sib tried to hold it in but caved within seconds, and soon was running and screaming into the folds of Rose's dress. Rose kissed Sib's ears; Rose's lips were sticky and gooey, but Sib cared less about how they felt than how they sounded, which was chiming and melodious, as if the sound were coming from one of Kieran's 45s. She almost wished a customer would try to steal something so that Rose would wield the whip and Sib could hear its glorious crack all the way out to Liberty Avenue. Over Rose's shoulders she shuddered as she looked toward the back and the listening booths, but they were gone, replaced by more albums and a room for blacklight posters. It was almost as if Rose knew, too, just like her dad.

"We need to celebrate, Chipper," Rose said. "You go and pick out any album you want."

Sib's face lit up, until her dad said from not far behind, "Uh, Siobhan, Christmas is in a couple of weeks. Maybe you should wait to see what's under the tree."

Sib somewhat glumly agreed and settled for a 45, Todd Rundgren's "Hello, It's Me," which she'd heard for the first time on the radio that morning and seemed a good choice for the first record she'd buy with her ears open again. The next few weeks she went up to everybody she knew, friends, neighbors, teachers and said, "Hello, It's Me," to all of them. As if she were a piece of art that had been restored and was worthy of another look. Another listen.

A reconsideration.

On Christmas Day, after early Mass — even the wheezing organ at I-Mac sounded sweet — Sib and her father visited the cemetery to lay wreaths on the grave. Sib had never wanted to go, and her father never forced the issue. But now she told him she was ready. "Let's go wish them a Merry Christmas," Sib said.

The silence came roaring back when they entered the gates of St. John's in Woodside. The place was vast, a rolling plain of gravestones poking up among denuded trees and dead grass, with visitors holding bouquets of flowers or pine sprigs or Christmas ornaments, live people floating around like ghosts, a city unto itself, a city of the dead. Sib couldn't even hear the car now as it wound its way around to the row where Kieran and her mother were buried.

She walked ahead of her father to the grave, with their last name, KELLY, loud across the top, in big capital letters, and, underneath, Eugenia M., 1932-1970, and Kieran J., 1956-1970. Sib had worried that all she'd be able to think of would be the loss of them, the silence, that horrible day of the accident. The grief and the guilt and the anger she felt. That she'd start screaming or wailing. Instead she thought of the dance parties in the basement, when Genie would sing and twirl them around. She said an Our Father and a Hail Mary, and then opened her coat and pulled out Kieran's copy of "He's So Fine," which she'd wrapped in plastic. She leaned down and started to dig out a narrow trench in front of the gravestone, then stuck the 45 in the ground where she'd dug the groove.

When her dad saw what she was doing, he touched her shoulder. "Don't leave that here, Siobhan. It will just get ruined."

"But other people leave stuff," Sib said. "This was one of his favorites. I wanted him to have it."

"Why don't you sing it instead?" her father said.

Sib picked up the record and stood next to her father. After a few seconds, she took a deep breath and tried to find the right pitch of those opening words, that refrain she'd known almost as long as she'd been alive. She squeaked out the first word a couple of times, then took another breath and started over, barely above a tree whisper. Then again, strong, hard consonants and pitch-perfect vowels.

The people visiting the graves in the next row turned around and stared at Sib. She stopped singing.

"That was nice, why don't you go on?" her father said.

"That's enough, Dad. Mom would just laugh at me, anyway. She always had the better voice." Sib put the record back inside her coat. "Merry Christmas, you two," she said.

Back at the house, after breakfast, Sib attacked the presents under the tree.

There was a pile of record albums: *Goodbye Yellow Brick Road* (a gift from Rose). *Band on the Run. Innervisions.* A tall box from Aunt Maddy, who was supposed to host them that year but hadn't been feeling well. Sib figured it was a bunch of dresses she'd never wear, but when she opened the box, she found a guitar. Nothing fancy, basic Sears acoustic, but it didn't matter. She took it out of the felt-lined case and strummed. Kieran, she knew, would have been able to pick out some kind of simple tune or chord progression right away. She just made noise. But it didn't matter. It was something that she could hear. Then she gave her dad his present, a framed picture of the 1973 Mets, who had won the pennant that year and got within a game of winning the World Series, their motto, "Ya Gotta Believe!" across the top.

Roy smiled when he opened the picture. "Ah, if only Yogi had started George Stone in Game 6," he said. But Sib knew that the motto, and the team, who had come from last place with a month left in the season, now meant something more to the two of them personally than the fact that they almost won the Series.

Sib thought she had saved the big box for last, but her father said, "Looks like there's one more under the tree." Sib looked toward the back and noticed what looked like another record album, with her name in the "To" field but no name in the "From." "Do you know who it's from, Dad?" she said.

"No idea," Roy said. The house had been filled the past few days with neighbors and friends and family members dropping by with trays of cookies and small gifts when they got the news that Sib's hearing had returned. "Could have been any number of people."

Sib ripped open the wrapping and stared down at the chocolate-brown cover. She was suddenly silent, everything was suddenly silent again. Her energy was sucked out, along with all the air in the room. Then she scanned the titles on the back cover. She felt some of her breakfast repeat on her.

It was the hateful duo's greatest-hits album. A couple of days earlier at Rose's store, Sib couldn't help noticing that it was No. 1 on the charts.

When her dad noticed her silence, he looked over and said: "Oh, boy. Whoever gave you that must not have known. I'm sure you can take it back to Rose's and exchange it for something else."

"No," Sib said. "I'll keep it." She was going to be tough, even if it meant keeping this godforsaken record. She put the album on the bottom of the pile, and Christmas resumed.

That night, Sib played all her new albums back to back, with her guitar slung over her shoulder. All except that one on the bottom of the pile. She put it away and forgot about it. She never even punctured the shrink-wrap.

Now, almost 10 years later, there was the word "bulletproof" again. "Yeah, whatever," Sib said to Timmy. "Where's Larry?"

"Right here," he said, walking over with a copy of Kid Creole and the Coconuts' "I'm a Wonderful Thing, Baby." "So, did we ever find out Rose's cause of death?"

"Cardiac arrest," Timmy said. "Probably from all those shakes and pizzas and tubs of takeout Chinese."

"That's not quite what it was," Sib said.

"Huh? She didn't die of cardiac arrest?" Timmy asked.

"Her heart was just too big," Sib said. "She had too much love for everyone. It just burst from being too full."

"Hey," Larry said, "there's a title for a song."

"What?" Timmy said.

"Too Much Love."

"Ha," Sib said, "maybe. Except who's going to write it these days?"

"Well, why don't we?"

Sib thought about it for a minute. She was always complaining that no one was writing great songs anymore, and so there were no great voices, or vice versa. She'd never written a song before, but Larry knew his basic music theory, and even though Timmy had no formal musical training, he had a good ear.

"Sure, why the hell not?" Sib said. If nothing else, it would be a tribute to Rose.

21. New York City, Summer 1982

The girl and her friends hadn't seen her. She'd heard the word "drafting" somewhere, meaning using someone in front of you in a race, on the street, as a human windbreaker. So she found customers in the store to do just that; she'd paint or sluice herself behind some biker type or some big suit who was close enough for her to hear what the girl and her friends were saying without letting them see her. She was practically slotting herself in behind her drafters.

They were standing in front of her section again, and one of the girl's friends called their big hits "bulletproof," and then they were all talking about some song called "Too Much Love." Great title, she thought. She'd make a note of it and tell the brother to track it down when they got back into the studio. After a few more minutes she realized it wasn't really a song, just a title they'd thought of. "Who would write it?" the girl asked, and then one of the others replied: "Why don't we?"

So they were thinking of writing a song. She'd been thinking about that, too. The brother was so good at it, the composing part anyway. She'd told her hairdresser that she was going to start writing her own material. Why couldn't she? Why did she have to be *just* a singer?

That night in the hotel, thoughts of the song title made her forget about dinner. She'd have to fudge her food log in the morning. She fell asleep watching a *Dallas* videotape. And she dreamed about the girl. She was wearing the same outfit from the first day she'd seen her: the denim skirt and the stockings with the sneakers, the backpack shed to reveal the muscled lats popping through her bra straps and top. Straight, light brown hair, in a bouncy ponytail. The girl was sitting in a parlor, with a wide bay window and sheer curtains that looked out onto a sloping bed of ivy. She was in front of something like a phonograph, a big box that she was looking down into. She still couldn't see the girl's face, only the same smudged rouge from the side.

Behind the girl there was a man, older, trim, in some kind of uniform, maybe a military guy or a groundskeeper. He unhooked the carabiner of keys from his belt and suddenly threw them to the floor. The girl didn't react. Then he picked up the keys and threw them hard up into the air. Still the girl didn't flinch, either when they hit the ceiling or when they crashed to the floor an inch away from her. The man moved away, while the girl kept staring into the phonograph. She grabbed the volume knob and turned it all the way up. She didn't recoil or even move when it got all the way to 10. Then she got up and stood next to the floor speakers, almost as tall as she was, and put her ear right up to the netting in front of the tweeter. The thing was pumping like a hydraulic piston, but the girl stayed still in front of it. She moved over to the next speaker and did the same. No visible physical reaction. She leaned so far into the cloth of the speaker cover, practically body-checked it, that it took on the shape of her. Finally she sidestepped from station to station — phonograph, speaker, the dusty upright piano in the corner — turned knobs, pounded her fists down from one length of the keys to the other, clawed at the strings on the guitar that was in another corner until one of them broke, banged on everything within arm's length. Nothing. She ran back to the phonograph and yanked the album from the spindle and flung it into the wall, where it smashed and then scattered. Finally the girl crumpled to the ground on the thick, fraying rug, raised her head up and from behind seemed to be screaming. The older man put a hand on her shoulder, and finally, after a mild flinch she uncoiled into his touch.

There was no sound at all throughout the dream. She realized that the girl was deaf.

Though she still never saw the girl's face, she was able to make out the fragments of the label on the record the girl had thrown into the wall. It was their Hits album, in black shards on the floor.

But the dream didn't end there. Suddenly she herself was pinned, against a chain-link fence. From the other side she could hear those hits from the collection, that first bulletproof 12 (or in music-biz parlance, "bulleted"), from "T." to "T." (chronological-ly), "W." to "C." (sequentially). She wasn't singing them, though. They were chirpy instrumental versions. She turned to see that they were coming from 12 soft-serve ice-cream trucks parked in a lot on the other side of the fence, all playing at the same time, louder now, bearing down on her in caloric measures. She tried to break free, but the wind kept pinning her to the fence. She was wearing the purple silk blazer that she wore during the photo shoot for the solo album, in the picture taken by the *Vogue* photographer, and it kept getting sucked through the diamond-shaped holes in the fence.

The only way was forward, but in front of her there was a thoroughfare with cars zipping by. In the inky half light she could make out a church on the other side of the street, a narrow crumbly brick structure with two slender stained-glass windows. In one there was an image of a young Latino man with a guitar; in the other an older, heavier white man with a leering smile and a tuxedo jacket. A procession was making its way into the church, hooded figures in chocolate-brown robes, cinched with belts made of lemons.

Then, a whistle. In the middle of the street there now stood a crossing guard, beckoning her. She broke free of the fence and started to move in staggered, windblown steps; when she got to the guard she realized it was the officer who stopped her that day in the subway, in full uniform now, but instead of a gun in his holster there was the paring knife he'd examined from her pocketbook. She thanked him, but he just smiled and waved her across the street.

She made her way to the end of the procession and was starting up the pyramided steps into the church, hay-colored grass and fresh tree stumps surrounding them, when she caught sight of the cornerstone — "Church of St. Blaise, est. 1959." She'd never heard of a St. Blaise. Or seen a church like this, so dark and gloomy. The churches of her childhood were bright places, simply adorned, blond-wood pews, the architecture of the major triad, apostles and saints with happy, picnic-going countenances, Jesus a genial master of ceremonies. These were the places where the brother played the organ; once during services he'd sneaked in a Beatles tune. She was the only one who noticed.

But this church was ornamented, sculpted, arted, bulky, with votive candles in every corner and alcove, booths with heavy burgundy curtains, and on the walls, six frescoes on each side, fog seeming to rise from below. Each fresco had a scene from one of their 12 "bulletproofs." Stars falling down from the sky. White lace. A sad guitar. Birds on a telephone line. A transistor radio from the '60s. And so on. Now at the back of the procession, she tried to focus in front of her. On the altar, facing the line and holding what appeared to be long candles tied in an X, was a hulking figure in a purple-and-gold chasuble. She couldn't make out his face, not yet. But the figure on the giant cross behind him was unmistakable. It wasn't Jesus, but someone with a similar frame, exposed ribs and oddly defined pecs. It was the cart guy from Sixth Avenue. Only now he was wearing horn-rimmed glasses.

The procession moved in jitters, fits and starts, as some of the hooded creatures stopped in front of one of those frescoes, kneeled, arms held out like a drummer reaching for the high hat or the free cymbal, and spoke, recited really, a few words from the song the fresco was depicting. As she got nearer the front she realized the hulking figure in the chasuble was putting those candles on the shoulders of each processor and chanting something. Finally there were just two left in the line, she and the processor ahead of her. The priest or whatever he was rested the candles on the leading processor's shoulders, so that the neck fit into the space on the top part of the X. And he said, "Through the intercession of St. Blaise, may you be protected from all diseases and afflictions of the throat." Well, she could go for that.

As the processor ahead turned to leave the altar, the hood fell off and she could see again the profile of the girl from the record store. When she got in front of the priest she stuck her throat out to receive the candles and the blessing. But the candles vanished. She looked and realized the priest was the subway busker. He had a small silver receptacle in his hand now, dipped his fleshy thumb and index finger in it and wiped some black substance on her forehead. In his basso profundo, he said, "Remember, woman, that you are moon dust, and to moon dust you shall return."

She woke up and reached for the laxatives behind the pillow.

Then a notepad on the nightstand. She wrote down the words "Too Much Love" and went back to sleep.

22. New York City, Summer 1982

Before the attack, Andy had worked seven days straight. A full week of scruff and city stink on him. In every borough, hours spent on the subway, following tourists in cowboy hats and chaps, a kindergarten class walking down Broadway, a drunken 20-something stumbling out of a bar in the West Village, a student on crutches outside Bronx Science, a trio in Astoria turning over and twiddling screwdrivers in their hands like majorettes, a parade of leering pervs in Hell's Kitchen. When he worked long weeks like this, he sometimes couldn't tell the potential victims from the potential perps, who were the truly vulnerable ones. As much as he liked being the lone wolf, mailing in his reports, getting his assignments on the phone, not even having to go into the station for his paycheck, the isolation that he seemed to crave his whole life had become a self-imposed solitary. The phone calls to his parents in Florida were the highlight of his week, practically his only opportunity to speak for days. "Are you dating anyone?" his mother asked the son who'd never brought home a girl, or went to a dance, or seemed interested in dating at all through high school and college. "Who's got time?" Andy said. "Too much work." It was a stock reply, but a true one.

But what was really getting to him, still, was the woman with the lemon. He didn't even know if she was the famous singer, but just the chance that she could be, that he could connect somehow to that day long ago, to that boy who made him feel, just for a few minutes, the way he'd never felt before or since, to that perfect music, kept her on his mind. But how was he going to find her?

And then there was the bump on the back of his head. He had her to blame for that too.

His obsession with her had led to his first big fuckup on his undercover assignment. He was on the Lower East Side, near a playground in East River Park where dealers were known to show up around midday. Squad cars did regular sweeps around the area but could never quite root them out; the dealers got used to the patterns and seemed to have a sense for when the cars would roll through. Andy figured he needed to keep the dealers guessing, make them less sure of their footing, mine the place to blow up their expectations.

The dealers would often case out the most vulnerable, the kids whose parents didn't come to pick them up or who didn't have travel buddies to get them safely home, which was usually one of the nearby projects. They'd hang out across the humid street, trail the kids to a nearby bodega, some as young as 8 or 9, strike up friendly conversations, show off their new high-tops or bling, hand out some candy or a soda, establish the trust, maybe offer some quick cash to run a bag for them. You can't save them all, he thought, invoking something he'd heard in some class in the academy. Crime will always exist. You can't stop it all. And, from long ago in church: The poor will always be with you.

Still, he did what he could, the usual getting in between when the kids were dismissed, or pretending to browse in the bodega so there could be no alone space for the kids and the dealers, intentionally dropping things, bumping, loud scuffs of his shoes on the floor, one time whirring a pocket New Year's Eve noisemaker, to break the flow, even dropping small flyers on the sidewalks around the playground, no bigger than the size of dollar bills, that said: Stay clean. Or, Drugs kill. He'd carry small packets of pepper to make himself sneeze, so that in the next aisle, the spiel of the dealers might be disrupted, if even for a second, to maybe allow the kids to escape the pull or, he hoped, even to let the dealers reconsider what they were doing, find for a few seconds their better angels. On his third day there, he was behind the Sixth Street overpass, close enough to hear the indistinct swell of kid giggles and shouts coming from the playground. It made him think of the singer's big hit with the kiddie chorus. His ears had flinched when he first heard it almost a decade ago — why is she singing a song from a children's TV show, he thought, and why is this la-la chorus taking up space where she could be singing? But the song grew on him; her vocal couldn't mask the sadness that made the song's cheer-up message so necessary and unfrivolous. He bought the single, the last one of hers that he took into his collection back then, one of the last records he bought before he turned off the radio for good, or what he thought was for good. He liked disco, which was getting popular then, but couldn't marry it, couldn't own or be owned by it. Anything new now seemed only to sully the purity of those good years, of those perfect records of the girl, of that perfect boy.

And the song was running through his head as he started to

move out from the bridge, occupying enough of his attention for him not to see, or to sense, the danger behind, the thwack out of nowhere to the back of his head. As he crumpled to the ground, he was barely able to pick up his chin and see a limo passing on the F.D.R., its window rolling up.

Andy could feel the warmth of the blood on the back of his head and consciousness slipping away, but he knew he couldn't pass out. And just as it was the song that might have dulled, or at least diverted, his senses long enough not to feel the attack coming, so it was the song that saved him. He played it in his mind to keep his focus as he dragged himself behind an ancient elm tree. Four bars of recorder. Four of the Bacharach-y trumpet. Then her voice touching the wound, a vocal Veronica's cloth, its balm nudging him back into consciousness, helping to heal him. When he got to the part of the song where the kiddie chorus was unleashed, he just went back to the beginning. Three, four, five times, and he was able to pull himself up against the tree trunk. Two or three more, and he pulled out a handkerchief and his water bottle to mop up the blood, which had slowed to a trickle. Three or four more, and he was able to rouse himself and stagger away from the park and toward a cab and an emergency room.

He didn't need stitches, but he was dizzy, and the E.R. doctor told him to take a few days off. Now on his couch, he touched the bump on the back of his head as the singer floated into his thoughts. You can't save them all, he thought. But maybe he could save her. He considered writing a letter. The fan-club address was listed on the albums. He scratched out a few lines:

Dear _____,

I know this might seem like an odd question, but were you stopped by a New York City cop in a subway station several weeks ago? You took a lemon out of your bag. . . .

If the situation seemed ridiculous and implausible, childish even, the letter was even more so. He balled up the paper and tossed it in the trash can.

He dozed off on the sofa while watching TV, and when he woke up, there was a Unicef commercial on with a half-naked, emaciated African child slogging through puddles, dark saucer eyes pleading and practically filling up her whole face, a pan with muddy gruel in her hand. The commercial gave Andy an idea. If he was going to find this woman, going to track her, he realized he needed to think like her. He'd already tried to piece together some kind of puzzle from the music. Yes, she was clearly trying to make herself disappear. But that didn't draw any bead on her potential behavior, where she might go, what she might do. He had to get further into her head.

He walked into the bathroom and pulled off his T-shirt. He ran his fingers up his torso, splaying his fingers slowly, pressing in, pincering his nipples in the valley of his thumbs and index fingers, almost a magnetic pressure between them, shooting a skein of pain down his side and leg on each side. Then he started his way again from the bottom and pawed and pulled the hair and flesh this time. There was too much fuzz on his torso for him to really tell if what he had in mind was possible. He got some paper towels from the kitchen and spread them into the sink. Then he took out his electric razor and starting trimming, slowly, evenly, in upward streaks from his navel, through his ribs and around his nipples, to where the hair stopped just below his Adam's apple, deeply breathing in and out to the mild buzz and cool steel of the trimmer. He shook off any loose hair and then coated his torso in shaving cream, put a new blade in his razor and worked it in the same direction he had the buzzer. Wiped it off, felt for any rough spots and did it again.

He sucked in his now-smooth stomach, such as it was. He could see the ribs through his arced, folded-in skin. But his pecs were still mini-mounds of muscle. Everywhere he pushed, poked, pinched, too much sinew was responding. And as much as he tried to straighten his arms at the elbows, he couldn't entirely de-emphasize the definition in his biceps either, somewhere between a ripple and a bulge. He ran his hands down the boughs of his legs, so thick from soccer and all the walking he did on the job that his fingers couldn't fit all the way around them until the ankles.

How long would it take him, he wondered?

It's not as if he ate a lot to begin with. There was food in his refrigerator, but it, like his cupboards, was a minimalist scape. He was no stranger to fasting, either. When he was a kid, there were always what he called the God gimmes, that is, what he gave up for Lent. Other kids at school joked about giving up spinach or liver or homework; Andy really gave up things he liked: Milky Way bars, ice cream, one year even TV. That weekend he spent at the seminary there had been something called a Poor Peter's fast, where you'd not eat all day and then for your evening meal have only broth or stale bread. Surviving the academy. The days when he was in uniform and had to work a double shift, or when a weekend soccer game ran long past regular mealtime, when he'd just forget to eat. Or a birthday party at the precinct, and he'd want to have some cake but got lost in his reports and missed it but then didn't miss it. Those five years when he stopped listening to the radio.

But still, to get to the starvation point? To look like that African kid in the commercial? To look like what he imagined the woman did underneath the layers of clothes? As he swept up the wiry clumps of his chest hair from the bathroom floor, he wondered again: How long would it take?

He tried it. He made fewer trips to the grocery store. Put small helpings on his plate, then moved them around, delayed eating as long as he could, then ate only half of what was already not there. Subsisted on nibbles and sips. Held his breath when he got near roasting nuts on the streets, backyard barbecues in his neighborhood. After a week of this he started to feel dizzy, overtired, irritable. But after the second week, he could also feel another muscle growing, flexing. It was the muscle of self-denial, the power of mind over body.

After the third week, he stepped naked on the scale in his bath-room. Only a couple of pounds down. And he looked in the mirror. No appreciable difference. He still had muscles. This was going to take some time, as the woman or maybe-woman once sang.

Then he put his clothes on and went out and got a pint of Häa-gen-Dazs mint chip and ate it all in one sitting.

So much for that experiment, he thought. But it did teach him something. To get to that vanishing state, the woman probably had to have been suffering from this affliction for months, maybe years, something that her gradual voice dissipation had already suggested to Andy. He didn't need any medical training to know that her body couldn't sustain that kind of abuse much longer.

Whoever she was.

23. Queens, N.Y., Fall 1982

Sib knew she could write. In her last semester alone, she did a 10-page paper on *Hamlet* and got an A from a tough Shakespeare professor. Her senior thesis for her American Studies class, "Why Disco Doesn't Suck: Sister Sledge and the Dissolution of the American Musical Conversation," was 75 pages long. Part I was "Racism and Homophobia: The Backlash." Part II, "Bad Apples: How Nixon and 'Baby Face' Spoiled the Whole Bunch." Part III: "All Politics Is Personal: The Pavlovian, Huxleyan, Pharmacological Effect of 'Rock the

Boat' and a Returning Sense." Another A, with comments from her professor — a graying ponytailed guy who moonlighted as a columnist for *The Village Voice* and whose gut seemed to thicken as the semester wore on — along the lines of "You make a surprising, compelling argument." Sib realized that her defense, her love of disco, was rooted in the fact that it was just gaining a foothold when her hearing returned. Even now, eight years later, "The Love I Lost" or "Rock Your Baby" or "Get Down Tonight," already premature musical relics to most of the rest of the world, would overwhelm her with happiness chemicals. Sure, some of it was terrible, but wasn't that true of any genre? The effect would wear off only when she would start to dance, and remember the basement parties, and start missing Kieran, and her mother.

How would they attack their very own song? It would have to be something like only 50 words long, maybe less, some of them probably repeated. She had two collaborators in Timmy and Larry. Timmy had a way with words; Larry could make up tunes on the spot. They had a title, and general musical and lyrical contours: Write a ballad with bite, not swill like Air Supply or "Endless Love." The theme of the words, that you can have too much of a good thing, should be complemented in the music, which should be catchy but not cloying. All the *ideas* were in place.

Yet there she was at 3 a.m., awake, after having stared at a blank page for hours. Not a note or a musical riff or phrase written down. She had her guitar, but she was just strumming aimlessly the few chords she knew — over the years she'd learned one or two songs but never put enough time in on it. She was much better with words.

Was it this hard for Smokey Robinson? she thought. How did prolific songwriters like him ever churn out hundreds of these things during the peaks of their careers, sometimes two or three in a single day? She finally wrote:

You can have too much of a good thing.
Much. Such. Touch. Dutch. Guts?

Maybe there was a book about how to do it. But when she thought about going to the library to look for one, she remembered one of her favorite episodes of *The Flintstones,* in which the characters Fred and Barney basically do the same thing, and the book they find tells them that the keys to writing a hit song include mentioning eyes, the color blue and the word "mother."

Too much love in your eyes
Too much blue in your eyes
Too much blue-eyed love . . .

Sib giggled to herself over that episode — she had always contended that "The Flintstones," which made its debut only about a month before she did, was underrated, that around every fifth episode the writers would kick it up a notch and produce something that transcended the charge that the show was nothing more than a *Honeymooners* knockoff. She remembered that the songwriter Hoagy Carmichael, who'd died not that long ago, appeared in the episode as his animated self. He'd written the music to "Stardust," which she knew was one of the most beloved songs of all time. Willie Nelson had had a recent huge recording of it. Sib had heard somewhere that it might have been the greatest pop song ever written.

Sib didn't necessarily want to write a song like "Stardust"; as timeless as it was, she needed a more contemporary lyric and rhythm. She didn't even care about writing "a hit." That would be another process, another of life's mysteries or algorithms that she probably couldn't find in a book.

But there had to be common threads among the greatest songs of every era. So she decided to choose one from every decade, starting with "Stardust" and the 1920s (she knew it was written then because she'd read Carmichael's obituary) and going at least through the '70s, and then analyze them, pull them apart and put them back together, pass them through some ricer in her brain to see what emerged, figure out what made them tick, what made them click. She was looking for songcraft, the art of marrying melody, harmony and words. A lost art, it seemed, lately. This might have made for an even better senior project than "Why Disco Doesn't Suck."

Sib had a pretty good idea of where she'd start with the '60s and '70s: Beatles, Beach Boys, Dylan, Paul Simon, Motown, Brill Building, singer-songwriters, Elvis Costello, Gamble-Huff. For the '50s, she could probably just pick any Chuck Berry song to get what she needed. She had "Stardust" from the '20s. But what about the '30s and '40s? What barometers were there for the songs from those eras? What songs resonated during the Depression? The war? The postwar, pre-*I Love Lucy* years? Those last pre-rock gasps?

Who was the best musical authority (besides herself) on music? That would have been Kieran, of course, and she still had his record collection, but it started in the early '60s. Rose would have been perfect, but she was gone now, too; maybe her husband the night-club owner, but she didn't know him well enough to ask. Then Sib shuddered, when she realized where she had to look.

The word "mother."

It had taken Sib some time, years in fact, to be comfortable with all the family memorabilia from before the accident. She avoided the framed photographs of the four of them, even as she insist-ed that they stay up when her father offered to take them down. She would avert her glance, or walk quickly past them, or sit in a chair that didn't face them. When she was younger, when she was a "they," she'd always dreamed of inheriting Kieran's perfect baseball glove, oiled and slept on, under his pillow, until it was broken in, soft and pliant, almost as easy to fold as paper. It had been on the handlebars of his bicycle that day. She just couldn't bear to have it on her hand after that, and so it stayed on top of the dresser in his room, which her father kept pretty much the same as it was the day Kieran died.

Sib had no problem playing Kieran's records, though. The collection was so perfect, in content and condition, that keeping them as part of her regular playlist, in regular rotation, became her way of curating her memory of him, of keeping a best part of him active in her life. Anybody could oil a baseball glove. Nobody could break in a record collection the way they could.

But there was a place in the basement that Sib had never gone since the accident, and now she knew it might be what held the key that unlocked the song she was trying to write. She slipped on her tube socks — white, thick, high, wrapping snugly around her calves. Even at this hour of the night, they provided a little adrenaline jolt, as if her body were now expecting her to go for a run or shoot baskets, and they'd also soften her footsteps on the stairs. Her dad was a light sleeper, and this was one night she really didn't want to wake him up, for him to find out where she was going.

She took a penlight from her night table and made her way out of her room, down the hall and to the stairs. The dark house, the limited vision, didn't scare or deter her. She'd had some experience with a diminished, deprived sense, after all, and never lost that ability to compensate with her others. She kept the lights off as she felt and listened her way, with what Timmy joked were her Bionic Woman ears, through the kitchen and down to the basement.

Still using only the penlight, she padded her way to the stereo. There was a cabinet underneath with accordion doors. They'd gone unopened since the accident, at least by Sib, much as she'd avoided the family photos or any reminiscing or dredging up.

Sib put her hand on the cabinet door and started to push it open. Then the face came back to her, from the one dream she could remember having while she was drifting in and out of the coma in the hospital.

All these years later, the face, looking down from her bedside, was sharp and clear, almost blunt, not hazy in that dreamlike way. And the voice was unmistakable, a soft clang.

Why wasn't it you?

Sib opened the door and saw them, the rows of binders, with gold embossing on the different-colored spines. She pulled one out and wiped off the thin layer of dust that had managed to accumulate through the closed door. God, it even smelled like her, beyond the must, that mix of her Dove bath soap and — what? Sib thought. Something outdoorsy. Newly mown grass? Country pines? Basketball leather? Axle grease?

Sib looked up at the corner of the binder she'd pulled out: There was a cracked, curling piece of masking tape, still with enough adhesive on it to stick. She drew the penlight closer to make out the faded writing: "Property of Eugenia Rooney," written in that familiar up-and-down, sticklike hand, like those readouts from an EKG she'd seen on medical shows.

She opened the binder, which was full of 78 rpm records in manila sleeves, just like the ones for 45s, only bigger and thicker, sturdier.

This was her mother's girlhood record collection. Sib couldn't remember her ever playing these records. Every time she or Kieran would ask about them, her mother would say that the 78s were too bulky, that they'd ruin the needle on the phonograph, that they were all so old anyway, why would anyone care about them now, let's play something new. And then she'd tear into "Downtown" or "She Loves You."

Don't dwell on the past, her mother had always said.

Sib carefully flipped through the bulky platters, almost as heavy as their good dinner plates. There were titles by the Andrews Sisters and Bing Crosby, the cast album from *Oklahoma,* jazzier stuff like Duke Ellington and Ella Fitzgerald. A version of "Stardust" by Carmichael himself. One entire book was dedicated to Christmas songs, Bing Crosby and Gene Autry and Judy Garland. In another she found Billie Holiday's original version of "God Bless the Child." And the last book, which got into the '50s, had 78s by Elvis and Buddy Holly. She took the copy of "Oh, Boy," out of the sleeve and put it on the phonograph. She slid the speed switch all the way to 78 and watched the thing crazily spin to life after more than 30 years. But when she put the needle down, all she got was static, chalkboard scraping; she'd forgotten that 78s needed a special, thicker needle. You always needed a thicker needle to get through to Mom.

Sib put "Oh, Boy" back in its sleeve. Maybe that would be her song from the '50s, if she decided not to go with "Johnny B. Goode" or "Sweet Little Sixteen." But as she closed the binder and started to tilt it back in the cabinet, a photograph fell out, a black-and-white snapshot with scalloped edges. There were six people gathered, all of them female, her mother and her three sisters, plus her cousin Colleen, who was probably about 7 in the picture, and, in the center, her ancient grandmother. They were in the front room of Constance's house, which had been their grandmother's, and they were all younger, brighter, somehow more vital than Sib usually thought of them (except her grandmother, who died when Sib was an infant and so in the family stories she heard was always old). Maddy, Constance and Bern were all dolled up and ballet erect, as was Colleen, who was wearing what looked like a Sunday dress and had her hair tied back in ribbons. And then there was her mother, on the lower outside perimeter of the photo, wearing a dress and a crucifix — a small static shock to Sib, who was used to seeing her mother in a blouse and pants — and looking as if she were in a three-point stance or a starting block, ready to bolt across the frame. Always the odd woman out.

Sib trained the light on the photo for what seemed like an hour, interrogating each face with the penlight. As usual, no men. Where were they? But the surprise was that for the first time, Sib had to admit the truth of what people had told her her entire life: She looked just like her mother, who, in the picture, was not much older than Sib was now. And there was no mistaking the round face, the slightly boxy but busty and athletic frame, the readiness to spring, the blunt, show-me-what-you-got expression.

Sib tucked the photo into her shorts and stood up, but suddenly felt a wave of something hit her and had to reach for the wall behind the phonograph to steady herself. Her knees buckled slightly as she walked slowly to the stairs, her socks sliding on the floor, and she gripped the side wall — there was no banister — up to the kitchen. She'd regained herself by the time she got back to her room and was in bed when she took out the photo again. Six women. She counted them over and over. But it wasn't just the number; there was something else about the photo that Sib couldn't shake. She'd always joked about "where the men were buried" on her mother's side of the family, until she thought of Kieran and then felt ashamed. But when Sib, in her bedroom in the dead of night, looked at this photo of her mother, her aunts, her grandmother, her cousin, she wasn't seeing the absence of men. She was seeing a band of sisters, self-reliant, proud, unlacking. *A girl group.* A coronet of light bulbs lit up around Sib's head. The picture practically had the same glow as Sib's favorite album covers — *The Supremes a' Go-Go* or the Shangri-Las' *I Can Never Go Home Any More.* The girl groups of the '60s might have been expressions of male fantasies, but in the pictures on those album covers anyway, the women, who were either dancing or simply drinking in one another's presence, didn't cry need, like some of the frillier girl groups, or throw confrontation, like some of the "womyn" groups Sib had seen in record stores. They were simply women with women by women for women.

And then she had an idea about what songs she had to study if she was going to write one of her own.

24. New York City, Fall 1982

She must have been to every store around Madison and Fifth a dozen times. Bergdorf's. Bloomingdale's. Prada. Chanel. "All the big ones," she'd told F. Mostly she just looked — she was still a Sears shopper at heart. And she'd learned her lesson after that Japan tour when she brought back an expensive, custom silk kimono for the mother, and the mother started complaining about the extravagance of the *box*, the cloth ribbon, the triple-weight, glittered cardboard, the plush pomegranate-colored tissue paper. When the mother finally got to the kimono, she picked it up by two fingers, held it at arm's length, thanked her, put the kimono back in the box and then asked the brother if he'd written anything new while they were away.

Still, she loved the fact that the best stores in the world were steps away from her hotel. In L.A., nothing was close; everywhere you wanted to go was a negotiation, a journey, an embarkment, and the excursions to and from were as much a part of the experience as the destination itself — how long it took, how much traffic you hit, where you parked, what the smog level was, what you heard on the radio, how many innings of the Dodgers game you missed, what lives you'd lived on the way there and back. In New York, especially if you had money, and she still had some, you could be anywhere, essentially, in no time. To others New York may have been the city that never sleeps. To her it was the city of no time.

"No Time" was also the name of a pretty good song, she often thought, by a pretty good group called the Guess Who, from back in their day.

She corrected the thought: from back in their *first* day.

She did buy a pricey Hermès scarf for F. at Bergdorf's, even though she realized F. probably had dozens like it already. Her credit card had her married name on it, but when she handed it over to the salesclerk, an older, sweetly imperious woman with her silvery hair in a bun, she still looked for the glint of recognition, that brief hold of the gaze that said, Don't I know you? Are you famous? The problem was, that could be said of maybe half the people who shopped in these stores. The clerk turned the corners of her mouth up slightly in a half smile while asking her to sign the slip.

They would be here soon, the parents and the brother, and like a single released in advance of an album, their admonitions were coming back to her ahead of their arrival. Repeating on her like some overplayed Top 40 ear worm. Of course they'd tried to talk her out of going all the way to New York for treatment. There are good places closer to home, they said. Fully tricked-out facilities where you can check in and the doctors can keep an eye on you (which she knew meant where we can keep an eye on you), not some outpatient therapy and overpriced hotel.

Wasn't it enough that she'd finally agreed there was a problem, that she needed help? Didn't she have the best doctor? What "facility" was more tricked out than New York City?

No, that wasn't enough for them. You should have learned your lesson the last time you were in New York, they said, all that money and energy for nothing. And now you won't have the record-company limo to chauffeur you everywhere. You'll be out on the mean, dirty New York streets, where cars run lights, people jaywalk, where they overcharge, where they bargain lives down. Potholes, manholes, cellar hatches to swallow you up, where people help themselves to a little something that's not really theirs in order to survive. One big collision course. In New York, they said, if something is worth having, rest assured that someone else, maybe hundreds of someone elses, wants it just as much or more than you do and will do anything to get it, sometimes just to stop you from having it. A place where people will block your way just because they can. That city will break every promise you ever thought it made to you. You'll never be skinny enough to fit through the eye of that needle. And now on top of all this, they have that new gay cancer out there, which they'll no doubt spread to everyone. You'll never get better there, someone told her, because you don't know how to cheat, how to protect yourself. Someone will lean out from a window, or across a sales counter, or from around a dim lamppost, or even down from your hospital bedside, and say, "Hey, fool." And you will turn your head and answer, "Present."

Well, the joke was on them. If she'd learned anything the past few years, it was that Los Angeles had more than its share of liars, cheats, disease and all-American scum. Strangers bearing jeweled ladles. The only difference was that in L.A. they had better tans and fatter asses. All those aerobics classes could never make up for the time spent in cars.

No, she was going to New York. Everything happened faster there anyway. And she needed to get well as fast as she could.

Now they'd be here in a few days. A different kind of showtime. Showtime, no time. And she was still not gaining, still hadn't had the breakthrough, still hadn't found the corner to turn. As she was out on Madison wondering how she would face them all, she found herself stalled in front of a building she'd avoided her entire stay. It was the building that held the offices of her record company. Its headquarters were still in L.A., but now that so many British acts were scoring for the label, the New York office had become a vital way station whenever these artists, especially those three cute blond boys, came to tour the U.S. It was as if the proximity to London gave the New York reps a better understanding of these acts, who were mostly male and new-wavish, as if the 3,000 fewer miles of ear canal made the New York team hipper and smarter, more in tune, helped them get this sound, which was grittier than the label's standard fare and not L.A. at all, sooner.

She stopped there finally because she needed to take her mind off the coming family session. She had some friends here still. The New York reps were the ones who actually liked those early tracks from her solo album. When the proofs for the solo-album cover came back from the *Vogue* photographer, she imagined a poster of one of them on a wall in the New York office.

What really gave her the confidence, though, as she rode the elevator up in the sleek building, was that she'd helped build it. This building. This piece of New York real estate. *Her* piece of New York real estate. She couldn't tell you anything about the architecture — she'd gotten through only a year of college when the career started to take off, and most of her courses were in music — and anyway her "piece" of it was probably the equivalent of a set of office suites. But she knew that her record sales had helped pay the rent, the salaries, the recording costs, had helped pay for the promo pics and

complimentary albums that went out to journalists, for every flack
pitch, for every flack. Had even made the signings and develop-
ment of those British acts possible. Some of the kinder suits at the
label had said as much to the trades, that she and the brother built
the label, that without them, there wouldn't have been a label. The
brother, even though he never thought they got their due from the
company and had implied more than once that it put out their records with held noses and then raked in the royalties, said this was
a bit of an overstatement. H. and his combo built the label, he said.
But they kept it going, took the foundation and built it up, and out.
Built it into a multimillion-dollar subdivision, he might have said.

It was undeniable that, more than a decade after they were
signed, they were still the label's all-time sales champs. All of their
albums had turned a profit, even the more recent, lower-charting
ones. Barely, those last few, but a profit just the same. All of them.
All the ones that came out, that is.

So yeah, she owned a piece of Manhattan real estate. Now she
was going to claim it, if only for a few minutes.

The elevator opened on a reception area with wavy, white, back-
lit walls. It looked like her dermatologist's office. It was all a little
vertiginous, the walls, the elevator ride; in L.A. their label offices
were on a lot, close to the ground, like everything else. It was a
latitudinal place. But New York was all about longitude, the dizzying ups and downs. She looked around and saw posters and displays featuring those three blond boys, and another, homelier British band who had just released a follow-up to their breakthrough
album from a few years ago (homelier in contrast of course; like
children and animals, those three blond boys were people you never
wanted to be hanging on a wall next to, or whatever it was that
W.C. Fields said about animals and children). There was the sister
of the Motown wunderkind, a teenager who had recently signed
with the label. And the lanky R & B guy who had gone solo from
his group. Gone solo. Imagine that.

But the big installation in the room was of the five power-pop women who had taken the charts by storm that year. They were on water skis and looked sun-kissed. Their debut album the year before, punky and beaty and surfy, had been released right around the time her vaunted comeback album with the brother was starting to tank. One of the women played drums.

Ah, well, she was always telling him they needed a little more zip.

She craned her neck around looking for a picture, or at least a framed platinum record, of theirs. She couldn't see one. But then this was just the reception area.

There was a young woman, a slip of a thing with spiky upswirled white hair poked through with cobalt-blue crochet needles, behind the reception desk, on the phone. She didn't have an appointment, but she figured the girl would realize who she was and key her in. "Yeah, so I'm probably going to have to start carrying Mace," the receptionist was saying. "Pervs everywhere in this city." The receptionist picked up her head, cupped the mouthpiece, raised her index finger and then mouthed to her, "I'll be right with you, sweetie." "So yeah, all five of them were here, and J. and C. were a little too cool for school, but B. came right up to me and told me she loved my Docs and asked where could she get a pair. I mean, just the fact that I was in the same room with them was, like, a heart attack. It was so rad. But when B. came over and started talking to me, it was the gravy. Or more like the gravy of the gravy."

When she heard the word "gravy," a little bit of her breakfast — the usual slivers of banana, half an egg white, eight sips of tea — churned back up.

The receptionist juggled a few incoming calls, punched a few hold buttons and then finally returned her attention. She asked to see Mr. _____ and gave her married name, figuring it was all just ceremony, a verbal wink, the usual dance. How could the receptionist, an employee of her record company, NOT know who she really was?

Then she saw the look. The eyes widening, the face rounding and filling up with expectation, the spiked hair standing even more on edge, the limbs both tensile and slack, that look that she had seen thousands of times when people realize they're in the presence of someone famous, and they think they've lost their own presence, when in fact what they've really done is create more of it.

She was getting ready to say, "Yes, I am who you think I am, how are you, love the crochet needles, I do needlepoint myself," and then have the girl usher her personally back to Mr. _____. The girl, after she gulped a few times, finally spoke.

"How do you do it?" she asked.

This wasn't the line she was expecting, but O.K. How do I do what, she wondered? Win Grammy Awards? Sell 75 million records?

The girl went on: "How do you get that body? I've been trying, for like, months, but I still feel so FAT."

She knew she should have worn that extra sweater, but it was especially warm that day, so she had just put on her satin baseball jacket when she was leaving the hotel, and had absent-mindedly unbuttoned it in the elevator up to the label offices, so that now her concave abdomen was right at eye level with the receptionist. And even if she had worn the sweater, her face, from under her baseball cap, had points so bony and sharp you could plot them on a graph and practically come up with something 3-D.

From a foot behind the desk, though, the receptionist had no such added dimension. The girl was willowy to the point of being diaphanous. Wick-thin. She felt as if she could have knocked the girl over just by breathing on her. Blown her out.

"I mean, I've tried every diet. Eating only red foods, green foods. NOT eating red foods, green foods. A coffee cleanse. A cucumber-juice cleanse. Avoiding carbohydrates after 6 o'clock. Half portions. Quarter portions. Eighth portions. . . . "

Keep going, she thought, 16, 32, 64, 128. She could play all of those notes.

"... Walking up the five flights of my apartment building a few
extra times a day. And still I can't get rid of these" — the girl stood
and pushed on her planar hips, so that her body almost formed
a sideways V or a less-than sign across the desk. "I mean, they're
just so big." She remembered saying more or less the same thing
to P. when they were watching footage of her on some TV special.
"They're so big," she'd said. And he'd replied, "Big where? In Aus-
chwitz?"

"If I could just lose a few more pounds," the receptionist continued, now hushed, intimate, conspiratorial, as if they were two teen-
agers sharing secrets long into the night at some sleepaway camp
or boarding school. "I might have to try, well, you know. . . ." She
pretended to stick her finger down her throat. "I did it once, and I
have to say, it wasn't bad."

Suddenly a phrase popped into her head, then that last scene
with the husband, which happened during a birthday celebration
for the father the year before: *You take back this bag of bones. I don't
want her.*

And then another: *body dysmorphic disorder.* She'd heard it said
about her, of course, along with that other term, the one she'd so
vehemently denied all these years. The Brits had a different name
for it: "slimming disease," which an interviewer confronted her with
on their last tour.

The girl took a sip from a glass cylinder of iced tea, or rather, a
cylinder of lemon wedges floating in ice and tea. "Seriously, what's
your secret?" she said.

She was usually quick to deflect any suggestion that she was too
thin, always had a rejoinder for the admonishment. But she'd never
had someone actually . . . praise her for being so skinny. For this she
had no ready response. By the time she came up with "clean living,"
the girl was already back slapping at the incoming calls. "Good afternoon, _____ Records, how may I direct your call? . . . Please hold."

Then she turned back and said: "I'll see if Mr. _____ is in. What did you say your name was again, hon?"

Someone will look at you across a reception desk and say, "Hey, fool."
And you will pick up your head and answer, "Present."

25. Queens, N.Y., Fall 1982

"So what we're trying to do here is write, what, the opposite of 'What the World Needs Now Is Love'?" Larry asked. "What the World *Has* Now Is *Too Much* Love"? He picked up his guitar and started playing the melody to the Bacharach/David classic, with the new lyric idea. "What the *world*/has *now*/is *too*/*much*/*love*."

They were gathered, Sib and Timmy (who was home from Bates for the weekend) and Larry, in the apartment on the Lower East Side where Larry lived with his mother, who always seemed to be out working whenever Sib visited. The job always changed. She was a substitute math teacher (though Larry could never say what school she was at on any given day). She sold cosmetics for Elizabeth Arden (though Sib never saw a travel case or any samples). She was a stringer for *The Staten Island Advance* (though Sib never saw a byline). Larry hadn't seen his father since he was 11 or 12. He was said to have a college degree in "statistical analysis," but when he was still living at home he was always on the phone talking about lines and spreads and "vigs." Later Larry would joke that he had a bona fide "by the book" childhood. Sib figured that Larry's dad was knocked off by the mob, or a spy, or in the witness-protection program, or just a loser who left.

Yet there was always money for rent and food and records — like Sib, Larry had been a precocious customer at Rose's shop, though they never crossed paths there — and music lessons, in which Larry applied his inherited facility for numbers — and weed, and later, for Larry to go to college, where he and Sib met. The dark apartment in the run-down, almost modern-*shtetl* stretch of Avenue B had a piano and sturdy furniture, and a sizable kitchen with full cupboards. Larry had the bigger bedroom of the two, and a D.J. setup with two pro Technics turntables and Sennheiser cans and crates of records stacked against every free expanse of wall. Larry's neighborhood may have been a bit of a danger zone for Sib — she always held her knapsack tight, stepped lively, kept her eyes in motion and "mug money" under the tongue of her running shoes, and she generally avoided the drugged-out Tompkins Square Park — but the musical bounty in Larry's apartment always made her feel at home.

"Something like that," Sib said. "Maybe not so on the nose." It had been a week since Sib found that picture of her mother and her family, her female family, and it had turned over in her head ever since, flicking and clacking like a baseball card attached to one of her bicycle wheels.

"Or maybe the opposite of 'All You Need Is Love,'" Larry of-

fered, and again strummed the melody of the song while impro-
vising the lyric. "*What you* need's not *love*," he sang. Sib knew that
Larry had smoked a joint or two before she and Timmy arrived, not
just because of his blissed-out, loosey-goosey frame of mind — that
could be Larry without the weed — but because of the skunky odor
that lingered like the smell of dead leaves after a November rain.
And that it was leading to all these cheeky parodies.

"Actually, it's already been done," Timmy chimed from the kitch-
en, where he was loading in peanut butter and squeeze cheese on
celery and Ritz crackers, and filling up jiggers of vodka. "Joy Division, 'Love Will Tear Us Apart.' All about the evils of surplus, you
know. I mean, the lead singer offed himself not long after writing
that song. A love song/suicide note for Lady Thatcher and a farewell to Old Britannica."

Sib had heard of Joy Division but had never heard the song;
she still got her music through mainstream channels, like radio
and prime-time TV, and Joy Division hadn't made an impression
there, at least not in the States. They were underground, heard in
the clubs and on the outlying frequencies, places like Area and the
Crop, and Sib was still very much aboveground, an inlier. Or maybe, considering her age and what her peers were into, she was the
ultimate outlier; most of her friends didn't care when WABC went
all-talk because they'd long abandoned it for other music portals,
like MTV, which a year into its existence still wasn't playing many
black artists. She always refused when Larry offered her a joint; she
had been drunk, stupid, silly drunk, only once in her life, after Aunt
Maddy died, from stomach cancer a few years ago, and even then
because she felt she was drinking the beer in tribute to her. It was
Schaefer, of course, just like that day in the kitchen, the day that
had bisected her life. Just smelling the foamy swill made Sib relive
the pain of the day, hit her like a ferocious wave she hadn't seen
coming, but for a while she could surf it, when she remembered
how happy she'd been at that lunch table, with Aunt Maddy and

her Mom and the good deli and the sunbeams through the kitchen window and the crisp dollar bills floating through the air and Freda Payne pulsing in her head.

Sib was able to get on a bike again eventually — necessity trumped trauma, in that case. But she never did get another copy of "Band of Gold."

She'd also never kissed anyone. She'd never been kissed. She never sought another pair of lips, and another pair of lips had never sought hers. She'd get around to it, she figured. Kissing, and sex. They just weren't a priority for her yet. And anyway, she never imagined that the real thing could be better than the Crystals' singing about it on "Then He Kissed Me." But whenever Larry mentioned artsy types like Keith Haring or Arthur Russell, Sib went blank.

"And there was 'Love Hurts,' too, which was kinda sorta the same thing." Larry must have said "kinda sorta" 30 or more times in the course of any conversation, initially to Sib's great annoyance. But she came to, if not like it, then not hear it. She was actually thankful sometimes for things she didn't want to hear. And the phrase made the usually cocksure Larry seem a little uncertain, which Sib found almost sexy. Everybody had a tic. Larry's were even more obvious when he was high.

"And 'Drowning in the Sea of Love.' Luther's 'Never Too Much.' But it really doesn't matter," Larry continued. "There have kinda sorta been only five pop songs ever written in the history of the world anyway. You just find a slightly new approach, or an old approach that's due for a comeback."

Five songs. Sib had that very phrase, that very construct, on her mind since they came up with the title "Too Much Love." Choose five of the greatest songs ever written, starting with "Stardust," and break them down, figure them out. But after she found that picture of her female family, she realized that she had to refine her approach. There was something about the sheer, undiluted musicality of those women who shared her bloodline. Sib had always figured that she owed most of her love of music to Kieran and his oh-so-perfect record collection and the passion he shared with her. But now she realized that it was women who were the main music supply in her life. Singers like Aretha Franklin, the Supremes, Dusty Springfield, the Shangri-Las. There was Rose, whose store had been a literal musical portal, a different kind of music provider. And her mother, with her silky, unwavering voice and impeccable taste. It wasn't just X chromosomes jumping out of that picture. There were a staff and notes and clefs and key signatures. Sib vaguely remembered her mother saying something about *her* grandmother writing a song, which would have been back in the Stephen Foster era. An original "Camptown Races."

So her new plan was to find five classic songs written by *women* and attack them from all angles, box them out the way she would an opponent on a basketball court, make them turn over the ball, yield their secrets.

She'd gone to the library and started learning about women like Kay Swift and Dorothy Fields, who wrote hits in the '30s; and she discovered that the Chad and Jeremy song from the '60s, "Willow Weep for Me," had actually been written in the '30s by a woman named Ann Ronell. But when she unearthed recordings of these songs, they made no impact beyond the fact that Sib recognized they were well composed. Good songs that sounded like other good songs of their era but that didn't especially move her. Sib had heard somewhere that your ears are shaped by your age; the fact that Sib had lost more than three years of hearing, during very impressionable years, made her wonder if her ears could be reset, if she could be receptive to anything new — or old — that she heard. But these songs still seemed from another time.

It wasn't until she got into the rock 'n' roll era that something started clicking. In 1958, just two years before Sib was born, a young woman named Sharon Sheeley had stalked the teen idol Ricky Nelson — as popular and heartthrobby as anyone in those days except maybe Elvis, who was in the Army by then — and played him a song she had written, music and lyrics, called "Poor Little Fool." It was about a recent breakup, and Nelson liked it enough to record it, and it went to No. 1. Her mother had the 45, and Sib fished it out and played it over and over. It was a simple tune, on the surface resigned and melancholic, a little lopey and folky, and yet Sib was sensing something underneath, not just a need to be heard but an insistence on it. The tune tugged at the listener the way Sheeley must have tugged at Nelson when she was trying to get him to listen to it. It was a laconic demand. A woman giving voice to a man. And then a man giving it back.

From there Sib came across a woman named Georgina Dobbins, who was a member of the Motown group the Marvelettes and, it turned out, a writer of the first Motown No. 1 hit, "Please Mr. Postman," though she'd long gone uncredited. Sib had a love-hate relationship with "Please Mr. Postman." The original was flawless, a template for all those dance records of the early '60s. Sib didn't know if Georgina Dobbins wrote part of the music or part of the words, but in that original Sib could hear the same chug, the same jab, the same sly in-your-faceness, the refusal to be denied, that she heard in "Poor Little Fool." And of course there was the connection to her father, an actual mail carrier. Sib's first day in the record store, Rose called him "Mr. Postman."

But then there was the cover version, the big hit remake, from six or seven years ago, by the duo Sib so loathed. Unlike most of their big hits, this one was on the radio after Sib's hearing had returned, and still the sound of that girl's voice made her retch. She always lunged for the radio to change the station whenever that version came on, and it was all she could do not to slug anyone in school who teased her about the song.

Why wouldn't they just go away, that awful girl and her dorky brother? Sib thought. Then almost as if she'd wished it, after a couple more hits, they basically did; the songs they put out weren't quite

so ubiquitous, not on the radio quite as much, and so they were easier to avoid. Sib did force herself to listen all the way through once
to some dopey song they had about Martians or extraterrestrials
or something, which came out around the time of *Close Encounters
of the Third Kind*, on Casey Kasem's show, which was still a Sun-
day-morning staple in her house, just for a laugh. The song didn't
last long in the countdown. "The public has finally wised up," Sib
thought.

"Earth to Chiffy, Earth to Chiffy," Timmy said through a mouth-
ful of Ritz and Snack Mate. "Where are you?"

"Sorry, must be the secondary smoke," Sib said. Larry hadn't lit
up his doob in front of her, but its punky aroma was still lingering. Sib figured that Timmy, who couldn't shovel enough squeeze
cheese down now, had taken a few tokes by then, too. "So what have
we got so far?"

Timmy had scribbled down a few potential rhymes. "Love can
overgrow. Love can overflow. Love can take you some places you
never want to go."

"Not bad," Sib said. "But they feel like the middle. Larry, anything?"

Larry played a few phrases, by themselves tuneful but all loose,
separate strands, none that seemed part of the same fabric. A mi-
nor-key triplety riff that had some potential but didn't lead anywhere. Larry shared Sib's contention that the reason pop music
sucked so much lately was that there weren't many great women
singing, and so the really great songs weren't being written. But
now they were finding out just how hard it was to get started themselves.

"What have *you* got?" Larry said, peering over to the notebook
Sib had in her lap, which had a doodle of a cat peering out of the
bottom right corner and a few random chord notations: Fmaj7, G6,
Dflat9.

Sib wasn't ready to talk about her overall strategy yet, but she offered a hint: "Do you know the Carole King chord?"

After all of Sib's research, hours of listening to songs written by women, she had narrowed her list down to Laura Nyro (intense almost to the point of spiritual, but too often unfocused and loopy), Joni Mitchell (poetic and gorgeous but, to Sib's ears, museum pop) and Jackie DeShannon (really, really close: A long arc of a career, and a song she'd composed in the mid-'70s, "Bette Davis Eyes," was a huge hit just last year. She'd even written it with another woman. But ultimately DeShannon had too diffuse a style for Sib to draw a bead on). So she ended up in the obvious place when it came to female songwriters: Carole King, the New York City girl (though she was apparently living in Idaho now), who had anonymously written songs for dozens of artists in the '60s, before scoring her own hits in the '70s, starting with her monster album, *Tapestry*. The record came out during the period of Sib's hearing loss but was still on the charts when her ears woke up. Discovering King's own recordings, after already knowing so many of her songs by other artists ("One Fine Day," "I'm Into Something Good," "Natural Woman" were all in her and Kieran's personal jukebox) was almost as thrilling to Sib as finding disco, a gift or reward she'd been given for suffering in silence, literally, for more than three years.

Tapestry ended up staying on the charts until the beginning of 1977, but now, only five years later, no one was talking about Carole King anymore. Reviews of her more recent albums, admittedly mediocre ones, Sib thought, referred to her as "rock's old lady," even though she was barely 40. Sib knew that King would never have to write or sing another note, and her place in the pantheon would be set. Same with Mitchell and Nyro and DeShannon.

"Yeah, sure, I know it," Larry said. "The tonic over the subdominant or dominant. Or just a 7 or 9 chord. Steely Dan used them all the time. Brian Wilson in 'Good Vibrations.' Jazzy. Upper level. Melancholy, tension. No one writes with them much nowadays."

"Right, that's the problem," Sib said. "Everything's way too simplified. And electronic."

"And here we are back to our theme, too much of a good thing," Timmy said. "Too much simplicity, too far a swing of the pendulum back the other way, it's all so . . . reductionist."

"Let me walk around a bit," Sib said, getting up from the couch. "Maybe I'll run around the block, jog something loose." But she got only as far as the kitchen, with the image of the *Tapestry* album cover following her there. A barefoot, frizzy-haired woman, wedding ring, jeans, needlepoint, cat in the window well. The sun not just beaming onto her face through the picture window but seeming to beam from it.

An unconventional-looking woman perched in the corner of a black-and-white photo, crucifix and Sunday clothes, shard of sun bouncing off her face, perched and ready for something.

The connection between the images seemed almost too obvious for Sib. But now she was even more sure that she'd picked the right song to analyze, a song from *Tapestry*. She first thought it would be "You've Got a Friend," which had become King's signature song, a Grammy winner, a feel-good standard so familiar now it was sung by grade-schoolers. But even though King had written both the music and lyrics, when Sib really thought on the words, she realized that there was something too navel-gazing about them. True, it came from the era of the introspective singer-songwriter. But to Sib the lyric was still way too self-celebrating, all about the singer: Here's what a good friend, what a good person *I* am, it was saying.

Instead, Sib picked another classic from the album, "It's Too Late." King wrote it with another woman, Toni Stern, and to Sib there was something deeper than "You've Got a Friend" about it. It was a breakup song, as "Poor Little Fool" had been, but this time the woman was leaving, and sounding compassionate and realistic as she was walking out the door. And it inspired the best composing from King on *Tapestry:* those jazz chords, and a subtle but bountiful melody that spilled out of the song even in the interstitial riffs. In the one music-theory class Sib had taken in college, the professor had said, "You can never have too much melody." There was the phrase again. "Too much." There were some things that you could never have too much of. Maybe that's the rhyme, Sib suddenly thought, or the refrain:

Melody, harmony, compassion, some things you can never have too much of

But still you can have too much love.

Sib, Larry and Timmy might never get anything close to "It's Too Late," but it wasn't a bad model to have, out of style as it might have been. If nothing else, the titles shared a word. Sib leaned over the kitchen counter and scribbled those lines in her notebook.

When she turned around, there was Larry, almost close enough to pin her to the counter.

"Is the Formica providing any inspiration?" Larry said.

"Well, maybe," Sib said, then threw her arms around Larry's waist and pulled his face close to her. Maybe it was finally time for this. Or maybe they'd get a few more lyrics out of it. Larry's shaggy curls brushed against her temples, and his scruff brushed her cheek. Up close Sib could see the beginning of mottled skin, which she'd heard happened to regular pot smokers, but Larry's lips were full and musical. She went for it.

Like most first kisses, this one was memorable more for the fact that it happened than for the particulars. Larry had been chewing some gum, so the herb smell was mixed with something minty. His lips were moist, not too hesitant, not too aggressive. Just a little tongue. The mustache bristly but not scratchy.

When he pulled back, he said, "Well, that was kinda sorta nice."

Sib was thinking then of her news-writing class, when she was learning how to write headlines, and composing one in her mind: "Finally Kissed," and the subhead: "Late-blooming Queens girl, 21, says she 'didn't hate it.'"

Sib thought about moving in again but just then Timmy charged into the kitchen. "What's all this folderol?" he said, with genuine surprise in his voice, as opposed to the mock surprise with which he greeted most everything else in the world. "Method songwriting?"

Sib released Larry from her clutch for the soft landing to earth. "Watch out, Sweeney, you might be next," she said. "Now let's get back to work."

26. Queens, N.Y., September 1982

Andy popped a fresh sheet of paper into the typewriter on his kitch-
en table. He'd gotten behind on his reports. His preoccupation with
the woman, with the maybe-singer, had much of his life skidding
off the rails lately, as he had yet to see her again. All his research had
led him back to the same two places: the Midtown corner where he
first spotted her, and the subway platform where he pulled her aside.
That was almost four months ago now. And even as he reacquainted
himself with her music over the months, there was nothing close

to a sighting again. Still, she was taking over his life. Had curiosity crossed over to fascination crossed over to concern crossed over to obsession crossed over to delusion?

He'd decided he'd try to get her off his mind, and to do that, he'd use the self-denial approach again. But this time instead of going hungry, he tried other methods of moving out of his comfort zone to distract him. He let papers accumulate, strew around his apartment; he went for hours using just one hand, which led to shaving nicks and more than a few stumbles and bumps and bruises. He wore an eye patch, which just made his "good" eye strained and tired. He plugged his ears with cotton balls for a day, which just gave him earaches. He ate foods he hated, like onions and beets, which just gave him gas. He even slept, on non-work nights, in sweats, which to him was like sackcloth that just made him itch and burn and toss and turn all night.

He smoked a couple of cigarettes. Smoke was something he negotiated all the time, in bars and on the street and in parks and parking lots, and never thought twice about. He almost sought it out. Where there's cigarette smoke. . . . But when he smoked off-duty, his body seemed to know it was being deliberately, willingly fouled, and so threw him into coughing spasms whenever he inhaled.

He rented a car and drove on the L.I.E. during rush hour. He removed as much space around him as he could stand.

And all to no avail. He couldn't get the woman off his mind. The questions churned in Andy's mind: Where was she? Was she even still in New York City? Was she even still alive? Was it even her?

He started to type out some notes.

OFFICER: Logan
PRECINCT: Various
PROJECT: Prevent
DATE: 9/3/82
Night surveillance on bicycle around shelter, may have scared potential

bad influences on runaways walking nearby. Whistles especially effective.

UWS 12 wallets pushed back into pockets.

LES Skimmed pebbles against telephone booth where legs were visible, flushed out potential perps.

FLATBUSH Lingered closing time dispensables solo female young clerk.

MIDTOWN No sight of possibly famous skinny woman in new sneakers.

Maybe some hair of the dog, Andy thought. He pulled out that Christmas album. Maybe that would shake the hold she had on him, turn his obsession into irritation. Just having to listen to it in September would be enough to irk him; he had always bemoaned to his parents how department and stationery stores started rolling out the Christmas merch right after Labor Day, sometimes sooner. By the time Christmas came around, you almost weren't seeing it, weren't feeling it anymore, couldn't smell the pine or hear the carols anymore, were already looking at store displays of suntan lotion. And this album wasn't even Christmas music that Andy especially liked.

But when he started to play it, all it did was make him think about the woman, the singer, more, because this time the experience was truly like a horror movie to him: not just the encroaching death in her voice, but the ghoulishly sweet, old-timey choirs, the overreaching arrangements, cutesy woodwinds lying in wait, strings shrieking, rivers of syrup everywhere.

He fell into a deeper funk; if this record could not purge her, could not exorcise her from his mind, nothing could.

It didn't.

Maybe he'd try another letter. He pulled the police-report notes out of the typewriter and put in a new sheet. He started this letter to her the same way he had the last one:

Dear _____,

I know this may sound strange, but were you in New York in May? Did you get stopped by a _____?

It still sounded ridiculous, even more so now because months had passed. He tried again:

Dear _____,

I've been a fan of yours since I was 14 years old. I remember the day I bought your first big hit. . . .

No, he couldn't go there, either. He'd held his experience from that day with the boy in the booth inside, kept it just between them all these years. And anyway this letter wasn't supposed to be about him or them; it was supposed to be a note of concern, a song of concern, for the woman. He'd keep it simple:

Dear _____,

Please sing out again. Sing low and sing strong and sing full. Sing through your phrases the way you used to.

But that was about him again. Who's to say he was right about her voice? Maybe she liked it better that way, lighter, softer, subtler. Weaker, is what Andy would say, but that was just his opinion. The Christmas album had been a big hit, their first substantial one in a few years, her and the brother's only substantial one in the second half of the '70s, and it had sold well every holiday season since it came out, so obviously the fans liked her voice this way, too. Maybe he was just wrong. Maybe this was the way she'd always wanted to sing. Or maybe there was even part of her that didn't want to sing at all. Andy felt selfish, and guilty, for wanting her to get better just so that she'd go back to sounding the way he liked.

Dear _____,

Please eat.

Better, but still not enough, he thought. She must have been hearing that a lot from everyone around, including other fans, if she'd been starving herself for as long as Andy suspected she had. Hearing it from some stranger probably wasn't going to have any effect.

Dear _____,

Please live.

He took that one out of the typewriter, signed it, "Your friend, Andy," and sent it to the fan-club address on the album covers, with just his street and city and zip, not his full name, in the return-address corner. He didn't expect to hear back, but two weeks later, an 8-by-10 manila envelope arrived (addressed just to "Andy"), marked, "Photo, Do Not Bend." The black-and-white picture inside was recent, and heavily airbrushed, with a stamped signature, "Best Wishes, _____ & _____." But no amount of retouching could disguise how thin the singer looked, or the hollowness in her eyes.

Still, Andy got a frame and put the picture up on his living-room wall. If nothing else, he figured, it would give him some inspiration. He wasn't sure what kind of inspiration — to pray, maybe? Since that weekend in the seminary, his prayer schedule had been inconsistent. Our Fathers and Hail Marys on the run, an occasional Rosary. Or maybe it was just a way of sending out a vibe to her, wherever she really was, to let her know that somebody still cared.

27. New York City, Fall 1982

Say yes to everything. Was it as simple as that?

Thanksgiving was around the corner. The holidays. Her favorite time of year. Her deadline for getting well. And yet, just after the family session, a few weeks ago, she was at her lowest weight, 79 pounds. Even she admitted that this was a serious problem. Tests were ordered, and her potassium was found to be low, which surprised her because she was always nibbling on bananas. This wasn't where she was supposed to be.

She was admitted to the hospital, only a few blocks from the park. Autumn in New York. The best time to be there, air cool and fresh and crackling, drained of its sludgy, sooty humidity, Central Park alive in living color. She could almost see it from the window in her room. When they lived back east, she liked autumn because she could wear sweaters and sweatshirts, just more clothes in general, and not actually sweat. Her chubbiness wouldn't be as obvious, she always thought. Then after they moved to California, where it was always warm, you wore less and people saw more.

The IV was put in, and after a few days the electrolytes and hydration normalized. While she was there, she asked, what about that other procedure?

She had to make things right with her family. The session with them and the therapist had not gone especially well. But then, what did she expect? That when they got out of the car from the airport, they'd feel anything different? That they'd take one look at her and wouldn't have the blood drain from their faces? 79 pounds! That the mother wouldn't say one more time, come home, roll up your sleeves and eat? That's how everything had always worked in their lives. That's how the country won the war, the mother said. Hard work and sacrifice. That's how we afforded all those instruments and music lessons. That's how you got a hit record. None of this fancy therapist and fancy city, the "Uptown East."

The therapist had called the mother by her first name during the session. The mother said, "Call me Mrs. _____."

Tell her you love her, the therapist said. That's *not* how we do things, the mother said. And besides, she knows we love her. She doesn't need to hear it.

The brother just looked angry. Especially when the doctor said that someday she might not want to sing anymore.

Hyper something.... That's what it was called. They just inject the calories, the pounds, the flesh right back into you. She remembered that episode from *The Mary Tyler Moore Show,* when the Rhoda character eats a piece of chocolate and says she should just apply it directly to her hips. Well, that's what this procedure would do. In her case, she was actually having the hips themselves applied, or reapplied. Or like that old line about having a weight lifted off your shoulders. Only she was having a weight put back on, though with the same dizzying relief.

Say yes to everything: Gain.

Autumn in New York. There was a famous song about it. Maybe she'd get to sing it someday. Her fans were always writing to say she should sing the entire American songbook. She'd get around to all of them eventually, she thought. To every season a song.

Say yes to everything: Sing.

Hyperalimentation, that's what it was. She consented. After a couple of weeks, she'd put on 12 pounds. North of 90 for the first time since, what, 1975? The year her body, and their career, started to collapse. The year of T., her one true love. They dated for a year. But they were both busy with their careers and so broke it off. He was married to somebody else now.

Say yes to everything: Forgiveness. Self-forgiveness. A new true love.

It was all so exciting, feeling her body return. The career would follow in step, she just knew it. At first the weight felt detached, burdensome, as if she were carrying around something separate from her body. She thought of that girl with the backpack, lugging around stuff. But after a couple of weeks, it started to feel like part of her, as if it were moving on some inner wheels. She had her drumsticks in the bed, and suddenly they weren't so heavy anymore.

Say yes to everything: Drumming.

Then, eureka! Her period. There it was. The monthly friend, that was always the joke in high school. But she did truly welcome it back, add it to the flood of life she was feeling again.

Say yes to everything: Motherhood.

She thought of I. almost the minute her own monthly fluid broke. I. was more than five months along now and just as active as ever, recording, jetting around the city with P., helping her move the hotel room into the hospital, video players and videocassettes and stuffed animals and running shoes and all. That's what she'd be like when she was pregnant, she thought, a dynamo with a fetus growing inside her, in the recording studio right up to when she went into labor.

She'd go home for the holidays and then be back in New York in early February for the birth. She told I. she knew it would be a boy.

Say yes to everything: Godmotherhood.

After about the third week, she was up to 95 pounds. I. had worried that maybe the weight was coming back on too fast. It took you years to get into this state, she said. Shouldn't it take at least a couple of years to get better? What about your heart? Can it stand the strain? I. said again and again.

I don't have years, she said. There's a new record to make, concerts to give. Besides, I feel fine. That's what she always said, but now she really meant it. Maybe it was the invigorating autumn air. Plus, her period had returned. Wasn't that a sign that her body was liking the treatment?

Say yes to everything: Commitments.

When the family was in town, she and the brother did get out to one club, to see a labelmate of theirs, a recent Oscar winner whose music and show were themselves as colorful as peak autumn. They ran into Lou Reed there, decked in his usual sunglasses and black. They nodded cordially to each other across the room. At least he still recognized her. It was a baby step back into the thick of things.

The brother checked out some studios — if she insisted on staying in New York, maybe they could record here, he told her. But he decided they weren't up to his standards. And she wasn't going to be staying much longer anyway.

Say yes to everything: The music business.

As her body filled back out, her daily, weekly, monthly planners did, too. That's how she knew she was really feeling better. Old business cleared up. New business scheduled. Papers from her law-yer arrived.

Say yes to everything: Divorce.

Even this she was pursuing with gusto now. Pay him off and send him on his way. For a year or so she'd gotten to wear a wedding ring and say, "My husband." Next time, it would be for real. And if her fans didn't like the fact that she was a divorced woman, then they weren't really true fans. No one was going to tell her she couldn't still sing about lace and promises anymore.

After she got up to 95 pounds, the IV was replaced with actual meals. Meals she actually ate. Roll up your sleeves and eat. If that's what it took. She started to look forward to Thanksgiving dinner. One whole list in her planner was devoted to the things she want-ed for the family meal: turkey and all the trimmings, maybe some wine. Writing it down was the first step to keeping it down. Going over it every day in her mind was like rehearsing for a big show.

Say yes to everything: Food.

She even found time, in between all the doctor visits, friend vis-its, treatments and list-making, to go back to that sheet of paper with the song title from the girl in the record store. One rainy day, out of nowhere, she just started scribbling away, so much that her pen started to run out of ink, and she had to double over some of the lines on the page. She looked for another pen in the room but couldn't find one. All that money, all this expensive video equip-ment, and not a simple pen to be found. Well, she had it all in her head anyway; she would finish writing it down some other time.

Say yes to everything: Writing my own songs.

By early November, she was up over 100 pounds. Mission accom-plished, she thought. She checked herself out, over the objections of, well, everyone. But she was just too excited. She'd make it back to L.A. for Thanksgiving. In less busy moments, she'd wonder how it happened so fast, what made her finally able to eat again. Was it the family session? Or seeing that bread line? Or the stick-figure receptionist at the record company? Her mind always got busy again, though, before she settled on an answer.

There were still a couple of weeks before Thanksgiving when she checked herself out, but she didn't head back to the West Coast right away. She had a couple of things left to do in New York.

Say yes to everything: The future.

28. New York City, Fall 1982

On his day off, Andy was in the library, idly flipping through *Bill-board* magazine. He'd long since given up expecting to find any news about her. After their last single fell off the Hot 100 in the spring (it was the lowest-charting of their career), he'd gone so far as to call her record company to see if there were any new releases on the way. The woman on the phone had to take a minute to process the name. Andy could feel her thinking, Are they even still on the label? But then he heard some papers shuffling. No, nothing new on the schedule, the woman said.

The trail had gone ice-cold.

Still, he leafed through the trades. Part of his cop training was that you just had to wait out the perps. They'd always play their hand. Now he really knew what a drill sergeant in the academy meant when he said, "Most of the time you'll just be bored."

November. She was probably long gone, he thought.

Then there it was, a small item in the "goings on about town" section. "Attending the ____ show at ____ were Lou Reed and _____."

She (maybe-she) was still in New York! There was still a chance.

Andy practically leapt up from his chair. The Midtown corner where he first saw her was only a few blocks away. He'd fade into the brickwork and wait for her.

The perps always play their hand, he'd learned. She would show up again. Andy was sure of it now.

29. New York City, Fall 1982

At one of her last sessions with the therapist, they didn't talk much about eating, or her family.

"I have a question," she said. "I was watching a cop show last night, and I heard the line, 'Did she sing?' Some witness was being interrogated, and later the other cops who hadn't been in the room said, 'Did she sing?' You know, like she was a stool pigeon or something. Why do they always call it that? *Singing*?"

"Well, what is it that singers do?" he said.

"Oh, come on, are you serious?" she said.

"Very. Can you answer?"

"Singers sing songs. They sing notes. Melodies. They make pretty noises. In tune and in rhythm. If they're good, and lucky, people listen. If they're really good, and really lucky, a lot of people listen."

"Is that all?"

"Isn't that enough?"

"What do witnesses do?" he said. "The 'stool pigeons.'"

She had to think about that for a minute. "They give up information," she said. "They reveal things."

"So, isn't that something like what singers do? Reveal things, in a song, that people didn't know before? Maybe tell even the people who wrote the song something they didn't know about it? Make the song give up its secrets, so to speak."

She'd never thought of it like that before. Stool pigeon. *Jailbird. Songbird.*

Giving it up. Giving it flight.

Singers reveal things.

30. Queens, N.Y., Fall 1982

Sib watched the numbers on the clock flip over: 3:45. She was now 22. She'd been thinking of the months between graduation and her birthday as a kind of grace period, when she could make some token efforts to find a job, help her dad around the house, listen to records, hang out with Timmy and Larry and not worry about the next phase of her life. But she couldn't avoid it anymore. She was officially an adult.

As if she needed something else to keep her up. The world wasn't about to suddenly throw open its doors to her just because she wanted it to or thought she was ready; jobs were still scarce. She was getting some record-review assignments for a few local music rags out on Long Island that paid maybe $10 a pop, when they paid at all, and she landed them mostly because she wanted to write about artists like Luther Vandross and Howard Johnson and Kashif, whom everyone else was too hip to care about (Sib liked these records even as she recognized that they were glossy collections of nice riffs and, in Luther's case, some virtuoso vocals, but not anything that was going to raise the tide of pop). She was filling in for Larry at the bar occasionally, and reluctantly taking the random $10 or $20 her father would throw her. But no job interviews. The temp places weren't calling back. She figured it was because she wasn't pretty or hip-looking enough. Her father even offered to get her some part-time work on a late shift at the Post Office. But she couldn't go there. She loved her dad and respected his work but going to work at the Post Office would be another of life's pause buttons that she just couldn't push.

Her dad. Eventually she would move out, and he would be alone, and lonely. For more than a decade their main purpose in life was helping the other survive, and even if her moving out wouldn't be as traumatic as losing his wife and son, she knew that he'd still have his routine upended. The Mets hadn't been any help; they finished the year with another abysmal record, their sixth losing season in a row, with not much hope for next year, save some sudden miracle trade, and her dad of course always watched until the last ugly inning. Now he would be facing another long winter of delivering mail in the cold and snow, while he was living for Opening Day. Even if he was in good shape for a man in his mid-50s (even for a man in his mid-40s), he couldn't carry that mail sack around forever, skate across icy sidewalks, trek for hours in summer heat, get drenched in sudden storms, dodge growly dogs or people complaining about checks or magazines that didn't come the day they expected them, averting his glance from the not-infrequent housewife (or -husband) who showed up at the door just when he was depositing the mail in the box in a robe too loosely tied. He'd have to retire one of these days. Sib had mentioned Mrs. Donovan from the bakery a few times again, but her father shrugged her off. Sib knew that she was mostly the reason; her father wouldn't think about getting his own life in order until he thought she was O.K. With all the key-jangling and foot-clomping and whistling and "accidental" banging into things, she worried that he really thought she was going to lose her hearing again, almost nine years later. He lived for routine.

Sib hadn't made much progress on the song either. Timmy was back at school, and Larry was off doing whatever Larry did when they weren't together. And now suddenly there was the kiss. What did it mean to her? Up to that point Sib hadn't even been sure about her own sexuality. Another thing she kept putting off, another matter she'd deal with when she was a grown-up, another bill that wasn't supposed to come due for a while. But the kiss had set something in motion. What was helping keep her up now was not the desire to kiss Larry again but trying to figure out what she felt at all. The kiss was pleasant enough, but it didn't give her the mild static-clingy electroshocks that she had when she saw that picture of her mother and her aunts and grandmother. Maybe Tuke, and not a few of her other "friends" and acquaintances, had been right all those years. But whenever those feelings would bubble to the surface, she'd pop them, just as she did when that vision of Kieran with the other boy in the booth flashed in her mind. She just wasn't ready to start sorting all of that out.

Music, like the Mets, still really sucked. The new Michael Jackson album was delayed again, but the first single had dropped, and it was some drippy duet with Paul McCartney. After more than three years, this was the best he could do? There was a new double album from Prince, but he seemed a little out there for Sib. Larry of course was raving about it.

Even with nothing she was really dying to buy, she needed to be in a record store. There was an unopened birthday card from Aunt Constance on the mantel downstairs; Constance, the last remaining Rooney sister, living alone in Flatbush, was still doling out her "loving" words of wisdom, even now that she was almost 75. There'd be something written in the card to the effect of, "How's the job hunt going, dear?" It was Sib's penance for the check that was enclosed. They'd most likely see her at Thanksgiving, when she'd bring seeded rye bread and a new tablecloth and suggest that they were the tastiest and nicest things there. And tell Sib that she should drink water because it "has a slimming effect." Just like when she and Kieran were kids and the brussels sprouts were never quite consumed with enough gusto, the shirt never tucked in quite neatly enough, the hair just a little too long.

Yet even with prospects on every front dim, or at best uncertain — work, sex, music, her father, the Mets — Sib felt that something big was going to happen soon. And that feeling scared her most of all, because it was the same feeling of anticipation she'd had that day in the kitchen with her mother and Aunt Maddy and the "elbow" and the magical dollar bills. That's why she knew she had to take another trip to a record store.

Sib got down on her knees. She prayed first to Rose. Then to Aunt Maddy. "Help me figure this out," she said. She'd often prayed to them over the years. But now, for the first time, she invoked someone else. "Mom, please," she said. "Help me with this music. *Our* music."

She crawled back into bed. At least her birthday gave Sib a plan. In the morning, she'd hit the bank first to cash the check. Then the subway to Downstairs. She pulled out the notebook and pen and dozed off, eventually writing and then crossing out lines and lines of lyrics for "Too Much Love."

31. New York City, Fall 1982

How those last two weeks flew. First moving back to the hotel from the hospital, then packing up for the trip back to L.A. All those running shoes. At least they were lighter now. She'd long since dumped the laxatives. Even the ones behind the drapes and the pillows. She hadn't taken them for months, but now she didn't even need to have them around anymore. The training wheels were off. It was her first official act on the outside as an (almost) normal-weight woman.

She revised her usual room-service orders. No huge meals that she would pick at or stare down or pretend-eat. Just sensible ones. Her eating was wobbly now but true. Nothing wasted or thrown away or pushed around or talked about. Just eaten, still a bit warily, the forks vibrating a bit as she lifted them to her mouth, tasting and chewing the food gingerly, then swallowing almost like taking a deep breath. But eating. Food didn't make her feel fat now, only tired. It was odd how it felt like a workout, even a salad or a bowl of soup. She had to rest after every meal.

Each day, each hour it seemed, she'd check the mirror, almost to make sure it was all real. Yep, there they were; her hips were back. They weren't imaginary now. She would slap and dig her palms in, giddily fill her hands with small globes of flesh. "Some people were just born hippy," she'd always heard whenever she complained about them. These days she just laughed. That was her. Never hip. Never a hippie. Just hippy. And she was mostly O.K. with that now.

Her front, well, even though her breasts had filled back out a bit, too, she'd never be chesty. That didn't matter now, either. It was the midsection. She still couldn't look in any mirror and not see the shadow of her chubby 16-year-old self lurking in there somewhere. That must never happen again, she thought. Sensible eating and exercise must never yield back to her fat DNA.

She could control it, with just a spoonful a day. Right in the drugstore. One bottle instead of the dozens of packages of laxatives. She bought some with the first box of tampons she'd actually be using in years. She could take it after meals but not too soon, so that only a little would come back. That way she could keep most of the food down, get the nutrients, keep the weight over 100 and not damage her throat or vocal cords. Just not let it get out of hand. Just a spoonful with each meal.

Her parents would be here soon to pick her up and fly back out to the coast with her. She'd take her last long walk around the city tomorrow. But first she pulled out a tape recorder and her tablet. She'd finished the song her last night in the hospital and had been humming the melody for days to keep it in her head. Now she was ready to put it down. The first song she'd ever written.

She sipped some tea as she looked over the words, made a few revisions, drummed out a few different tempos on her knees. How hard it had been. All the cross-outs, the false starts, the ideas that seemed to hold promise but went nowhere, dribbling off the page like some wayward doodle. She respected the brother even more now that she had written her own song. And all the songwriters they'd worked with and she'd just taken for granted, how she'd assumed they'd always come up with something great for her, that it would magically appear on her music stand. "Thank you," she whispered across the side table toward the window, and picked up her hands to push the words out into the world, swooping her arms in a full drum fill, hoping that somewhere all the songwriters who'd ever written something she'd sung would hear them, or at least feel them. She'd get around to thanking as many of them as she could in person once she was back in L.A. again. And let them know she was back, and ready again to give their songs flight. *Songbird.*

She looked over the words one last time, then hit the record button. The key she'd picked — she wasn't sure what it was, maybe D-flat major, but it wasn't too high or low, a nice midrange, just like that first hit of theirs. She flubbed the lyrics a few times and had to start over. The first time she got all the words, she still wasn't happy with the tempo. Just a smidge slow. The song wasn't a ballad per se. She knew things had to move a bit these days. Then when the tempo was good, relaxed but sprightly, she thought her pitch was slightly sharp, and she had no pitch pipe to help her correct.

But after an hour or so, she had the song down. She listened to the playback a few times. Was it a hit? Well, who knew what made a hit anymore? If that "Tainted Love" was a hit, who could predict? And it was only her first try. But she'd done it. She'd written a song, and here was the evidence on the tape. She wrote the title on the white strip, stuck it to the cassette, put it in the case and dropped it in her purse.

The next afternoon she checked three times to make sure she had everything. Small bills for the crazy cart guy. A subway token and a 50 for the busker's finale, her final finale. And the tape.

That morning she'd woken and felt something babbling, burbling in her chest. Something trying to get out. Must be all those songs I haven't been singing all these months, she thought. Putting down her song last night on the tape must have loosed all of them inside her.

F. had called that morning, while she was lying down after dressing, showering, eating. "Won't be long now," she said. "All these months, all this time, all that I've lost. Time for some things to come back to me now."

"Honey, are you sure you're ready?" F. said. "The holidays, there's so much pressure, there'll be so much. . . ."

"So much what?" she said.

"You know."

"It's all right. You don't have to dance around it. Go on, say it: The F-word. . . . Food! *Food. Food. Food.*" Shouting the word gave her a rush, a burst of energy to sit up in bed.

"Oh, honey, I'm sorry."

"Don't be sorry. I'm not afraid of it anymore. And anyway, I have all these contracts to sign, things to get in order. Gotta ditch the creep, too. And see my godchildren. How are the little munchkins?"

"They can't wait to see you!"

"Well, tell 'em I'll be there soon, with lots of presents for them both."

Her godchildren, were they really 5 already? She'd missed a big chunk of *their* lives too. Another reason she had to get back to L.A. Hell's exit gates were finally opening for her, and she had to pass through them while she could.

She tried on a few different outfits for her last walk around New York. The usual sweater-and-jeans ensembles, but in about six different color combinations, with her pink satin jacket. She enjoyed trying on clothes now, playing a little dress-up, loved the fact that the clothes actually fit, didn't fall off her anymore. Some of them, the smaller pieces, were actually a little snug. But after a half-hour or so, she finally just picked some blue jeans and her usual merino sweater. Then she put on her baseball cap and the one pair of Nikes she hadn't packed. She was ready.

On her way out the door she felt a little dizzy. She was so used to bounding around. Her doctors said she had to remember that she'd just put the equivalent of 25 percent of her weight back on. Imagine someone who weighed 200 suddenly going to 250, they said. She needed to take it easy, to let her body get used to the extra she was lugging around. When she got outside and started walking, the weather seemed to change on her every block, the wind like icicles slicing through her on one, the next the heat beating down on her from above and steaming up from the pavement below, trapping her in a pressure cooker. Still, she pushed on. Her body would adjust, she thought.

The walk felt like a farewell, even though she knew it wasn't. She'd be back in February for the birth of P. and I.'s baby. Just as soon as the business affairs were in order. Maybe she'd move to New York someday. Her walk felt like the last date of a tour before they headed home, knowing they'd be back again when the next album came out.

She thought she might actually talk to the smelly guy with the cart this time, to tell him she was leaving and to wish him well. But as she approached his usual corner on Sixth Avenue, she didn't see him. Maybe he was marching up and down the block. She turned the corner, but he was still nowhere in sight. She looked all the way up Sixth Avenue as far as Radio City, and down toward Macy's, but he was clearly not around today. Then she looked down and saw a few crumbly flowers and votive candles ringed around a 45, perched up against the corner building, a store that sold tourist tchotchkes, almost like a mini-shrine. She bent closer. The 45 was Diana Ross and the Supremes' "Someday We'll Be Together."

She was sorry to miss him. She thought about leaving some money under the record in case he came back, but she knew he'd probably never see it. Maybe they'd meet again the next time she was in the city.

When she stood up straight, she had to steady herself on the wall of the building, press her hand into the cement slab. The burbling in her chest again. It's nothing, she thought. Her body would get used to this.

Her next stop was the subway platform. The finale. She hadn't been around to hear it in weeks, since before the hospitalization and the family visit. She wondered if the man would even be there, especially now that the days were getting colder. Maybe buskers had seasons, too, like crazy guys with carts. She would try the same time as always: 3:20. Even with her slower gait, she still had a good 15 minutes to go just a few blocks.

But as she crossed Sixth Avenue, she felt her mind moving faster, her body lagging behind it, trailing it again, as if all the new weight she was carrying dropped down her legs and into her feet, turned her sneakers into solid lead blocks, the air in front of her something she had to break through, pierce. The more she pressed, the harder it seemed to move. People passed her, bumped her, jostled her. She had to stop several times to catch her breath. It was never like this when she was thinner.

She got to the subway hole at 3:10, still in plenty of time, but it was closed off, with yellow police tape spread from railing to railing. Construction or crime scene or something. She tried another opening a block over but wasn't sure where it took her when she got down the stairs. The extra steps fatigued her, and on the way down another set of them she got caught going against the current of school kids emptying out and up. By the time she got her bearings, it was already 3:23. Maybe the busker would have been late himself that day.

When she finally got to the platform, she was relieved and elated to find he was still there. But he was already starting to pack up his keyboard and his shoebox earnings. She must have just missed the song, if in fact he had sung it. She decided to give him the 50 anyway. He might need it for the cold winter ahead. She moved close to the nearby magazine kiosk to open her purse — all that time in New York, maybe even being stopped by the cop months ago, had taught her some street smarts, so she knew not to take out the money in the open space. She clasped the 50 in her fingers and started to move toward the shoebox, which was still on the ground. She crept right next to it and opened her fingers, looked around and got ready to drop the bill into the box, less than a foot from the busker.

"Put your money away," he said suddenly, in a deep, resonant whisper, his body a monument, his face locked straight ahead.

"I'm sorry?" she said, bolting upright and closing her hand around the bill.

"You heard me. Keep your money." She stared at him. Was he really blind or another city hustler? His eyes didn't seem to move toward her, and yet the sheer shiny hulk of him held her there.

"You haven't been around here in a while," he said. "Where'd you go?"

"I'm sorry, you must have me mistaken for somebody else," she said, trying to back away from him.

"I don't think so," he said, his voice now a confident burring bass, intoning both below and above the rumble of the unseen trains coming and going in other tunnels. "I know exactly who you are. Always here for the last song." He paused for a beat. "Your song."

Now she was frightened for maybe the first time since she'd been in New York, much more than the day when the cart guy spit on her. Did he really know who she was? Had he known the whole time?

"I have to be going," she said, but before she could move very far, a train emptied, and the people pouring out of it pinned her close to the busker. She lost her footing a bit trying to move, to mix in with the crowd, but somehow ended up right before him. She took a step toward the shoebox again.

"I told you, I don't want your money," he said. "But there is something else you can do for me."

Could she scream if she needed to? This wasn't on the itinerary for the day. Improvisation still didn't come naturally to her.

She turned to face him, but far enough away to run if she needed to. "What . . . what do you want?" she said.

"I want you to sing with me."

"What?"

"Sing with me. You know something about that, don't you?"

She couldn't, didn't want to believe that the man knew who she really was. He'd probably just heard her humming along all those times she came to hear the finale. Could she risk it? She hadn't sung in public in months. Most of those last TV performances they did, they lip-synced. It's true that she had been able to sing into the tape recorder the night before, but that didn't mean she was up to it now on a New York subway platform. Maybe F. and I. were right. Maybe this was all happening a little too fast.

The busker unfolded his keyboard stand again and placed the little piano on top, and soon his meaty, ringed fingers were gliding over the keys. She thought he'd choose the finale again, but once he stopped noodling and played the opening bars of a song, it wasn't the finale at all. It was another one of hers, though. The one about the groupie. So there was no doubt now. He knew.

Say yes to everything: Singing.

She steadied herself, letting him vamp over the opening eight or 10 times, and started to take the first breath before the first note, but then stopped every time.

"Whenever you're ready," he said, not breaking the vamp.

A small crowd was forming now, slowing, in that blasé New York way, to absorb a little of the scene without seeming too interested.

He played the opening riff a few more times, and finally she started. "*Long ago. . . .*"

After the first phrase, the busker stopped playing.

"What's that?" he said.

"You asked me to sing," she said.

"I did. But I want to hear your real voice. Not that ap*prox*ima-tion."

"I, I don't think I know what you mean."

The busker lifted his left hand from the keyboard in a slow, grand sweep, moved it next to his mouth, and closed his thumb and forefinger next to his lips. Then suddenly his other hand joined it, and they moved in reverse directions along his body from the top of his head to the end of his torso, his bottom arm suddenly dropping untethered.

"Use all of your voice," he said. "Like on the record." He started to play the intro again. "Put the soul back into it."

Why am I standing here, putting myself through this? she thought. Isn't it enough that I put the weight back on my body? Do I have to put it back on my voice too? But as the busker played a flurry of arpeggios, leaving her lots of room, she realized something: She'd been making her voice smaller because she thought it was the only way she'd be noticed inside her brother's bigness. Or because she'd felt guilty for crowding him out of what was supposed to be his spotlight. His *life*. Now, with just a single piano, no strings, no four-part harmony tripled over, she didn't have to make her voice disappear anymore. Or herself.

Singers reveal things.

She started again. It was almost like that first take of the song all those years ago, reading the lyrics off the napkin, when she wasn't thinking that that would be the take they kept, when she wasn't concentrating too hard, when she was slightly spilling over the words, making them give as much as they had. The busker stayed with her, shadowed her, followed a baby step behind her so that she knew she was the star of this show. As things heated up around the first chorus, they were both almost attacking the song. But she led the charge. The final line of the chorus brought things down to the earth, and by then he practically wasn't playing at all. It was all her, and she didn't back off. She leaned into that last line the way she used to, her own low voice now seeming to push against the wall on the other side of the subway tracks.

She figured she'd catch her breath for the second verse and chorus, regather her voice, but the busker never got there. He just ended the song. She looked again for some recognition. There was a smattering of applause.

He just nodded at her. "Now *that*," he said, "is what I've been waiting to hear."

32. New York City, Fall 1982

Andy watched the E.M.T.s load the body into the ambulance from across the street. He'd seen the man collapse, one minute striding with his cart, again in camos, chanting something about all going down together, and the next minute actually going down, dropping so fast, rag-doll-like, almost as if he'd been shot or had fallen out of a window, that he couldn't even try to grab the handle of his cart before he landed on the pavement. Andy called 911 and started toward the man — he'd had extensive CPR training in the academy — but by then a beat cop was on the scene, waving the crowd back and trying to revive the man himself. The cart, with a small tub of cigarette butts and crushed pizza boxes on top, rolled back and forth, as if searching for its master's grip. Andy stepped away as the sirens of the ambulance got closer.

And still there was no sign of the woman. With the cart man almost surely dead now, there was one less reason for her to pass by this corner again.

She was somewhere close, though. He could feel it.

He kept watch on the block a few more times, when he could get there on his days off. Someone left a 45 and some flowers on the corner near where the man was frequently stationed. Andy always made sure the thing was in place when he walked by. The record was by the Supremes. Their last No. 1. The last No. 1 hit of the '60s. It seemed a proper shrine for someone who never got out of the '60s himself.

Andy spent the time he was waiting thinking of what he would say to her when she showed up. Always be prepared for the perps, who had the litany of excuses, versions of "the dog ate my homework." "I was only here for a minute, Officer." "I didn't see the sign." "I thought I had the light." "My old lady is really sick, gotta get to her." "I don't know how that got there." "I never smoked a joint in my life." "There's no problem, Officer, really." The usual comebacks were just as programmed: "So you're telling me I'm wrong, is that it?" "You're saying that I'm not seeing what's in front of me?" "Telling me I need glasses?" Get them back on their heels. Get in front of them. Let one go every now and then with a stern warning, especially the ones who admitted they'd done something wrong. Andy's firm but gentle manner was usually such that they felt sorry for him; by the end people he stopped often sounded as if they wanted the ticket. "A natural confessor" is what his partner once called him.

But what to say to her now if she actually showed up? It was easier when he was writing a letter and could keep that distance, that artificial intimacy, between them. Was he ready for the reality

of her? Could he really say anything to help her? What more than
"Please live"? Would he come off as an interrogator? Would she
think he was just another New York crazy? Would she remember
him from the last time? What would she have to confess? Andy's
thoughts were crowding him, making his heart race, sucking up the
air around him.

And there was still the chance that it wasn't the singer after all.

Another week went by. Andy was almost starting to feel stood
up. And hungry. He'd been subsisting on coffee and carrots, the
occasional bagel or banana or Snickers bar. It was easier to go hungry when you weren't really trying. He'd be a sight for her now,
disheveled and unshaven and looking not much different from the
cart guy.

It got well into November. Even in the bull's-eye of Midtown,
of city grime and junk, a million heart-attacks-waiting-to-happen
walking by him every day, there was something calming in the autumn light to Andy, in the way the sun caressed the buildings now
instead of pouncing on them, bounced gently off the pavement,
everything low to the ground. The crackling melancholy in the
air. He thought of the singer's second big hit, so full of spirit and
promise and yet also embracing, not confronting, a song of perfect
autumn harvest. So full of her. At her best, he realized, she had an
autumnal voice, deep and dark-hued, yet fluttery. Even the first hit,
the big summer song, had that shading, that warmth of a sweater
about it, a low but steady fire. He thought of that boy in the booth.
The way the baseball cap, wrapped backward on his head, seemed
almost sculptural, ingrained, part of the boy's skin, as if it couldn't
be knocked off no matter how anyone tried. That day they'd met
was over 10 years ago now, and still Andy occasionally wondered
where he might be, what he looked like, if he was listening to her
still.

Andy got so lost in his thoughts of the boy that he almost missed
the bright Nikes and the forward-facing baseball cap moving up

45th Street. From behind he could just about see the brown hair tucked between the cap and the jacket. The hips seemed slightly bigger than those of the woman from the spring. But at this point he had to follow every lead.

He trailed the figure, walking west, just far enough behind to keep her in sight. The woman was sauntering, not moving at an accelerated New York City clip, and even stopped a few times. Andy did, too. He didn't want to catch her right away; maybe he'd pass her and then face her on the corner. Maybe she'd remember him. Or, if he realized it wasn't her, he'd know not to reveal himself to her.

He lost her between Broadway and Seventh, when a theater let out after she'd passed it. Matinee-day crowd. By the time Andy made his way through the lingering crowd of blue hairs in shawls and wool coats, the woman had disappeared into the maw of Times Square. Andy stood among the bustle and the street vendors looking as lost as a tourist, crossing the same blocks a few times over, looking as suspicious as the potential perps he monitored.

Let her go, he thought. Get on with your life.

He drifted almost absent-mindedly toward the subway. He would probably come back again tomorrow, but something felt finished now. That might have been his chance.

Just as he was near the token booth at 41st and 7th, near where he'd spoken to her all those months ago, he thought he heard something coming up from the platform, different from the rumble of trains and the hum and buzz of the crowd and yet too far away to really be intelligible. He drew closer. It almost sounded like one of her songs.

Boy, you really have lost it, he thought.

The sounds sorted and separated themselves out. Not only did it seem to be one of her songs, but it sounded like her singing it. With her old, full voice. The voice from that golden day.

As Andy charged down the stairs, he told himself the song was still going, that the phantom second verse was actually happening. It was only when he got down to the nearly empty platform, with the usual assortment of students, hangers-on, pole lurkers, one truck of a blind man carrying a large case, nothing but train sounds, that he realized he must have been imagining what he heard.

And even if he hadn't been, he was too late. Either way, she was gone.

33. Queens, N.Y., February 1983

━━━

SOUL TO SOUL

A publication from the young adults' corner of the Church of the Immaculate Conception.

Issue of February 3, 1983

REVIEWS

Michael Jackson, THRILLER

By S.V. Kelly

Today is the feast of St. Blaise, the guy who something like a thousand years ago saved a kid from choking on a fish bone with a proto-Heimlich maneuver and since has been the patron saint of throats. So if you get to church today to have your throat blessed, when the priest rests the crossed candles on your shoulder, presses the opening next to your throat and says, "Through the intercession of St. Blaise, may you be protected from all afflictions of the throat," you might want to say a prayer for Michael Jackson's throat too.

Yep, he's finally back, three years after the brilliant Off the Wall, *a jumping soulful mélange that was the last great blast of the disco era. "Don't Stop 'Til You Get Enough" was not just the best thing to hit dance floors since "Get Down Tonight"; it was also a funk fire sale: The '70s are over, here come the '80s, get everything while you can.*

Thriller *isn't nearly as joyous or liberating as* Off the Wall; *it's only nine songs long, and most of them have some kind of weight to bear, some emotional baggage to lug around. And yet once again it's about the most vital record you're likely to hear in a very long while.*

Rat-tat-tat. The opening drum riff of "Wanna Be Startin' Somethin' " fires off and announces that you're in a new landscape, one of smoke and mirrors and hazardous turns and twists, a dance floor littered with broken glass and landmines, with Manu Dibango's 1970s hit "Soul Makossa" as inspiration and road map into the perilous '80s of oil embargoes, hostage crises and long recessions. Jackson spills so much energy in this opening track that he needs a couple of songs to recover, including the limp duet with Paul McCartney, "The Girl Is Mine" (which works if you take it as a joke), before he's back to paranoia central with the title track, whose flourishes come on you like a sudden dousing on a street curb. Life as horror movie, or at least as fun house, and once again, the only way to outrun the zombies is to outdance them. Jackson growls and yelps and hiccups his way through the danger zone until Vincent Price, the king of horror movies himself, comes along to relieve him with a goosebump-drawing narration/rap, while the beat keeps going, kind of like Edgar Allan Poe meets Chic.

Jackson really ups the ante on the Side 2, starting with "Beat It," featuring a 12-hammer guitar solo by Eddie Van Halen. Yeah, that Eddie

Van Halen. Then along comes "Billie Jean," a tale about a love affair on the dance floor, or with the dance floor, that might have gone terribly wrong, which slinks and creeps along as Jackson keeps ducking and feinting, almost singing into himself. Here is a man who feels besieged from every angle, and he's essentially fighting for his life by the end. Not as easy as A-B-C, but just as funky.

He lightens up for the rest of the album. "Human Nature" is, if not quite innocence regained, then at least a chance for him to catch his breath and his hope (it was co-written by one of the guys from Toto, and almost makes up for their recent bloodless radio hits); then there's some candy floss ("P.Y.T.") and a sweet if unessential ballad to close the record, "The Lady in My Life."

All in all, maybe not the album we were expecting, or hoping for, but more than the record that we, you know, need. Some of you may be aware that this day, Feb. 3, is not only the feast day of St. Blaise but an important day in rock 'n' roll history, the day that Buddy Holly, Ritchie Valens and the Big Bopper were killed in a plane crash in 1959, the day that Don McLean sang about in "American Pie." They were something like the Shadrach, Meshach and Abednego of rock, martyrs for the rock 'n' roll cause. Now, 24 years later, it might be time for another veneration, but not because of something or someone lost, but for something found: Michael Jackson may just have brought pop music back to life.

Sib read the review on the mimeographed sheets from I-Mac four or five times as she sat propped up in bed in her sweats, the smell of apple-pectin shampoo hanging in the air, replacing the secondhand smoke and stale beer from spinning that night at Whelan's. She'd wanted to get Marvin Gaye's "Sexual Healing" and Prince's *1999* (which she had warmed up to) into the review, too, but figured that would be too much for a church publication; even Michael Jackson was a gamble for the director of the youth group, a young priest named Will, who agreed to let her write it because he'd been a big fan of the early Jackson Five hits.

But she'd take it for now.

She'd had a good night at Whelan's, her fourth consecutive Thursday spinning since Larry had given her the night permanently after he started getting some gigs in Manhattan. The bar had been steady, the crowd mostly the club kids and the late-shifters and a few random guys in down vests slowly cozying up to a winter weekend, cold but not frigid, no snow on the ground. No meatheads like Tuke. No foosball-table tremors to make the records skip. No snorters in the men's room. With the regular gig, Sib finally had some dependable money landing in her pocket, even if, with the occasional tip, it was only $50 a week.

She had five requests for Michael Jackson's "Beat It" that night, which was a lot for a four-hour shift. At most she'd play a song twice in one night, but she was in a good mood, and got to it three times before she ended at 2. "I can't believe that's Michael Jackson," a lumberjacked guy with a silver rope earring named Travis said to Sib. "But if he's good enough for Eddie, he's good enough for me." And then he dropped a five in her tip jar. Whenever she put on one of the songs from *Thriller*, suddenly the D.J. booth, the bar, Sib's life didn't feel so cramped and shabby.

Sib had been to church that day and actually offered up a prayer of thanks for *Thriller*. She also got her throat blessed; Sib wasn't sure if it really protected her, but the ritual was comforting. And the day, February 3, was always something of a turning point for her. It meant that Christmas was finally, officially over — there were still the straggling trees on the curbs up to then — and that Lent and spring and baseball, her own personal crocuses, would be popping up soon.

Sib couldn't remember the last time she felt this good, and couldn't begin to figure out why. She still didn't have a full-time job. She still worried about her dad — when she got home that night, she found him asleep in the living-room chair, waiting up for her, her review of *Thriller* splayed across the afghan he had pulled up around him. "Oh, fell asleep watching TV," he said as he stretched his legs and pushed himself out of the chair. "Nice review," he said. "Michael Jackson and St. Blaise, there's an odd pairing. Good night, Siobhan." And she still hadn't figured out who she was sexually. There hadn't been another kiss with Larry. They just avoided the subject of the first altogether and went back to being pals. It was easier that way. Sib still wasn't sure if she liked boys or girls or both or neither. That would be all her dad needed. She could just hear herself having *that* talk with her father. "Uh, Dad, you might want to forget about the grandkids." She wondered if her parents ever knew about Kieran, or knew what she thought she knew about Kieran, based on that day in Rose's store. She'd never told anyone but Timmy, and now it was so long ago she wondered if she was even remembering it right. The present was already muddy enough.

But tonight something was lifting her. Sib glanced over at her nightstand. Was she finally ready, she wondered? Should she risk the natural buzz she was feeling? Just cash out the good feelings of that day and night and face the rest tomorrow?

She opened the drawer of the stand and pulled out the cassette. She'd had it in there since before Thanksgiving, since she found it in Downstairs Records that day around her birthday. It had been sitting at the front of the section, of *that* section, wedged in before the first record, and at first she just thought someone had left it there randomly. Then she picked it up and saw the title handwritten across the top: "Too Much Love."

What was this? A joke, she figured, played by Larry and Timmy, but they never said anything about it at the next songwriting session, and she never brought it up. They basically abandoned the project after that, as none of their promising leads — the odd riff, the snatch of lyric, the elegant bass line, the Carole King chord progression — ever knitted together. Sib's songwriting career lasted all of two months.

Sib's first inclination was to toss the tape, but every time she started to, some pang of guilt would stay her hand. What if it wasn't a joke? What if by some weird cosmic turn, there was a real song there? A song with her title? Yet she couldn't bring herself to play it. Something was going to be revealed, and she wasn't sure she was ready for it.

She'd gotten a Sony Walkman for Christmas — among other things, it let her listen to music late into the night without worrying about waking her dad. Should she risk the vibe she was feeling? Maybe there *was* a song. Maybe it was bad. "Get used to the idea of things going wrong, dear," Aunt Constance once said.

Finally, some of Constance's advice that might come in handy, Sib thought. She popped in the tape.

Almost a full minute went by. Sib kept fast-forwarding, but heard nothing. Maybe it *was* all a joke. But then just when she was ready to give up, she heard four finger snaps counting off, and then a solo voice, no accompaniment:

Just a glance my way
Floods my senses
Just a sliver of your day
Kicks down my fences
Just the thought of your touch
It's all too much

Every step you take
Feels like a mile
My heart can break
At the crack of your smile
Just the thought of your touch
It's all too much

It's a drop it's a flood
It's a stride it's the tide
It's a note it's three

It's a mile-wide melody

A word you send my way
Can rend all my seams
A hint of your someday
Can mend all my dreams
It's all too much
It's all too much
It's too much love

The song stayed a cappella all the way through, with just the finger snaps. Sib listened a dozen times. She wasn't sure that "rend" or "fences" were such great words for a pop song, though she liked the rhyme with "mend." The snappy, jaunty rhythm could have almost been sister to Doris Troy's "Just One Look." Sib recognized the fact that, as in all good pop songs, the music was actually listening to the lyrics. Could her title really have inspired it?

For now, though, it had to be reduced to the basics, to the things that grabbed Sib the most. The lowish voice dabbing itself on the melody, and the bouncy rhythm. Sib thought it could have been written by a drummer.

No way, she thought. It couldn't be. This might really have been the greatest cosmic joke of all.

Sib got out of bed, taking the Walkman with her, and tiptoed down to Kieran's room. She didn't venture in there much, but every time her dad talked of breaking it down, maybe putting some of his things away, Sib always protested. His glove was still on the dresser, along with his grammar-school yearbook, the stereo system he'd gotten for 8th-grade graduation, still on the low shelves next to the bed. Sib opened the door to his closet, dove into the shirts and sports uniforms still on the rack and parted them, wincing at the whiff of a decade of must and mothballs. In the back was the album she'd gotten from the mystery donor the Christmas right after her hearing had returned. She'd put it in Kieran's closet, shrink-wrap unpunctured, and not looked at it since.

Now as she considered the solid brown cover, the letters of the group's logo stenciled in gold, she remembered how she could barely stand to hold it all those years ago, how it sickened her, how it *frightened* her, as if it were wired and she'd get some shock just touching it. When she picked it up now, the shrink-wrap crumbled a bit under her fingertips.

She slit the side and pulled out the album. The booklet with the lyrics spilled onto her lap, and when she opened the fold of the cover, there was a picture of the two of them on a bridge somewhere, looking flush, bell-bottoms and bangs on her, very '70s, sheepish grins on their faces, as if they'd realized they'd pulled something off, gotten away with some kind of cultural heist.

She slid the shiny, virgin vinyl out of the sleeve and placed it carefully on the turntable that Kieran had barely gotten to use.

She sat on Kieran's bed. She didn't bother to start at the beginning; she went straight to the end of Side 2, to the song that she'd gone out of her way not to hear for more than a dozen years. There was that opening piano riff, tickling her in unpleasant spots. The day, the kitchen table, the bicycle, the booth at Rose's, the garbage strewn in the gutter on Liberty Avenue, the sight of Kieran flying headfirst toward her bicycle, all of it contained in those first few notes.

Sib fully expected unbroken misery once the girl started singing, but instead she found herself fascinated, to the point of aural gawking. There was a geeky kind of warmth, depth in a shallow pool. An acquired taste for sure, but now, for the first time, acquirable by Sib.

And maybe it *was* the same voice on the tape she'd found at the record store. She listened to the song on the record a few times, then rewound and replayed the tape. They were very similar, in tone, in range, in the slightly halting phrasing, the newer voice on the tape sounding both older and younger, lighter and yet wiser.

Still, there was something beyond the vocal similarities. Some quality that Sib couldn't put her finger on. Some music critic you are, she thought. She turned off the record player and, Walkman still attached, went back to her room and the drawer in her nightstand. She pulled out the picture of her mother and her family. Her female family.

Then the word came to her: *diapason*. Tuning fork. A musical completeness.

***

The late-morning sun coaxed its way through the curtains on Sib's window, and the warmth on her cheek woke her, the youth newsletter with her review of *Thriller* next to her on the bed. She uncurled her arms and legs under the Mets comforter and turned to look at the clock. 11:00! She'd slept more than eight hours for the first time since before she could remember.

When the cobwebs cleared, she pulled open the drawer in the nightstand. There was the tape, just where she'd left it weeks ago. Had she dreamed the whole thing?

She went down the hall. Kieran's room. Looking just as it had for years. No warm impression on the bed, no residue of anyone other than a 14-year-old ghost. The record player was covered.

She pulled on her hoodie and made her way downstairs. It was her father's day off, and she figured she would find him in the kitchen reading the paper or tinkering with something in the yard. "Dad?" she called. No answer. She saw a bakery bag on the table. "Dad?" All quiet. Maybe Mrs. Donovan had made contact finally.

She went down the stairs and onto the pavement in her sweats and socks. It was a brilliant, dappling day, cold but invigorating. The outdoor thermometer on the side of the garage said 32 degrees, but it felt warmer, especially in the unshaded parts of the driveway. "Dad?" she called. No one in the yard. As she turned to go in, she caught a glint from the basketball hoop and walked toward it. At the base, she noticed for the first time that the fissures had been filled.

34. Outside Los Angeles, February 1983

She slept in the brother's old room that night. All the good video equipment was there — she still had some episodes of *Dallas* to catch up on, or to watch again — but part of her also knew that she needed one last rest stop in the past. A place to validate all the good things in her life. A place where the future would officially start. A place to let go of the hate.

Thanksgiving, Christmas, seeing her old friends, showing off her new body, it had all gone mostly according to plan. Even if a lot of the new plan seemed to be the old plan, the four of them sitting around the dining-room table, talking about big things for the future. It was a much larger house, and the clothes were a little nicer, and the parents a little grayer and more wrinkled, and she was rid of those awful bangs, and they had been around the world a few times. But now, after a decade of dreams realized and revoked and redreamed, here they were again, ready for another go-round. The brother and the father talked about cars. The brother raved about the new CD technology, how he couldn't wait for them to have their catalog digitally remastered, how he could get rid of "all the imperfections." The mother, as usual, was no-nonsense. "Every time I look at those damn charts. . . . " the mother said. "Makes me crazy. That should be you up there." A dozen or so years ago, around a similar table, she was saying: "Those damn charts. That will be you up there soon." She made eye contact with the brother, though without looking at her, the mother did sweep her arm in her general direction.

And that was the difference. Now even the mother knew how much hinged on her. And not just her voice this time, but her health, her very being. At the therapy session in New York that summer, the mother also talked about business. "Young man," she said to the therapist, who wasn't that much younger than she was, "we need to be done with *this business* and get on with things."

Thanksgiving was the start of that process, of "getting on with things." And so the plates were passed around and filled that day as if all that business had been concluded. "Turkey?" "Yes, please." "Dressing?" "Yes, please." "Green beans?" "Yes, please." "Wine?" "Yes, please." And she could feel everyone looking sideways, as if *their* very existences depended on every spoonful. Every time a loaded fork approached her mouth, she could practically feel them holding their breath.

The food went in. In fact she cleaned her plate. "That was good," she said, the way she would after a satisfying take in the studio. The applause was both implied and inferred.

Everyone did *ooh* and *ahh* audibly at her new look. She and F. went shopping on Rodeo Drive for new clothes. And she even sang in public again, a short Christmas concert for her godchildren's kindergarten class; she wore a red silk blouse, white jacket and red shoes and called the brother to get the keys for the school's accompanist. It wasn't the *Saturday Night Live* spot she'd imagined when the solo album was still in the chute, but it was a start.

They signed a new contract with their longtime label. "You look wonderful," H. said. "Let's make some more hits." The terms weren't as good as the last contract's, but that would make them hungry. And one big song would change all that anyway. That hit was going to come.

Her 33rd birthday was only a month away. Plenty of time.

Her divorce was about to be finalized. She couldn't wish him ill, much as she tried.

She'd gone to her parents' house the day before her divorce papers would be ready to go shopping with the mother for a new washing machine; they couldn't find a good deal, so she decided to stay overnight and continue the search the next day.

They went out to dinner. She had a shrimp salad and then a taco on the way home. Part of it was show; after years of their watching her not eat, she figured they still didn't believe her. Sometimes eating now felt like checking in with a parole officer (whatever that felt like). But she actually enjoyed it. The crunch of the shrimp, the melting cheese from the taco breaking over on her tongue, were like good memories that she got to relive again. The hating *had* stopped.

Just one spoonful afterward to keep it under control.

It was all a little dizzying. She'd sign those papers tomorrow and then get on the plane to New York over the weekend. I.'s baby was due any day. She was going to be a godmother again. And maybe, now that she had a working body, a mother herself someday. She called I. and P. that night. They spoke of the album, *their* album, how good it was, how "F-ing great" it was.

P. said: "I was talking about you with a friend recently. He said you're like the New York Mets. People will flock to you again if you just field the right team."

She laughed. She thought she was done with baseball years ago.

She would never leave the brother, though. To her, he was still a genius. They had a legacy. She liked the records they made. She *loved* him.

But some things had to change now. She wanted a greater say in how they made their records. And she'd want some time to do solo projects. It was probably too late to resurrect the last one. But P. was always telling her that she was capable of so many different styles. Bob Dylan songs, country, jazz. And hey, didn't their longtime lyricist have a song on the hot new album by the former Motown wunderkind?

She'd try to write a few more songs of her own. She liked how the first one turned out. She wondered if that girl ever found the tape. She'd go looking for her again when she got back to New York.

That night she dreamed of Champagne, corks popping at some star restaurant like Chasen's. It was a party for a record release, for *her* record release. The early chart numbers were very good. "Who Knew?" was the headline for the review in *Rolling Stone*. The brother was there. The parents. P. and I. (with her new baby in tow) and F. and H. And the girl with the backpack, whose face she could finally see, cracking a smile. Her face was sharp but friendly, full and fresh, recognizable somehow. The girl raised a glass to her.

When she woke up that morning, her heart was fluttering, buzzing, tiny fireworks going off, darting about. There was so much ahead.

She went downstairs to put on the coffee. The parents weren't up yet. From the kitchen, she thought she heard something, a shaker or a soft reed. It drew her back to the stairs. Every step up felt like three; the whole morning seemed to be consumed by the ascent. At the top, she could feel the imprints her feet were making in the plush carpet as she made her way to her bedroom in a slow shuffle, the same rhythm her brother imagined on that first gigantic hit of theirs. She stepped into the walk-in closet, slipped out of her dressing gown and lay down on the floor, on her left side. Six months ago she would have keeled over, but now, almost at normal weight, her body was firmly sunk into the carpet. She closed her eyes and put her ear close to the ground. There it was again, finally, loud and clear. Somebody somewhere was playing one of her records. Listening to her.

35. Queens, N.Y., Summer 1988

Sib felt the pang in her back, short and sharp, as she bounced up from the front of the gravestone, where she had been pulling stray weeds and buffing the area around the names. Seven months along, and she still often forgot that she was pregnant. The first question she asked the doctor when she found out was whether she could stay active, and when the doctor gave her the O.K., she continued to run, to shoot hoops, to swim a few times a week. For the first six months, even as she gained weight, nothing felt especially different, or slower, or more exhausting. But lately the baby was reminding her, with a swift kick, a sudden twinge, just the jutting second-personness, that maybe she shouldn't throw their weight around so much or so fast.

It was the 18th anniversary of the bicycle accident, and while Sib and her father had visited the cemetery many times, this was the first year that Sib had gone on the actual day. Her father and Mrs. Donovan — now Mrs. Kelly — and Larry had come with her, and they all stood around the grave and said a few prayers, the usual rosary trio, plus a few words from Larry that seemed a medley/remix of the *Kaddish* and Bob Marley's "Kaya," which earned him a sidelong smirk from Sib. After Sib's father laid a bouquet of roses on the grave, Sib asked to be alone for a few minutes, and as the other three were retreating, Larry threw his arms around Sib from behind, pressing his small, strong palms against either side of Sib's bump.

"Dude, what are you trying to do, fit her for headphones?" Sib said.

"Never too early," Larry said.

Headphones. Sound. It was still something that Sib didn't take for granted. Sib remembered that first time she and her dad came to the grave, and how sound all fell away, the way it did when they fell away. But today the place was a riot of noise, at least to Sib. Birds, the wind, the distant cars, the half-life of the songs they'd heard on the radio, even the grass pushing up through the ground and the thick, slow blasts of heat seemed to be registering raucously in her ears, and she couldn't take it in fast enough. Sound restored again, just as it had been when she was 13, or as it had been on the radio since *Thriller* kicked in the doors five years ago. Prince, the Pointers, *Graceland, Control.* Crowded House, De La Soul. Music, glorious sound spilling everywhere again. Even the great '60s singer Dusty Springfield had found her way back to the Top 10 after almost 20 years, hitched to the Pet Shop Boys. Sib was at Larry's when she heard that record, "What Have I Done to Deserve This?" for the first time earlier in the year — and couldn't remember when her ears had tingled with such excitement. Larry saw the sudden stop-time look on Sib's face.

"Pretty good track, eh?" Larry said.

"It's not pretty good," Sib said. "'There's not a single thing wrong with it. It's fucking perfect.'"

"Such language from a Catholic girl! But what do you *really* think?" Larry said. He often razzed Sib for her sliced-ribbons opinions, but they had made a name for her in the male-dominated rock-crit world, where most everyone else wanted to write about U2 and Springsteen and R.E.M., but where she found a niche writing about pop and soul. Her reviews were noticed by a junior exec in the publishing division of a major label, who was looking for a song doctor for some of his acts. Sib got the job when she told him to simply change a pronoun in a Britboy track from "them" to "we." More recently she had rewritten practically the entire lyric of an arena-rock band's power ballad and helped them land their first No. 1 single. Sib didn't receive any label credit, but she got a bonus check that was more money than she'd ever dreamed of. Money that more than paid for the obstetrician and baby stuff and then some.

Midsummer and the Mets were comfortably in first place.

Sib and Larry hadn't married. They still thought of themselves as best friends who occasionally had sex, and the sex itself was almost like foreplay for their shared music passion, for the nights they stayed up listening to records or spinning the radio dial. They would raise the baby together but would live apart, at least for now.

They were even going to try the songwriting thing again. Sib hadn't listened to the tape in a while, but the song, she knew, was timeless. With the right production, anything could be a hit, so why not an actual quality song? Dusty Springfield's recent comeback only confirmed Sib's faith.

Alone now at the grave, the singer on the tape came to Sib's mind. Was it really the singer Sib had detested all those years, who had died shortly after Sib found the tape? Or just a soundalike? She had never resolved the question, and sometimes thought she didn't want to; when she heard that the singer had died, and then learned how the singer had suffered from that strange affliction, she felt guilty for all the rage she'd had toward her all those years, realized that it was a stand-in for the guilt she felt about the accident. At some point she had pulled out that greatest-hits album from Kieran's closet again and listened all the way through, to the songs she had avoided for so long. She thought some of the arrangements were cheesy, but she had come to realize that the singer had something singular, something happening in the grooves, and in between them.

Sib stared at her mother's name on the gravestone. "Of course you knew," Sib said. "You always knew." Then she looked at Kieran's name. "The two of you always knew," she said. "I still don't quite get it the way you did, and I'll never sound as good as either of you, but here you go."

Sib felt a wave of queasiness go through her, like morning sickness, only she was too far along for that. The song she was thinking of still had that unsettling effect on her. But now, she knew she could keep the song down. She knelt to one knee, slowly, lest the baby protest. She took a breath, swept her head up from the gravestone into the cooling blue-and-white floes in the sky, and started to sing. "*Why do birds . . . ?*"

36. Chelsea, New York, January 1990

Sean was panting by the time they got to the fifth floor and Andy's door. "I see why you have such good glutes," Sean said. Andy just shook his head at the line, and they went in. A second after Andy turned on the lights, Sean said, "Oh, my God, this place is so . . . tidy."

It was true. The railroad apartment was clean and airy, like every place Andy had ever lived. Open spaces, minimal furniture, dish rack emptied, counters gleaming, rugs vacuumed, masculine, wood-lined, understated in its charms, a nonworking fireplace taking up half a wall and high, beamed ceilings giving the illusion of space.

Soccer ball tucked neatly in a corner. Zero clutter.

"Can always be tidier," Andy said as he hung up his coat and went to his tiny kitchen to put on the teakettle. Out in the living room, he found Sean, who had shed his down vest and was wearing a blue canvas button-down with cartoon characters all over it, splayed on the couch. He'd flung a pack of cigarettes on a side table. This is going to be a challenge, Andy thought.

They met a few weeks earlier at a gym in Chelsea called Good Bodies. Once AIDS had secured its vise grip on New York, all the bathhouses were closed, and gay men were flocking to gyms not just for anonymous sex but to build muscles as a first line of defense against the enemy. Andy had gone that day not to work out — he still preferred outdoor runs, even in the cold, fewer people, more space — or to hook up but instead to drop condoms and literature about safe sex and ACT UP in the locker room and steam room, at least what he could fit under his towel without being too conspicuous or weighed down. He'd fashioned a rubber stamp with his mantra-phrase — BE SAFE — and emblazoned it all over the fronts of the pamphlets. The steam and his constant movement, his strategy of going during the off-hours, his refusal to return or even notice any cruises, kept him focused, ahead of his mission.

But one afternoon the steam was so thick that Andy walked right into a guy about his age, a little shorter, in a towel and glasses with gold frames. "That's quite a package you've got there," the man said, having felt the condoms and cards and pamphlets under Andy's towel. The corniness of the line, and the man's buzz cut, café-au-lait skin and smirky-friendly face disarmed Andy, and when the man nudged him toward a bench in the steam room, Andy found himself following. "I've seen you here a few times before," the man said. "I'm Sean. I was just on my way out. What's all this stuff?"

"Andy. Condoms, information about H.I.V. and AIDS, safe sex, ACT UP," he said. "Want some?"

"No, thanks. I've got it all already, engraved in my skull in fact.

Too many friends gone in just 10 years." Sean seemed focused on the BE SAFE stamp. "I do want something else, though," he said

"What's that?" Andy said, ready to bolt if Sean made a move.

"Your number."

Andy had almost forgotten Sean by the time he called a few weeks later. They made a date. But then Sean didn't show up at the coffee shop, and Andy was almost back at his apartment when he heard someone calling his name from down the block, clopping and zigzagging toward him in the light coating of snow on the sidewalk. It was Sean, who apologized and said he had been visiting a friend in the AIDS ward at St. Vincent's, which was just a few blocks away from Andy's place. "Please, can I come in, just for a few minutes, to get warm?" Sean said. "I won't keep you long."

Andy's inner flares went off. He didn't really know this guy, and at least in the coffee shop he might have been able to figure him out a bit, get ahead of him. Now he'd be right in Andy's space. But if he'd had a long night at the hospital. . . .

"O.K.," Andy said. "Just for a little while." He still had his gun, safely concealed under a side table. He'd still never fired it.

Now Andy sat at the other end of the couch and tried to make small talk. In the light, with clothes on, still a little breathless, Sean came into more focus, as he wasn't enveloped in steam or winter night air. He was a little meaty but defined, confident in his slouch, brown eyes that seemed fully open and focused on everything except what was right in front of him, like most of the men Andy had dated.

"So tell me about your friend," Andy said as the kettle started to whistle.

"A buddy from the old 'hood in the Bronx, Frankie, Italian, sweetest guy ever," Sean said. "We called him Sugarcube."

Sugarcube. Some guys on the force used that word for smack. "Drugs?" Andy said.

"No, no, not Frankie, he was a good kid, wouldn't know a packet of cheer from a packet of Cheer." Sean saw the recognition in Andy's eyes and went on. "We called him that because he had the biggest sweet tooth in the Bronx. He could wolf down the cannolis and never put on a pound. His mother always knew where to find him most days: near the bakeries on Arthur Avenue.

"When I heard that he was in the hospital, I went back to one of those bakeries and got him some Italian cookies, jelly-filled minitarts, chocolate dips, sprinkles, rainbows, in a white box with a string, just like the old days. But he couldn't bear to look at them, or at me. He couldn't even really talk. He just seemed so shriveled and scared. I mean, he's barely 30." Sean gazed out Andy's window, into the tall grid of lights of the old Port Authority building on Ninth Avenue. "I'm sorry, I can't go there right now," Sean said, his voice cracking a bit. "I've been eating, drinking, sleeping, breathing this plague all week, all my life it seems. . . . How long have you lived here?"

"A few years," said Andy, who had retrieved two steaming mugs from the kitchen. He'd stayed in Bellerose for a little while after he resigned from the force, right after he heard that the singer had died. His experimental undercover program had been discontinued — inconclusive data was the conclusion — and he couldn't bear the idea of going back in the squad car.

When Andy told his parents over the phone that he was leaving the force, his father said, "Son, I think you have a problem with completion." His mother just sounded relieved. "I read that the library is hiring," she said.

He lived off his savings for a while, then, when his father died a few years later, a decent-size trust fund, which paid his basic expenses and allowed him to volunteer at the Gay and Lesbian Center in the Village, where he manned the hotline in the late hours, talking to men worried about the disease, about coming out, about finding safe space. And he often thought about the singer, the one he might have seen, when he didn't kick himself for not finding her,

or at the very least despair over the fact that she didn't get to have
one more moment in the sun. There was always something there
to remind him: a new pair of sneakers, a baseball cap, a percussive bounce in someone's step. The lemon wedge on his teacup. He
still went to record stores and made sure her albums were stocked
prominently, called oldies radio stations and requested her songs,
wrote to music magazines and suggested articles about her. The
one thing he didn't do that often was actually listen to her records.
Hearing her voice only collapsed the space between Andy and the
loss of her. It was coming up on seven years now.

When the conversation with Sean stalled, Andy moved over toward the fireplace, next to the stereo equipment, the same good
components his parents had given him years ago, only now with a
CD player add-on. There was a single cube on the floor filled with
about 30 albums; he was still selective about the music he would
actually buy. He pulled out one of his few recent purchases, Janet
Jackson's *Rhythm Nation 1814*, which proved to him yet again that
you could have good songcraft with modern production, and that
a smallish voice with attitude and heart could carry farther than a
barnyard bellow.

"Wait, wait!" Sean said, suddenly behind Andy and reaching
into the cube. Andy jumped back, cop reflex, space expansion. Sean
pulled out a few of the singer's albums. "I can't believe you have
these," Sean said, fingering and flipping over the covers of, first, the
silver-and-blue album and, then, the tan.

Another come-lately fan, Andy suspected. In the past couple of
years, there had been that movie about her with the dolls, and a TV
biopic, and singers like Madonna and Chrissie Hynde professing
their admiration for her. It was almost as if her disease had giv-
en her some street cred, turned her into an ironic icon. Andy felt
some validation for her, and even a little for himself, but mostly
he couldn't help wondering where all this love was when she was
dying.

Andy reached for the silver-and-blue album, which had those first two big hits, figuring that's what Sean would want him to play. "No, no, I need to hear something else," Sean said, and stuck his hand back into the cube, pulling out the singer and the brother's "progressive" album. "Side 2, Track 1."

Andy looked at the titles on the cover. Sean had asked to hear her country hit from later in the career. Not one of Andy's favorites — it was from her lighter period — but what the heck. He put the record on, turned around and saw that Sean had stripped down to his thermal T-shirt, boxer briefs and socks, and when the song began he started pinging around Andy's living room like a pinball. Andy's unease with Sean, and with the song, dissipated as Sean, twirling and pogo-ing around his living room, got lighter himself, having shed not just some clothes but the heaviness, the heartache of his day, the agony of life during the plague. And for the first time Andy noticed that the singer actually sounded happy in this song, unlike most of her others. Sean was soaking up her joy and spraying it back across Andy's living room. Somehow the record didn't skip.

When the song was over, Sean spread the albums on the floor and said, "Play this cut, then this one, then this one." So maybe this guy wasn't just a fly-by-night fan, Andy thought. Andy just started the silver-and-blue album from the beginning, and they sat back on the couch. Suddenly Sean was pouring out details of his life: He was half Puerto Rican and half Irish, he worked in fashion — that would account for the designer glasses and the quirky shirt and the hint of snark — and lived just outside the city with a younger sister, whose two young children he was helping to raise. In the past 10 years, he'd buried more than three dozen friends, but had so far escaped the disease himself. "Sometimes I wonder if it would be easier to just get it and be done with it," Sean said.

Andy snapped to, upright now on the couch, boring into Sean's eyes with the same look of disapprobation and concern that he'd give someone he'd pulled over. "Please, please don't," he said. *Please live.* Sean looked right back at Andy for the first time all night.

"You're handsomer than I remember," Sean said. "Of course it was hard to tell in all that steam."

Sean reached for Andy's hand, then moved in for a kiss. Of the few men Andy had dated over the years, he'd never really found a good kisser, one whose lips just matched his, weren't too dry or too moist, didn't freeze up or engulf or slide around or slam on the brakes, but interlocked like moving puzzle pieces. Sean's, though, were a perfect fit. He still might be a psycho, but Andy had the hot tea next to him just in case. And the gun wasn't far.

Andy offered a few details of his own life. "An ex-cop who thought about the priesthood?" Sean said. "Got a thing for uniforms?"

After a few more songs and some heavier petting, they moved into the bedroom, and as their T-shirts and socks were hitting the floor, the medley of songs by the famous '60s songwriters came on.

"You know, the thing about this medley," Andy said, in anticipation of the zippy, stitched-together snippets of hits, "is that it starts in the heavens, and then — "

"I know, I know," Sean said. "The slathered harmonies, that loungy piano solo, the brother's voice . . . . Pretty goofy. But still somehow charming. And isn't she just — " Sean popped up from his pillow — "spuh-*len*-did all the way? That warmth, that quiet control, that impeccable rhythm. . . ."

***

At 10 o'clock the next morning, they were still in bed. Andy had been dozing on and off until he was awakened for good by the bells from St. Peter's on 20th Street, a smidge out of tune but still one of the things he liked best about Sunday mornings in Chelsea, reminding him, as they often did, of that one blissful Saturday morning in the seminary. He really ought to get up, he thought.

Sean, who was still sleeping, would probably be gone soon, and if things went the way they usually did, he wouldn't be back. They'd had a memorable night, but she had been the conduit — her voice lingered in the morning-after air like the smell of sex and tooth-paste, lingered just as it did that day years ago in the record-store booth — but how many more times could that happen? Sean might have just needed a shoulder and a warm bed, a warm voice, after a rough night in the AIDS ward. Andy thought about how he never even knew the name of that boy in the booth. Be safe, wherever you are, he thought.

Andy leaned toward the edge of the mattress, and his legs started to swing toward the floor. Just then Sean, still on his side facing away from Andy, reached behind and pulled him back into the bed, cradling Andy's right arm against his chest.

"Where are you going, Andy?" Sean said. "Get closer. Close to me."

And so Andy did.

Acknowledgments

With gratitude, for their eyes and ears, time and talents, across the decades:

Frances Scully Abbott, Herb Alpert, Mark Ansell, Eileen Benjamin, Paul Bresnick, Colin Bridgham, Marie Scully Browne, Ted Casselman, Tom DeBona, Gladys Eldred, Wm. Ferguson, Frenda Franklin, Ben Grandgenett, Paul Grein, Michael Hanrahan, Gerald Hoerburger, Mary Hoerburger, Peggy Hoerburger, Virginia Scully Hoerburger, Bill Holland, Marjorie Holt, Russell Javors, Bill Kelley, Jon Konjoyan, Robert LaForce, Kyle Ligman, Robert Liguori, Linda F. Magyar, Arthur McCune, Michele McKenna, Tausif Noor, Derek Petti, Karen Ichiuji Ramone, Phil Ramone, Aaron Retica, Joe Rucci, Daniel Rushefsky, Christopher Schelling, Randy L. Schmidt, David Scott, Alice Scully, Jane St. John, Adam Sternbergh, Doug Stewart, Andy Waldron, Carolyn Waldron, Rachel Willey, Alex Witchel.

CPSIA information can be obtained
at www.ICGtesting.com
Printed in the USA
LVHW051112110819
627235LV00006B/882

\ \

9 781532 38